JURASSIC NIGHTMARE

"We'd better get a move on if we're going," Remo said.

Professor Stockwell stood erect and glassy-eyed, as if he'd been hypnotized. "Incredible," he said, and then repeated it for emphasis. "Incredible."

"Unfortunately, we are not inedible," said Remo. "I'm afraid we must leave right now."

With Audrey's help, he hustled Stockwell off the dais, toward the wings, with Sandakan behind them. Nagaq let out a screech. No, no special training course on dinosaurs was needed to recognize the sound of big feet slapping on the stonework, gaining on them in a rush.

It would be snack time any moment now, and Remo felt a little like an appetizer, destined to be eaten raw.

Other titles in this series:

Created by
WARREN MURPHY
and RICHARD SAPIR

THE

Destr☯yer™

BAMBOO DRAGON

A GOLD EAGLE BOOK FROM
W☯RLDWIDE®

TORONTO • NEW YORK • LONDON
AMSTERDAM • PARIS • SYDNEY • HAMBURG
STOCKHOLM • ATHENS • TOKYO • MILAN
MADRID • WARSAW • BUDAPEST • AUCKLAND

First edition July 1997
ISBN 0-373-63223-1

Special thanks and acknowledgment to
Mike Newton for his contribution to this work.

BAMBOO DRAGON

Printed in U.S.A.

For Eva Kovacs, one of the best.

And, as always, for the Glorious House of Sinanju.

1

The cursed jungle had invaded Hopper's dreams. It was bad enough that it had made his every waking hour Hell on Earth, but now he could find no respite even in his sleep. His private nightscape stank of rotting vegetation, hummed with biting insects, seethed with wriggling vipers. Always, in the murky background, he could hear the rumbling snarl of larger predators, unseen but waiting for the false step that would make him theirs.

Instead of waking up refreshed each morning, ready for another grueling workday, Hopper found himself exhausted, haggard from the nightmares that pursued him once he crept inside his sleeping bag and pulled the beige mosquito netting down around him like a giant spider web. The past few days, he had forsaken shaving, not because the simple operation sapped his energy, but rather to avoid the face that greeted him each morning in his mirror—gaunt and dark, with sunken, bloodshot eyes and hair like straw that stubbornly defied the comb. His cheeks were hollow, mottled with the pox of insect bites, and Hopper didn't like the blotchy tan that made him look like an escapee from a lab experiment. His gums had started bleeding Tuesday night—or was it Wednesday? Not a lot, but still enough to stain his teeth, and that had been the final straw. He left his mirror for the monkeys when they broke camp in the morning, and he wished them better luck. He wouldn't shave again until he had hot water and a proper bathroom, possibly a barber to perform the ritual, so he wouldn't have to face himself.

A lady barber. She could shave his whole damned body if she wanted to, and scrub him clean until he started feeling human once again.

It was peculiar, this reaction to the jungle and the job that had been paying Hopper's way for close to fifteen years. He didn't like to think it was the work, for that meant starting over, finding something new if he couldn't perform, and that was never easy for a man of his restricted educational achievements.

No, it couldn't be the job. That never changed. He used the same equipment each time out and knew the drill by heart. He could perform the simple operations in his sleep—had done exactly that, the past ten nights or so—and there were only two ways it could go. Success or failure. Either way, he still got paid for making the attempt.

It had to be the jungle, then, and that was strange. In his time, he had been sent to every stinking pesthole from the Congo to the Amazon. He had communed with pygmies and the wild men of the Mato Grosso, sharing meals that would have gagged a maggot, pumping the locals for information that would help him do his job. He knew about the spiders, snakes and scorpions, and had learned to wear his jockey shorts while bathing, so loathsome parasites and tiny spike-finned fish wouldn't invade his genitals or rectum. On the flip side, he had trekked through deserts where the ground cracked like old leather and the temperature topped 120 in the shade—if you could find the shade at all—and even biting flies had sense enough to hide until the sun went down. At the other extreme, he was no stranger to the Arctic tundra, and had dined on frozen mammoth steaks with blubber on the side and watched his piss freeze in a golden arc before it hit the ground.

But he had always done his job.

So what was different now? What was it that repulsed him so about this place?

He didn't think it was the climate, which reminded him of Indonesia at the height of summer, hot and humid, sapping the vitality of anyone foolish enough to labor in the daylight hours. Still, a man could fortify himself with salt and special beverages, restoring lost electrolytes. He knew the tricks, all right. Indeed, he had invented some of them himself.

The teeming insects? Hopper didn't think so. Granted, the mosquitoes were particularly large and vicious, rivaling the worst that he had seen in Africa, and there were flies that felt like hypodermic needles when they hit you, always from behind. But Hopper had been vaccinated for a whole list of diseases, from malaria to filariasis, and he was armed with bug repellent tailored for the military. As it was, he suffered only twenty-five or thirty painful bites per day, and he could live with that.

What, then?

Eleven weeks of speculation and analysis led Hopper to conclude that it must be the place, some nasty combination of the climate and terrain, plant life and skulking fauna, that conspired to put his nerves on edge. It seemed ridiculous, but there it was. This place was evil, pulsing with malignant undercurrents that invaded blood and muscle tissue, wormed their way inside the human brain.

Or maybe he was simply going mad.

Eleven weeks.

They were supposed to finish off the job in half that time, but someone upstairs had clearly underestimated the jungle, basing their timetable on bland tourist guidebooks and maps that shrank the country down to postcard size, reducing mighty river networks to a web of slender threads, the all-devouring jungle to a green blotch you could cover with your hand. The "planners," as they liked to call themselves back in the States, were absolutely ignorant of what it took to ford a river when the crocodiles were waiting, scale a hundred feet of crumbling shale or wade through miles of reeking swamp with stagnant water up around your chest and leeches squirming underneath your sodden clothes.

All this he had been willing to endure, as on his other expeditions, for the payoff. Half up front, the rest when he was finished, with a handsome bonus if he scored. Around Los Angeles—where he made his home of sorts—and in the industry at large, there was a saying that what Hopper didn't find could not be found. Hyperbole, perhaps, but no one ever lost his shirt by cultivating an impressive reputation.

It could get you killed, though, if you didn't watch your step.

The job had sounded perfect when they laid it out for Hopper at the briefing back in March. Not easy—that would be too much to hope for—but at least it didn't sound impossible.

The planners had a fix on what they wanted him to find, spun off from a potpourri of native legend, secret military documents, some wishful thinking based on satellite photography and laser tracings from the past two shuttle missions. What it added up to was a fortune…maybe. All they needed was a pro to carry out the groundwork under "primitive conditions."

In the field.

He had to smile at that, the way they made it sound as if he were being sent to walk around a meadow, someone's open pasture land. "The field" was in fact something else entirely: jungle, desert, maybe rugged mountains where you knew damned well a mining operation would be difficult, if not impossible, to organize. It wasn't Hopper's job to rain on anyone's parade until he had a look around and scouted out the territory, looking high and low for the elusive pay dirt that would fatten up his bank account along with everybody else's.

That was one good thing about his job: instead of working free-lance, for himself, he went out on retainer for the companies with deep, deep pockets, and they had to pay him, win or lose. It pissed them off whenever Hopper came up empty, but that didn't happen often. By the time a sponsor needed him, the ground had been examined from a distance, probabilities determined by the kind of high-falutin math he never even tried to understand. From that point on, the job came down to Hopper in the field, pursuing fame and fortune on behalf of men who didn't have the skill or courage to go out and grab it for themselves.

And he had done all right...until this time.

He told himself that he was being foolish; there

was nothing in the jungle hereabouts that he hadn't previously encountered somewhere. Same snakes, or close enough. Same frigging spiders, ants, flies, gnats, mosquitoes, body lice. Same natives, more or less, with their innate suspicion of outsiders who had screwed them in the past and might again if they let down their guard.

It wasn't anything, in fact, that he could put his finger on. But beneath the sweat, sunburn and jungle rot that came with any mission to the tropics, there was…something else.

A nagging sense of dread.

And he wasn't the only one who felt it, either. Starting with the local tribesmen who had balked at sharing information, much less renting guides out to the expedition, forcing Hopper to pay well beyond the going rate for native help. He didn't mind—it wasn't his cash, after all—but their reluctance, verging on a state of superstitious terror, set the tone for everything that followed.

Eakins, the geologist from Houston, had been first to show the signs among the three of them who counted. You could see him getting edgy, checking out the shadows while they marched and staring past the firelight into darkness when they camped. Before the second week was over, he had started dropping hints and questions, getting curious about the natives, predators, whatever. Still, it was his first time in the heavy bush, and there were bound to be some nerves involved.

The fear crept up on Hopper next, and took him by surprise. So far, he thought that he had done a fair job of concealing it, though the lack of decent sleep was wearing on him in the stretch and threatening to breed mistakes. He wrote it off to age at first—the big four-oh was coming up in August—but there had to be some other reason for the nightmares and the grim, oppressive sense of doom that dogged his waking hours.

Now, unless he was mistaken, even Sparks was feeling it. Sparks was their troubleshooter, muscle with a military background who had drifted into mercenary work and on from there into the nebulous preserve of what they liked to call "executive security." For fifty grand a year, plus traveling expenses, Sparks might be dispatched to twist an arm in Washington, tap phones in Birmingham...or baby-sit an expedition slogging through the shit a thousand miles from anywhere.

Sparks knew his job and calculated the attendant risks before he made a move. When there was danger brewing, he could kick ass with the best of them. There was a hazy but persistent rumor, stateside, that his killings weren't confined to Third World civil wars.

But he was getting nervous now, no doubt about

it. You could see it in his eyes, the way he kept his rifle close beside him, with the safety off.

It had to be imagination, Hopper told himself, since nothing much beyond the ordinary had occurred so far. There was continued reticence among the guides and porters, but you got that sometimes, where taboos and superstition were involved. The trek itself, while beating any Hopper could recall for sheer exertion and fatigue, wasn't otherwise especially dangerous. The nearest he had come to outright peril was a close encounter with a cobra on the fourth day out, when he had left the trail to take a bladder break.

Shit happened in the field, but he couldn't escape the nightmares, even so.

They always started out the same way, Hopper tramping through the jungle, lost, with darkness coming on. He knew the camp should be ahead of him, another hundred yards or so, but when he called to Sparks and Eakins, no one answered. Haunting bird calls echoed through the forest, unseen rodents scuttling in the undergrowth, but nothing human seemed to share his space.

Time was elusive in the dreams, but after a while Hopper would gradually come to understand that he was being followed. Something large and hungry stalked the trail behind him, keeping out of sight but coming close enough that he could hear it breathing. Christ, it must be huge, with lungs like bellows. Now and then, when trees got in the way, it snapped them off and sent them crashing to the forest floor. In panic, Hopper would start running aimlessly, with thorny branches slashing at his clothes, his face. The scent of fresh-drawn blood inflamed his nemesis, producing snarls of hunger that reminded him of King Kong on the prowl. At last, he'd glimpse the camp ahead, apparently deserted. Sprinting for the tents and the illusory protection of the fire, he always stumbled at the far edge of the clearing, sprawling on his face. The massive predator behind him, bearing down on top of him, until he smelled the foul rush of its breath. The teeth—

His eyes snapped open, just like always, saving Hopper from the moment when he had to face his terror in the flesh. Between the nightmare and the sleeping bag, his body was awash in sweat. And he was trembling like a little kid.

He sat up on his cot, the metal legs spiked into cans half-filled with water to defeat the creepy-crawlies, swung his legs out of the sleeping bag and glanced around his feet for safety's sake before he put them down.

The dreams were getting worse, goddammit. This time he could feel a tremor in the earth as his pursuer closed the gap between them. Jesus, if he didn't shake these nightmares soon—

A tremor in the earth.

No way, he told himself. No fucking way at all. It had to be a muscle spasm in his legs that made him feel as if a giant was approaching, almost close enough to burst upon the camp, with the vibrations registering through Hopper's naked feet.

The scream brought Hopper vaulting off his cot, snared in the mesh of the mosquito netting till he ripped it down and struggled free. By that time, he could hear the guides and porters shouting gibberish, a startled curse from Sparks.

The echo of his rifle sounded like a thunderclap.

Outside the tent, Hopper stumbled into pandemonium. The natives were evacuating, running every which way, two of them stampeding through the fire and out the other side without a yelp of pain to mark their passing. Fear would do that to you, numb the other senses, a survival mechanism saved for desperate times.

He looked around for Sparks and Eakins, and located the troubleshooter standing near his own tent, dressed in boxer shorts and crew socks, with the rifle at his shoulder, pointing skyward at an angle close to forty-five degrees. Another crack, and Hopper saw the red-orange muzzle flash.

What was he shooting at? And where was Eakins? It had sounded like his scream, if Hopper had to guess, but what—?

He saw it then. The hulking shadow-figure from his nightmare striding forward, beckoned by the firelight, swiveling its head to scan the camp. A rag-doll figure was suspended from its gnashing jaws, blood streaming down across the lips and chin. The flaccid doll wore khaki pants, a matching shirt, all stained with crimson.

Eakins.

Sparks cranked off another shot, to no effect. The walking nightmare turned in his direction, shook its head and spit the bloody rag doll out. Sparks had to jump aside, the body bouncing once before it wound up in a twisted, boneless heap. The troubleshooter was about to fire again, but he never got the chance.

No slouch, this shambling nightmare, when a bit of speed was called for. It appeared to hop, the motion almost birdlike, but its landing caused the ground to tremble under Hopper's feet. Sparks didn't notice, since the monster's bulk came down on top of him and crushed him to the earth, arms splayed, the rifle spinning out of reach. The demon beast ducked low, like a giant chicken pecking corn, and found him with its flashing teeth.

It took a heartbeat for the scream to register, another beat for Hopper to discover it was coming out of him, then he clapped both hands across his mouth.

Too late.

The living nightmare made a wish and ripped Sparks down the midline of his body, spilling him into the dirt. It had a mouthful when it glanced around at Hopper, following the sound of his demented scream.

Oh, Jesus! Run!

He ran.

There was no conscious planning, no time left for that. A part of Hopper's mind knew he was barefoot, fleeing in his underwear, but there was nothing he could do about it. If he stopped to grab his clothes, much less to put them on, he would be caught inside the tent, join Sparks and Eakins as a tasty midnight snack.

The clearing wasn't large. A dozen strides brought Hopper to the tree line, and he kept on going, heedless of the rocks and thorns that gouged his feet, ignoring the potential threat of serpents. He knew well enough the danger waiting for him if he stuck around the camp. All else was secondary, something he could deal with if and when it came along.

The urge to run was instinct, something primal, triggered by adrenaline. His mind was barely functional, still dazed by the transmission from his eyes, part of him hoping this would prove to be a dream within a dream, the latest in his panoply of nightmares.

No such luck.

He stumbled in the darkness, threw both hands out in a desperate bid to catch himself and felt a jagged branch sink deep into his palm. Blood marked the spot as Hopper freed himself, the sharp pain banishing all hope that he was still asleep.

Was he insane? Had fever and fatigue snapped his connection to reality? What if he stood his ground and waited for the monster where he was?

A heavy thrashing in the jungle answered that one for him, kept him moving as the beast pursued him. Could it see him in the darkness? Was it following his scent?

He ran as if his life depended on it, lost, surrendering to panic. Part of Hopper's mind was still coherent, though, and it was telling him that he'd been mistaken in his dreams. The dark, relentless hunter didn't snarl and roar. It hissed. A great steam engine racing after him, immense and indestructible.

He thought about the river, which lay somewhere to the north of camp. If he could only get his bearings, make it that far in the dark—a mile or two at most—he still might have a chance. It worked with bloodhounds in the movies; water threw them off the scent of their intended prey and gave the hapless fugitive a break. If nothing else, the river might be deep enough to slow his adversary down, perhaps dissuade the demon altogether.

His lungs were burning, and a rush of dizziness came close to overwhelming him as he stumbled to a halt. He braced himself against a tree trunk, leaving a bloody palm print as a signature, bent double to reduce the stabbing pain from stitches in his side. His feet were torn and bleeding. Hopper felt as if he were standing on a bed of razor blades.

And silence.

Had he done it? Was he safe? It seemed impossible, but how could anything that large move silently?

He felt the strike, a stirring in the air above his head, before the gaping jaws descended. Hopper squealed and threw himself aside, rolled over twice and vaulted to his feet. It was impossible for him to choose a direction; there was only life and death to think of as he turned and sprinted through the trees.

Behind him, hissing its rage, the predator came on, its nostrils flaring at the scent of blood and warm, wet flesh. It recognized no law but hunger, no imperative except to feed.

The forest swallowed Hopper up alive.

2

His name was Remo, and he reckoned it should be a serious felony for any person weighing upward of three hundred pounds to wear the kind of skintight stretch pants that looked painted on, revealing every dimple, lump and divot on their grotesque derrieres.

The two Americans in front of him were prime examples of the problem. Matching rings told Remo they were married, and the way they clutched each other's hands suggested they were either newlyweds or else intimidated by the act of wandering around a foreign city on their own. So far, they had confined themselves to window-shopping, browsing at the sidewalk stalls that offered everything from hand-stitched clothing, jade and native handicrafts to cobras stuffed and mounted in the posture of attack.

Between them, Remo guessed they must have weighed at least 650 pounds, most of it lodged below the waist. With matching horn-rimmed glasses, frizzy hair and garish tourist clothes, they looked a bit like cartoon figures, something from "The Far

Side,'' and a number of the street merchants couldn't keep from giggling after they had passed. It would have been bad form to laugh in a potential buyer's face, of course, but after they were gone...well, what was there to lose?

He didn't know their names, but Remo thought of them as Fred and Freda Frump. It was a fluke that he had crossed their path, but Remo's tagging after them wasn't an accident. He was concerned about his cover, shaky as it was, and shied away from prowling through the city on his own. One round-eye in an Asian city was a curiosity, while three or more together made a tour group.

He hadn't spoken to the Frumps and didn't plan to. Remo didn't need a friend to help him see the city; he was merely riding in their slipstream for a while to see if he was being followed and avoid attracting undue notice to himself. The less his hefty escorts knew about his scam, the better it would be for all concerned. Let them draw the attention, while he moved unnoticed in their wake.

Malaysia had become a tourist destination almost by default in recent years. It had a hard time keeping up with Thailand, where the lures ranged from ancient culture—monks in saffron robes, surrounded by impassive gilded Buddhas—to the cutting edge of sex and drugs. Hong Kong and neighboring Macao eclipsed Malaysia when it came to international finance, and Taiwan offered more in

terms of cut-rate souvenirs. Exquisite dancers stole
the show in Bali, while Brunei hogged much of
Southeast Asia's oil and gas. The Philippines and
Indonesia offered island living at its best, for those
who could afford the going rate.

Malaysia, in comparison to its successful neighbors, was a relative late bloomer in the rush for
tourist dollars, and was better known from dated
novels by the likes of Ambler, Black and Maugham
than from reality. Of late, though, it had grown into
a favored destination for the sort of tourist anxious
to relax in an exotic land without the worry of out-
rageous prices, crowded sight-seeing attractions and
daunting language barriers. Whatever might be
lacking for the die-hard culture vulture was made
up, and then some, by the first-rate service in hotels
and some of the most striking beaches in the world.
An additional benefit for safety-minded Western
tourists was that Malaysia was also rated as the only
Southeast Asian country where a round-eyed tourist
could feel truly safe while touring in a private rental
car.

No wheels for Remo, though, when he set out
from his hotel to see the nation's capital. Kuala
Lumpur—or ''K.L.'' to its familiars—was a rapidly
expanding base of education, politics and industry.
The latest guesswork census placed the city's population at one million, but the tourist guidebooks
estimated nearly twice as many residents packed

into the onetime colonial town that had initially grown around tin mines and kept going from there.

Kuala Lumpur's name translated literally as "muddy river junction," for the nearby merger of the Gombak and Kelang, but there was little to recall those early years in modern-day K.L. The architecture was a blend of early-weird and modern-functional, the arabesque atmosphere of Kuala Lumpur's public buildings—the central railway station, town hall and national mosque—contrasting sharply with the sweeping, functional lines of the newer high-rise school. Both styles collided in the neighborhood of Market Street, along the banks of the Kelang, where the central market drew tourists and locals alike in search of bargains as iron filings are drawn to a magnet.

It was several hours before Remo had to meet the others. Wasted time if he remained at the hotel and tried to guess which way the game would go. He and Master Chiun had a nice room at the Hotel Merlin, on Jalan Sultan Ismail, and he couldn't have dragged Chiun out with a team of horses while the reruns of his beloved soaps were on the tube, much less to mingle with a population that was heavily Chinese in origin.

"At least they are not half-breed Japanese," Chiun had remarked while they were waiting for a taxi at the airport. From his tone, a perfect stranger could have guessed the frail Korean's view of half-breeds generally and the children of Nippon. For Chiun, the Japanese invasion of Korea, back in 1910, had more immediacy than the latest rumbles in Kuwait and Bosnia.

"It is unfortunate," he liked to say, "that they remember nothing of the lesson taught them in Korea."

"Back in 1945, you mean?" asked Remo. "When the U.S. Army and the Russians threw them out?"

"Your textbooks are predictably inaccurate. It was the Master of Sinanju who convinced the foul invaders to depart."

"And how did he accomplish that trick, Little Father?"

"Through a bargain with their emperor," Chiun replied. "The occupation troops withdrew, and Hirohito was permitted to survive."

"What took so long?"

Chiun's expression conveyed disappointment. "You still think like a white man when it comes to time. What is thirty-five or forty years compared to all eternity? The immortal House of Sinanju had more-important tasks than dealing with a few barbarian usurpers of the throne."

"Like earning gold?"

"The second-most-important task of any Master."

"And the first?"

"Pursuit of personal enlightenment," said Chiun, "about Sinanju."

At the moment, Remo would have settled for enlightenment about his current mission, but the final show-and-tell would have to wait a bit, until he met the others at the Shangri-la. Meanwhile, he had some time to kill before that rendezvous, and it would help to put his mind at ease if he could satisfy himself that he hadn't picked up a tail within the past two hours.

The Frumps would help him there, and all they had to do was be themselves.

THE CONTRACT WAS a relatively simple one. It called for one dead round-eye, half the payment in advance, the rest when Sing Hop Ma returned with proof of execution.

Easy.

It could even be a pleasure.

He had picked up half a dozen Malay thugs to do the dirty work and make the hit seem like a random street crime. The police were strict about this sort of business, and the locals worked for pocket money—what the Yanks called chicken feed. If they were caught, he trusted them to keep their mouths shut, out of fear and the survival instinct.

Sing Hop Ma had been a red pole—an enforcer—for the local Ben Hoa Tong these past

eleven years, since he turned twenty-one. He was a
Malay-born Chinese whose father and grandfather
served the tong before him, raising Sing to honor
the traditions of his clan. The first time he had
killed a man, at seventeen, he had been feted by
the tong and welcomed to their brotherhood with
open arms, a celebration that had nearly made his
father weep with pride. Now, as a full-time soldier
for the tong, he handled jobs and problems that required a certain killer instinct. Most arose from
matters of internal discipline or economic competition, but a few—like this job—were accepted on
a contract basis from outside. Another family, or
even round-eyes, could procure the services of an
assassin if they had sufficient cash in hand.

The target this time was a nondescript American.
Six feet, dark hair, brown eyes, no visible tattoos
or scars. Sing had a candid photo, taken from a
distance at the airport as the target passed through
customs, but it told him nothing of the stranger. He
looked fit enough, without the bulging muscles that
would mark a bodybuilder in the States. Only his
wrists looked unusual, huge and sturdy. Perhaps he
was a businessman or lawyer, dabbling in some en-
terprise that earned him lethal enemies.

It made no sense for Sing to speculate. He had
no personal investment in the contract, other than
the payoff for successful execution. Sing wasn't
concerned with what may have provoked the kill-

ing, or the impact it would have on foreign shores. His reputation was at stake, dependent on attention to the technical details, but he had supervised this kind of work a hundred times before.

He was sure that nothing could go wrong.

His mark was staying at the Hotel Merlin, one more piece of information from his sponsors to facilitate the work. It had been simple for the Malay thugs to follow him when he went out, along Jalan Ampang, beside the river, walking south until he reached the central marketplace. Most round-eyes hired inexpensive taxis to conserve their energy, but this one liked to walk. He browsed in several shops, paused now and then to speak with sidewalk vendors, but he purchased nothing, even waved off the advances of a stylish prostitute on Market Street.

It would be best to kill him in or near the central market, Sing decided, passing the instruction to his Malay go-between and watching as the man slipped off to find his soldiers in the crowd. The kind of mugging Sing envisioned was uncommon, but it happened. Deaths were rare—the random murder of a round-eyed tourist almost unheard-of—but the only fair alternative would be a manufactured accident, and Sing Hop Ma did not trust his associates to pull it off. That kind of ploy would force him to recruit more soldiers from the tong, and thus reduce his private income from the contract. Better to be happy with the Malays, keep it simple and collect his payoff when the contract was fulfilled.

He could have done the job himself, enjoyed it for the rush of pride he felt whenever he was able to defeat a round-eye, but he didn't care to risk his life and freedom on a mission that had no importance to the family. If this man had done something to invite the wrath of the tong, it would have been a different matter. There would be no need for payment, nothing but a word from his superiors to send him on his way. Sing Ma still executed contracts on his own from time to time, when summoned by the hill chief of his tong, but that was always family business, when the master wished to send his enemies a special message. This was something else, a job for hire, and no sworn member of the tong would soil his hands if it could be avoided. Let the Malay mongrels do it for him, while he split the cash with his superiors.

He was a businessman, no different than a banker or attorney, with the sole exception that his stock-in-trade sometimes included sudden death.

What difference did it make? The men and women he had killed were all deserving of their fate, sworn enemies of Sing Ma's family. They were informers, turncoats, thieves, assassins, spies for the authorities—no good to anyone, themselves included. As for contract killings hired from the outside, he reckoned there must be an urgent motive—fear, perhaps, or hatred, even jealousy—to make a stranger part with so much cash.

Sing Ma was watching when his target fell in step behind the two obese Americans. They weren't friends, from what the tong enforcer could discover, watching from his vantage point across the street. In fact, they didn't speak at all, the two in front ignoring Sing Ma's target absolutely while they bartered with a sidewalk vendor over trinkets.

Three could make the job more difficult than one, if they were fighters, but a passing glance was all it took for Sing Ma to dismiss these bloated round-eyes as potential threats. In this case, he suspected that their presence might prove beneficial. Afterward, when it was done, police would think his hirelings had gone trolling for Americans in general, instead of picking out a special target from the crowd.

Another glance around the marketplace confirmed no uniforms in evidence. Unless the Malays bungled it supremely, they should have no trouble closing in, accosting the Americans, demanding cash and jewelry. There would be a struggle, with the target trying to defend himself, and one or more of the Malays would stab him. Once would be enough, if he was working with a skilled assassin, but Sing Ma had specified no less than half a dozen wounds, to guarantee the job was done. His proof would be the fanfare of publicity attendant on the slaying of a round-eye at the central market.

Perfect.

Sing Hop Ma didn't approach the target personally, hanging back a constant fifty yards to watch from a respectful distance. There was still a possibility, however slight, that something could go wrong. The Malays would be on their own in that event, with nothing but a heartfelt guarantee of slow, protracted death if they betrayed their master. Peasants that they were, they knew the reputation of the Ben Hoa Tong and would do nothing to provoke the massacre of their extended families.

Sing Ma was ready for the trap to close.

LET THE FESTIVITIES begin, Remo thought. He'd felt the executioners before he picked them out by sight; nothing about their superficial looks that would have made them stand out in the crowded marketplace. If pressed for a description of the feeling, Remo might have said they broadcast raw hostility, the same way other human beings radiated fear, anxiety or confidence. It took conditioning and practice to revive the special sense that most men lacked, an edge they had surrendered quite unconsciously along the evolutionary road from "savagery" to "civilization," but the study of Sinanju opened many hidden doors.

Before they came in striking distance, Remo knew that there were six of them, all Malays, traveling in pairs. They weren't total idiots, no shouting back and forth to keep in touch, but once he had them spotted he could read the glance they exchanged while closing for the ambush.

It was fairly well coordinated: two in front of Fred and Freda Frump, two more in back of Remo, with the final pair approaching from his right, across the open marketplace. The hunters broke formation as they closed the gap, forming a semicircle that enclosed the three Americans but allowed other Malays to slip through the cordon when they recognized the danger.

It took another moment for the Frumps to realize their path was blocked, so taken were they with the handmade jewelry offered by an aging sidewalk vendor. Only when the merchant started packing up his wares in haste did either of them realize that something was amiss. They looked around the ring of hostile faces, blanching at the sight of knives and bludgeons, trembling like two effigies constructed out of Jell-O.

"Kasi kita wang segala engkau," one of the assassins ordered. *Give us all your money.*

So, it was supposed to look like robbery, thought Remo, with the sidewalk merchant serving as a witness for police. No matter that a daylight mugging was among the city's rarest crimes. Assassination would be rarer still, and it required at least a nominal diversion if the killers meant to stay at large.

He tried to picture Fred and Freda as the targets, but dismissed the thought at once. They were innocuous, despite their violation of prevailing fashion codes, and they didn't look prosperous enough to make six hardened thugs risk prison for their pocket change. If anything, bad luck had brought them to their present circumstance.

Which meant the killers had been sent for Remo. That, in turn, suggested strongly that his cover had been blown, but he couldn't address that problem at the moment.

Not until he dealt with more-immediate concerns.

"Kasi kita wang segala engkau," said the leader of the thugs once more. He punctuated the command by jabbing with his wavy-bladed kris in the direction of the Frumps. They squealed in stereo and clutched at one another, sweating through their polyester outfits with the sudden rush of fear.

"Don't move," said Remo, stepping forward to confront the ersatz muggers as he spoke. His next words were addressed to the apparent spokesman for the group. "You're making a mistake."

The blade man stared at Remo, took a moment to absorb the warning and dismissed it like the oaf he was. His forward lunge was telegraphed by twitching muscles in his jaw and the shift of balance to his forward leg before he struck. It was too late to save himself, once he committed to the strike.

One moment, he was thrusting forward, on the verge of burying the kris in Remo's gut; the next, his striking arm was twisted out of shape, the elbow shattered, shoulder dislocated, forming crazy angles, and the blade he meant for Remo slid between his sixth and seventh ribs. The man was dead before he knew it, lurching several steps past Remo, toward the cringing Frumps, before he fell.

The others rushed Remo then, and while his physical reaction was instinctive, nothing but a blur to those who watched dumbfounded from the sidelines, Remo's senses broke the action down and analyzed each movement as a master choreographer reviews a complicated dance routine.

The two goons on his left were close enough to merit an immediate response, one brandishing a dagger, while the other swung a length of chain. He crushed the blade man's larynx with a floating strike that killed him where he stood, continuing a single fluid motion as he spun the standing corpse around and used it as a shield. The oily chain whipped out to wrap itself around the dead man's skull, and Remo met his startled adversary with a snap kick to the face, explosive impact shattering the lower jaw and driving bony needles deep into the soft flesh of his palate.

That left three, and he was ready for them as they tried to mob him, getting in each other's way. He hardly seemed to touch them—Fred and Freda would babble to the police that their attackers almost seemed to turn on one another, it had taken place so quickly—but dramatic roundhouse punches aren't required to kill. A fingertip behind the ear will manage very nicely, or an open palm below the chin, delivered from perhaps a foot away.

The work was done in fifteen seconds, give or take a heartbeat, then Remo stood perfectly composed amid the bodies of his fallen enemies. He faced Fred and Freda, stepping close enough for them to smell his aftershave.

"What did you see?"

Fred blinked at him behind his horn-rimmed glasses. "Hell if I know, mister. It was all so fast."

"So fast," squeaked Freda, echoing her man.

"That's fine."

A dozen witnesses would offer vague descriptions of the round-eyed warrior to police, but none of them could say exactly what he wore or how he vanished from the scene within a few brief seconds of the massacre. It had been self-defense, of course; they all agreed on that score, but investigators were concerned about the presence of a stranger in their city who could wreak such havoc, even if the late recipients of his attention had been gutter trash with records that included sixty-five arrests in thirteen years.

Who could predict what such a man might do?

As for the object of their urgent curiosity, he was intent on getting back to his hotel before he had to meet the others. There was still some time remaining, and he wanted to consult Chiun before the rendezvous.

It was a long shot, granted, but he hoped the two of them could figure out who wanted Remo dead.

3

"What do you know about Malaysia?" Dr. Harold Smith had asked him two weeks earlier.

"It's hot there," Remo answered after due consideration. "And it rains a lot."

Smith frowned, his face like an animated lemon. "And to think we marvel at the sorry state of modern education," he remarked.

"It's been a while since I read up on my geography," said Remo.

"Obviously. May I bring you up to date?"

"Please do."

It was Smith's specialty, in fact—not world geography, but bringing Remo up to speed on areas where major problems had arisen, sometimes overnight. In fact, the recognition and solution of those problems was the only reason Dr. Smith and Remo came together. Viewed another way, it was the only reason Remo was alive.

Harold W. Smith was the chief officer and sole surviving staffer of what had to be the smallest and most secretive clandestine-operations unit in the world. Created by a former President of the United States who had the foresight to predict a law-enforcement crisis in America before it came to pass, the unit—known as CURE—had been specifically conceived in an attempt to "save the Constitution by unconstitutional means." Behind the double-talk was a tiny, supersecret strike force, primed to deal with enemies and problems that the law couldn't legitimately touch.

CURE was an assassination squad, and Remo was the assassin.

He worked without a net, no backup teams, support divisions, agents standing by to bail him out if things went wrong. A job like that demanded special skills, a special man, and so it was that CURE had chosen wisely, reaching out for Remo when he least expected it. The group—if such it could be called—had engineered his "death," revived him and presented Remo with an offer he could not refuse: take on the troubles of the world, or die for real, while Dr. Smith went shopping for another paladin.

So Remo took the job, and while he would have liked to say that nothing could surprise him anymore, the world still held its share of mysteries. And some of them were served up to him on a silver platter, courtesy of Dr. Harold W. Smith.

"If you were asked about the state of global exploration in the nineties, Remo, what would you reply?'' Smith asked him, rocking backward in his high-backed swivel chair.

"We've pretty well disproved that flat-earth thing, unless you're one of those who think the moon walk was a sci-fi special filmed at the Nevada Test Site.''

"You've been watching Oprah.''

"Montel Williams,'' Remo said. "The smaller shows pick up a better class of flake these days.''

"And otherwise? In terms of exploration?''

Remo thought about it for a moment. "Looking at your average map,'' he said at last, "I'd have to say, 'Been there, done that.' ''

"Exactly. Looking at a map.''

Smith's lips turned upward in a small, uncustomary smile. He held it for perhaps three seconds, but the silence stretched between them for a good half minute, until Remo understood he was expected to respond.

"Okay, I'll bite. What's wrong with maps?'' he asked.

"They represent a combination of research and educated guesswork,'' Dr. Smith replied. "To start with, eighty percent of the planet is covered with water—oceans, seas, lakes, rivers. In many places, the oceans are well over six miles deep, and the average depth is about two miles. Divers rarely venture below fifty fathoms—about three hundred feet—and even then they seldom leave the continental shelf. Who really knows what's happening in the Pacific Ocean, for example? Who can say what's living down there, at the bottom?''

''Jacques Cousteau?''

Smith blinked at Remo and ignored the comment. He was on a roll. ''It would appear, despite our glaring ignorance of life beneath the sea, that we've at least explored the land we live on, yes?''

''I'd say.''

''Consider this—the greatest waterfall on earth is found in Venezuela, on the Churun River. Angel Falls, 3,212 feet in height. It was unknown until a pilot crashed his plane nearby, in 1937, and discovered it by accident. Thirty years later and not far away, cartographers discovered that a major mountain range, the Cerro Bolívar, had been misplaced by some two hundred miles on every map in print around the world.''

''That's sloppy work,'' said Remo.

''But it's not unusual,'' Smith told him, warming to his subject. ''Why, in northern California alone, we have seventeen thousand square miles that were last surveyed by land in 1859. Today, cartographers rely on aerial reconnaissance—they've even got the shuttle beaming lasers down to chart topography— but none of that says anything about what's going on beneath the forest canopy.''

''In California?''

''Anywhere!'' Smith answered. ''We've got scientists who sit in sterile labs and tell us Bigfoot cannot possibly exist in California, when their last excursion to the area took place before the Civil War. Imagine, Remo!''

"Bigfoot?"

"An example," Dr. Smith replied. "An archetypal mystery of nature."

"Ah."

"Which brings us to Malaysia."

"More or less."

"Are you familiar with the Tasek Bera region?"

Remo thought about it for a moment, frowned and shook his head. "I must have missed it."

"You and damned near everybody else," said Dr. Smith. "It's sixty-five miles due east of Kuala Lumpur as the crow flies, but sixty-five miles in the Malaysian jungle feels more like a thousand. Suffice it to say that the region is poorly explored."

"Fair enough."

"The name translates literally as 'Lake Bera,' but it refers to a much larger region, several hundred square miles of the worst swamp and jungle Malaysia can offer. The lake is a centerpiece, surrounded by the kind of wilderness white hunters used to call Green Hell."

"That's white men for you," Remo said.

The doctor's frown was there and gone, a flicker at the corners of his mouth. Smith never knew quite what to make of Remo or the changes that immersion in the secrets of Sinanju wrought between one meeting and the next.

"What do you know about uranium?" Smith asked him, shifting gears.

"Expensive, toxic, not approved for costume jewelry," Remo said. "I couldn't tell you who discovered it."

"Klaproth," said Dr. Smith, "in 1789. He's not our problem at the moment."

"I'm relieved to hear it."

"You are aware, I think, that weapons-grade uranium is not the most abundant element on earth."

"It rings a bell," said Remo.

"Hence the current seller's market in a world where everybody wants the Bomb," Smith said. "If you have access to uranium in quantities, you've got it made."

"Until your stash is confiscated by the government."

"Precisely." Dr. Smith seemed pleased. "Which leaves uranium prospectors in a kind of legal no-man's-land. They have to find the stuff—no easy job, at that—and try to sell it off for what they can before the nearest sovereign moves to seize the property and add it to existing stockpiles."

"We were getting to Malaysia," Remo interjected.

"Quite. About four months ago, a freelance expedition made its way into the Tasek Bera, looking for uranium where no man's gone before, that kind of thing. Officially, they were a group of birders. Phony papers from the Audubon Society, the whole nine yards.''

We're coming to the punch line, Remo thought, content to wait and listen while the doctor spelled it out. He would receive his marching orders soon enough.

''The team was out of touch for thirteen weeks,'' said Dr. Smith. ''That's verging on excessive, even for a jungle expedition, but security is paramount in operations of this type. You don't want anybody listening when you report a major find.''

''Okay.''

''Eight days ago,'' Smith said, ''some natives found a member of the expedition wandering along the Pahang River, ten or fifteen miles above the Tasek Bera. Terrence Hopper was his name, a veteran prospector with several major strikes behind him. Africa, Australia, South America.''

''Uranium?'' asked Remo.

''Most recently,'' Smith said, ''but Hopper's hunted everything from oil to gold and platinum. Not much on formal schooling, but he had a major reputation in the field.''

Past tense. That meant the man was dead, and Remo would not be required to send him on his way.

''What happened?''

"When they found him," Smith elaborated, "he was nude, malnourished and delirious. The fever spiked around 106, I'm told. It's not important. What concerns me—us—is Hopper's story, pieced together by a nursing sister in Bahau before he died."

"You said he was delirious."

"Indeed. That should not be confused with incoherent, though. Our Mr. Hopper, better known to friends and competition as 'the Mole,' had quite a tale to tell."

"I'm listening."

Smith paused a moment for effect. "He said his expedition was annihilated by a monster."

"So we're back to Bigfoot?"

"Worse. A dragon."

"I assume you've got a call in to Saint George."

"It's not a laughing matter, Remo."

"I can see that."

"As it happens, there have been reports of large reptilian creatures from the Tasek Bera spanning close to half a century. I don't suppose you've read Wavell's *Lost World of the East.*"

It was a rhetorical question. Smith knew before he spoke that Remo's reading was confined, by choice, to information necessary for successful execution of his latest mission. That and certain comic strips.

"Why don't you fill me in?" said Remo.

"Back in 1951, Stewart Wavell explored a portion of the Tasek Bera, interviewed the natives, observed the culture. He brought back stories of a massive predator the tribesmen call Nagaq. That's 'giant cobra,' more or less."

"A snake?"

"A reptile," Dr. Smith corrected him. "Descriptions vary, and it's understood that few who see the beast survive."

"Sounds like a fairy tale."

"Except when you evaluate the witnesses. Wavell himself heard eerie snarling sounds and spotted giant tracks."

"Without a camera handy, I presume."

"Malaysian soldiers and policemen have reported sightings," Smith went on, ignoring Remo. "Back in '62, an expedition from the Royal Air Force went looking for the creature."

"Let me guess—they didn't find it."

"Actually, no."

"In which case—"

"The reports continue. Every year or two, some filler item, mostly in the British press."

"I think that's what they call the silly season," Remo said.

"It hardly matters at the moment. Hopper's story—ravings, if you will—have sparked new interest in the Tasek Bera. There's an expedition forming as we speak, with funding from the Museum of Natural History, to check the region out once and for all.''

"Sounds like a tax write-off to me.''

"In any case, the expedition will be striking off from Kuala Lumpur in fifteen days, bound for the Great Unknown.''

"That's fascinating,'' Remo told him, stifling a yawn.

"I'm glad you think so. You'll be going with them.''

"Say again?''

"They need a herpetologist,'' said Dr. Smith.

"Who doesn't?''

"Dr. Clarence Otto was their first choice. He's a Ph.D. from San Diego State, affiliated with the zoo at Buena Park. If you've read anything significant on reptiles in the past ten years or so, you'll recognize the name.''

"Of course,'' said Remo, smiling through.

"Unfortunately for the expedition, Dr. Otto had an accident last weekend. Hit and run, I understand. The cast comes off around Thanksgiving.''

"That's a shame.''

"Which means our dragon hunters need a quick replacement.''

"And?''

"You're it.''

"I don't know how to tell you this,'' said Remo, "but I'm not exactly Mr. Lizard.''

"You have time to study up," Smith said. "I've requisitioned all the standard texts. It shouldn't be too difficult for you to pass."

"Depends on who I'm dealing with," said Remo.

"All right here." Smith nudged a thin vanilla folder toward the center of his desk. "The other members of your team are mostly into fossils, working on the supposition that Nagaq—if it exists—may be some kind of dinosaur. You'll be the only one on hand who works with living animals."

"In theory," Remo said.

"That's all you need," Smith told him. "Drop a Latin name from time to time. Sound educated."

"Right."

"You have my every confidence."

"Did it occur to you that someone on the team may want a name they recognize?"

"You have a name," Smith told him. "As of now, you're Dr. Renton Ward, from the New Orleans Serpentarium. You've published in the field— one book on New World vipers and a dozen monographs. You'll have a chance to read those, too. No photos with those publications, by the way."

"That's handy. What about the doctor?"

"He'll be taking a vacation in Tahiti, courtesy of CURE. If anybody calls to check on him, you're covered."

"So, you fixed the serpentarium?"

"They needed help with export permits on a couple of endangered specimens from Thailand. Also some assistance with their new construction budget."

"One more question—why?"

"Uranium," said Dr. Smith.

"I'm guessing you watch Abbott and Costello every chance you get."

"Why's that?"

"Third base," said Remo.

Smith considered that from several angles, finally dismissed the riddle as insoluble and let it go. "We think the expedition—or at least some members of it—may be more concerned with tracking down uranium than dinosaurs. If they can pick up Hopper's trail, find out what he was working on, they could be close enough to bring it home."

"What makes them think he had a lead? You said yourself he was delirious."

"With fever, right." Smith stared across the desk at Remo, hesitated once again before he spoke. "I may have failed to mention that his illness was not caused by any virus or bacteria."

"I'm waiting," Remo said.

"According to the autopsy report," Smith told him, "Terrence Hopper died of radiation poisoning." With that final enlightenment, Remo had been released to bone up for his task.

THE NEXT TWO WEEKS found Remo back in school. He waded through a dozen books on reptiles and amphibians, retained the information more or less verbatim with the tricks of concentration he had learned while studying Sinanju through the years. Before he finished, Remo knew that reptiles and their kin weren't ''cold-blooded''; they were poikilothermic, dependent on ambient heat for their own body temperature. He learned the difference between vipers and the older, more primitive *Elapidae,* with their short fixed fangs and neurotoxic venom. He knew the range and breeding habits of the major species, focusing on Southeast Asia, and could spot the difference between an alligator and a crocodile in seconds flat. If necessary, he could read a turtle's gender from the structure of its carapace and differentiate between the two suborders. A fat encyclopedia of prehistoric animals provided balance, filling in the background of an age when giant reptiles ruled the planet. By the time he polished off his ''own'' book—Renton Ward's *Revised Taxonomy of New World Vipers*—Remo felt he knew the subject inside out.

Which helped him not at all with explanations for Chiun.

In fact, the reigning Master of Sinanju seldom asked about the details of a mission, and he never asked about the motivation. For Chiun, it was enough that Dr. Harold Smith—whom he regarded as a powerful, albeit senile and demented emperor—had chosen special targets for elimination. The assassins of Sinanju had been mercenary killers for a thousand years and more. The very motto of Sinanju—Death Feeds Life—spoke volumes from the heart of the assassin's craft.

Still, Chiun was curious about the pile of weighty reading matter that distracted Remo from the proper study of Ung poetry and breathing exercises. Remo caught him paging through a sixty-five-page monograph on Asian tree frogs, noting Chiun's reaction in the almost microscopic elevation of an eyebrow.

"I have to play a new role for my latest mission, Little Father," Remo said.

Chiun responded with an airy wave, dismissing the remark. "Whatever is required," he said. "Emperor Harold Smith knows best." And to himself added, The idiot.

"What can you tell me about dragons?" Remo asked a moment later.

"Dragons?"

"You know, giant lizards breathing fire, that kind of thing."

"Sarcasm is a poor excuse for discourse," said the Master of Sinanju.

Remo rolled his eyes at that one. "You've been known to use your share."

"Nonsense. The Master of Sinanju does not bandy words with fools. I offer wise instruction and correct the faults of those who fail through negligence, stupidity and arrogance. If my instruction shames them, it is only through a private recognition of their own unworthiness.''

''About those dragons...''

Chiun considered Remo's question for a time before he spoke. ''In ancient days,'' he said at last, ''before the Supreme Being attained his pinnacle of achievement by creating the first Korean, it amused him to place monsters on the earth. Their forms were varied and diverse, but most of them were stupid creatures. It is written that a few possessed low cunning and the sort of greed that plagues most non-Koreans to the present day. They killed for sport, as some men do, and hoarded skulls as if old lizard bones had some intrinsic value. Finally, when the creator tired of watching them, he slaughtered most of those he had created to make way for human beings.''

''Slaughtered most?''

''It is my personal opinion—and most probably the truth—that the creator, driven by his need to see perfection in the flesh, neglected to exterminate the monsters thoroughly. A few survived and hid themselves away in caverns underneath the ground. They watched as men began to multiply and reap undreamed-of harvests from the earth. In time, they threatened man, collecting tribute in the form of gold and silver, precious stones and virgins.''

"Virgins?"

"Even monsters have to eat," Chiun replied.

"Of course. I wasn't thinking."

"A lamentable consistency," the Master of Sinanju said.

"So, you believe in dragons?" Remo asked.

"Belief implies a matter of opinion," said Chiun. "A wise man is conversant with the facts of life, reserving his belief for matters of the heart."

"Excuse me, Little Father. What I meant to ask—"

"You meant to ask if there are dragons in the earth today," Chiun finished for him. "My experience as Master of Sinanju offers no solution to the question, but there is a story...."

"Yes?"

"Before the days of Tamerlane, when Master Kim embodied the perfection of Sinanju, it is written that a foolish dragon tried to victimize the people of my village. He was old, this scaly worm, and knew the ways of lesser men from feasting on their brains. Of course, he did not know Sinanju, any more than a gorilla in the zoo can speak Korean."

"So, what happened?"

"Master Kim prevailed with only minimal exertion," said Chiun. "Have you not learned that size means nothing in Sinanju?"

"Kim went out and killed the dragon?"

"Master Kim," Chiun corrected him. "If you

peruse the early scrolls, you will discover an amusing recipe for lizard stew.''

"I'll pass," said Remo.

"Such disdain from one who has been known to gorge himself on charred cow's flesh." Chiun scanned the stack of books in front of him. "Is there no information here on dragons?"

"The authors aren't Korean."

"And still, their scribblings are accepted as the final word? Incredible."

"I'm going on a dragon hunt," said Remo. "I'll be gone awhile."

"It will be difficult to find one in the modern world," said Chiun. "Perhaps impossible."

"It doesn't matter," Remo told him. "Dr. Smith is more concerned with ringers and uranium."

A total lunatic, Chiun thought. Aloud he said, "The emperor is always right."

"I don't suppose you'd want to come along?"

"Will we be stopping at Sinanju?"

"Not this time. I'm sorry, Little Father."

"Is there television?"

"Almost certainly."

Chiun thought about it for another moment, finally nodding. "I shall go. If there are dragons to be slain, the Master of Sinanju should be there."

"My thoughts exactly," Remo said.

"Of course," Chiun replied. "You recognize perfection, even when it stands beyond your grasp."

4

It was a mile-long walk from the chaotic central market back to Remo's lodgings at the Hotel Merlin, on Jalan Sultan Ismail. He made the trek on foot, preferring crowds for cover. Also, he wanted to avoid taxis, because he didn't believe in coincidences. And in that case, he could expect other stalkers searching for him on the street. He wasn't followed from the marketplace, but that was little consolation in the present circumstances.

He was blown. Someone had tried to kill him, and even if the effort was clumsy it was proof positive that Remo's cover had been shot to hell. Logic called for him to scrub the mission, which had been compromised, take Chiun and fly back to the States as soon as possible, but Remo knew he couldn't run away.

His pride was part of it, a failing that Chiun and all the wisdom of Sinanju were unable to eradicate. And there was Remo's patriotic fervor, still a mystery to Chiun, who couldn't understand why any man—much less a trained assassin—would be anxious to surrender life for something so abstract as "God and country."

"What is it you love about America?" Chiun had asked his pupil in the early days of their association.

"I believe," Remo answered, "that this country has given so many people so many chances that it deserves to be protected."

"Why?" the Master of Sinanju prodded.

"Because I'm an American."

And that was that. Despite Chiun's admonitions that a man owed nothing to the country that had framed him for a murder he didn't commit, then staged his execution, drafting him into the service of a cause he didn't choose or fully understand, Remo wouldn't be shaken from the basic tenets of his faith in the United States.

America was threatened by the proliferation of nuclear arms in unreliable hands. If there was weapons-grade uranium available in the Malaysian jungle, it behooved America's defenders to ensure that none of it wound up in Baghdad, in Tehran, Beirut or any of a hundred other places where an A-bomb could ignite the fuse of global holocaust.

The job came down to Remo by coincidence, or maybe it was Fate. In either case, he viewed the execution of that duty as a privilege.

Chiun was watching television in their suite when Remo got there, seated on the floor, a perfect lotus, while he indulged his blossoming fascination for "Love's Secret Flame." This afternoon, it seemed that Whitney Calendar must finally decide between her husband, the philandering Arturo, and the handsome lawyer, Stetson Keating, who admired her none too subtly from a distance.

"How's it going with the Calendars?"

"Arturo is an idiot, enslaved by alcohol," said Chiun, "but he has possibilities. This Keating is not good for Whitney."

"Never trust a lawyer."

"You state the obvious."

Remo sat down on the nearest bed and waited for the next commercial break. "Somebody tried to kill me in the marketplace," he said when Chiun was momentarily distracted from the tube.

"A foolish bandit?" Chiun inquired.

"It was supposed to look that way," said Remo, "but they were assassins."

"Common thugs," Chiun replied. "If they had truly earned the designation of assassin, they would not be dead."

"How do you know I killed them?"

"You are not entirely foolish. Also, you are still alive. How many were there?"

"Six."

The Master's smile was tinged with pride, but he recovered in the twinkling of an eye. "So, they were clumsy thugs."

"I'd like to know who sent them," Remo said. "Right now, I'm flying blind."

"Trust no one," Chiun advised him, "and you won't be taken by surprise."

The douche commercial faded and resolved itself into a close-up of a frowning Whitney Calendar. The camera panned across to find Arturo staring at her, sipping from a whiskey glass.

"The curse of self-indulgence," said Chiun.

"I'm going now," Remo announced. "Time to meet the others."

If Chiun heard Remo speak, he gave no sign. His sparkling eyes were focused on the television set once more, his every sense apparently in tune with the fictitious trials and tribulations of the Calendars, McGreevys, Potters and their ilk.

Chiun's devotion to the soap opera had never ceased to baffle Remo, taken in conjunction with that fine disdain the Master of Sinanju demonstrated for most other things American. If he had not been so familiar with Chiun, the old man's crystal clarity of thought, he might have misjudged Chiun's preoccupation with the soaps as a precursor of senility. Instead, he took it simply as another part of what made Chiun the rare, complex, sometimes infuriating person that he was.

The door closed softly, locking automatically as Remo left the suite. Behind him, seated on the floor, the Master of Sinanju turned away from Whitney Calendar and faced the door.

"Trust no one," he said softly, in Korean. "And take care, my son."

THE SHANGRI-LA HOTEL was situated some four hundred yards beyond the Merlin and southward, where Jalan P. Ramlee crossed Jalan Sultan Ismail. It ranked among Kuala Lumpur's newest, most luxurious hotels, with several restaurants and more than seven hundred rooms.

It seemed to Remo that he wasn't followed on the walk between hotels, but then again, there was no point in tailing him if he was blown. His enemy—or enemies—would simply have to wait for Remo to present himself, an insect blundering into the spiderweb.

Except that he was not an ordinary insect, this one. He could sting, as they had learned with the attempt on Remo in the marketplace.

The message had been waiting for him when he checked in at the Hotel Merlin. Dr. Safford Stockwell, Ph.D., requested the pleasure of Dr. Ward's company at 5:00 p.m., to introduce the other members of the expedition and discuss last-minute strategy before departure, first thing in the morning. Remo hadn't bothered to return the call, preferring to remain aloof for now, but he wasn't about to miss the first glimpse of his fellow jungle travelers in the flesh.

Especially now that one of them had tried to have him killed.

The expedition's leader occupied suite 413. There was enough time left for Remo to bypass the elevator, taking to the stairs. As he ascended, Remo summed up what he knew of Safford Stockwell from the information passed along by CURE.

An eminent paleontologist with numerous publications and several major fossil discoveries to his credit, Dr. Stockwell was a Harvard graduate who did his alma mater proud. Of late, his specialty was Asian dinosaurs, which made him perfect for the Tasek Bera expedition. On the downside, he was fifty-eight years old and had confined himself to teaching, with sporadic forays into print, the past six years. Depending on his physical condition, Stockwell might become a burden once they left paved roads and riverboats behind. He didn't figure as a killer, but it was impossible to say with any certainty before they met in person. Age and dwindling economic prospects could be ample motivators for a change of character in later life, especially if the rumors about Stockwell's private life were accurate.

The rumbles out of Washington, where Stockwell taught at Georgetown and donated time at the Smithsonian, suggested an affair—some said a soon-to-be-announced engagement—featuring the veteran dinosaur hunter and his protégée, one Audrey Moreland. Blond and beaming in the snapshots Remo had examined, Moreland was a paleobotanist out of UCLA, some twenty-five years Stockwell's junior. They had formed a bond of sorts soon after her arrival on the teaching staff at Georgetown, and it had been only natural for Stockwell to select her as his number two when he was tapped to head up the Malaysian team.

As for the rumored romance, Remo didn't know or care if the reports were accurate. On balance, he imagined it would make things simpler all around if Dr. Moreland was in love with Stockwell. That way, she would be less likely to go into business for herself and start prospecting for uranium—or hiring killers on the side.

The fourth floor might have been deserted, judging from the traffic in the hallway. Remo closed the stairwell access door behind him, checked the numbers visible from where he stood and set off to his right, in search of 413. He knew that he was truly in the Orient, when large hotels ignored the superstitious Western terror of "unlucky" numbers.

"White men," Remo muttered, constantly amused—or angered—by the eccentricities of his own race. But oddly, he was less amused when Chiun made his biting observation.

He stopped at 413 and hesitated for a moment,

listening, his head turned slightly to one side and tilted toward the door. Other people would have heard a murmur of voices and the occasional word, but Remo's senses were heightened through Sinanju training, and the conversation came through, distinct and clear. Four people talking: two of them American, one British, by the sound, and one that could have been a native. Asian, anyway. One of the two Yanks was a woman, with a sultry voice that still possessed a cutting edge.

"What do we really know about this Dr. Renton Ward?" she asked the others. "I mean, we've never even seen him."

"Equal footing, there," her fellow countryman replied. "He hasn't seen us, either."

"You know what I mean," the woman answered, sounding peevish.

"We were fortunate that anyone could make the trip on such short notice," said the older man who must be Safford Stockwell. "Anyway, I've read his book and several of his monographs. He knows his subject."

"Even so—"

The subject of their conversation rapped three times against the door, imagining how easy it would be to put his hand and arm completely through the flimsy wooden panel. That would give them something to discuss around the campfire, but Remo wasn't prepared to discard his cover yet, despite the fact that it was evidently blown. They had a jungle trek ahead of them, and he would have to stay in character as long as possible.

The door was opened by a walking slab of muscle dressed in khaki. Jungle Jim on steroids, with the sickly sweet aroma of a full-time carnivore exuding from his sunbaked skin. The man was six foot five or six, with sandy hair combed straight back from a face that looked like sculpted leather. He was looking down his nose at Remo, literally, with a pair of cold gray eyes. That nose had taken brutal punishment at one time, and an impressive scar ran from the left eyebrow to the jaw hinge, just below his ear.

"And you are?"

Here's the Brit, thought Remo as he answered, "Renton Ward."

An older man stepped forward, easing past the hulk and offering his hand. The grip was firm enough, but there was no real strength behind it.

"Dr. Ward, come in, please. We were just discussing you."

"That explains it, then," said Remo.

"Sorry?"

"Why my ears were burning."

"Ah." Confusion flickered for an instant in the aging academic's eyes before he shook it off and introduced himself. "I'm Dr. Stockwell. Safford Stockwell."

Fearless leader, Remo thought, as if I couldn't guess. The man was fifty-eight, according to his file, but could have passed for ten years older at a glance. White hair, receding in a George Bush pattern, and a face that seemed to droop, with wattles showing underneath his chin. Whatever muscle tone and color Stockwell had acquired from years of fieldwork, chasing dinosaur remains, had long since vanished under the fluorescent classroom lights. He might be stronger than he looked, of course, but Remo guessed that he would burn out early on the trail, become a major burden if their group encountered any major obstacles requiring physical exertion.

"My assistant, Dr. Moreland."

Stockwell made the introduction with a flourish, not quite showing off his prize, but close enough.

And what a prize she was. A honey blonde, blue eyes that gave her angel face a hint of something more sophisticated, verging on exotic. World-class breasts, unfettered beneath a Thai silk blouse. Legs better suited to the runway at a fashion show than any jungle game trail.

"Call me Audrey, please."

"My pleasure. Renton Ward."

Her mentor stepped between them, steering Remo toward the hulk who manned the door. "Pike Chalmers," Stockwell said. "Our designated troubleshooter, if you will."

Some kind of military background there, thought Remo. Maybe service as a mercenary, once he pulled the pin. Pike Chalmers had the look of someone who enjoyed the act of killing for its own sake, as a form of sport.

The hand he offered Remo could have doubled for a catcher's mitt. His grip would be a calculated crusher, showing off, and Remo braced himself, prepared for anything.

"So, you're the reptile man," said Chalmers, tightening his grip.

"That's right."

The trick was not resistance or brute force, but a strategic application of sufficient pressure to the carpal nerves and tendons. Remo felt the big man's knuckles crunch together like ball bearings, but restrained himself from breaking any bones. The big man grimaced and retrieved his hand, concealing it behind his back as he began to flex the fingers, testing them for damage.

"And, of course, our escort from the Ministry of the Interior," said Stockwell, guiding Remo toward a slim Malaysian in his thirties. "Second Deputy Sibu Bintulu Sandakan."

The small man bowed ever so slightly from the waist in lieu of shaking hands. Ordinarily Remo followed more-casual American manners, but some past drilling by Chiun prompted him to follow suit. So he took care to show the proper courtesy, his

bow a bit more solemn and pronounced, accentu-
ated by averting his gaze. The second deputy of
who-knows-what seemed pleased.

"I hope you will accept the greetings and best
wishes of my government," said Sibu Sandakan.
"It is my privilege to accompany such fine, distin-
guished guests on their excursion to the bush."

"The privilege is ours," said Remo, wrapping up
the niceties.

He glanced around the room at each face in turn,
alert for any sign that one or more of them were
disappointed or surprised to find him still alive.
Pike Chalmers, glaring back at Remo like a
wounded bear, would require watching, but there
was nothing in his manner to suggest that he had
hired the gang of thugs to waylay Remo in the marketplace. If anything, he seemed more like the sort
of man who would enjoy attending to the dirty work
himself. As for the others, Sandakan and Stockwell
seemed innocuous enough, while Audrey Moreland
favored Remo with a smile that stopped just short
of flirting.

So much for deduction.

Simple logic told him that some person in the
room—and possibly some two- or three-way combination—had conspired to rub him out before the
expedition left K.L. Whoever was responsible was
more adept at covering than Remo had expected.
There would be no giveaway disclosures, nothing

to betray the ringer here and now, before they hit the grueling jungle trail.

But Dr. Smith's suspicions were confirmed, at least, if nothing else. There obviously was a ringer on the team, or more than one, who meant to safeguard what was perceived as a potential fortune by eliminating any wild cards from the deck.

How had the ringer penetrated Remo's cover? Was the bungled hit a simple effort to ensure that no untested strangers joined the team? Were all of them involved, including the unfortunately sidelined Dr. Otto?

"Shall we get to business, then?" asked Stockwell, bringing Remo's thoughts back to the here and now.

"Suits me."

Five chairs had been positioned to surround a glass-topped coffee table, where a two-by-three-foot topographic map lay open, anchored on the left and right by ashtrays. Remo took a seat with Audrey Moreland on his right, Pike Chalmers facing him across the table. Dr. Stockwell took a folding pointer from his pocket, snapped it open and craned forward in his chair to start the briefing.

"We are here," he said, the pointer tapping a spot on the map that was named for Kuala Lumpur. "And our final destination...is...here."

The pointer slid a foot or so to Stockwell's left and settled on a patch of blue that had to be a lake, its several fingers splayed as if to mimic the impression of a malformed hand.

"The Tasek Bera," Stockwell said, his voice pitched low to emphasize the drama. "It's 64.7 miles due east, in Pahang Province. It appears to be an easy trip on paper."

"Easy, nothing," Chalmers said. "That jungle's broken more good men than I can name."

"As I was saying—" Stockwell caught himself just short of glaring at the hulk "—it seems an easy trip on paper, but we have our work cut out for us. We'll have to make the trip in stages, starting with a flight tomorrow morning, up to Temerloh. From there, we take a riverboat due south, another forty miles, to Dampar. That will be our jumping-off point, as it were. No airstrip at Dampar, you see."

"No bloody road worth mentioning," Chalmers added.

Dr. Stockwell cleared his throat before continuing. "We'll meet our guide in Dampar. Deputy Sandakan has taken care of the arrangements there."

"Indeed," the little Malay said to no one in particular. "We have engaged one of the best guides in the province for your expedition."

"From the time we leave Dampar," Stockwell went on, "it should take perhaps three days to reach the Tasek Bera proper. We will travel by canoe as far as possible, but I'm afraid there'll be some hiking at the end.''

"A bloody lot of hiking," Chalmers said, still glaring hard at Remo.

"I'll keep up the best I can," offered Remo, smiling at the hulk.

"You haven't spent much time in Asia, have you?" Audrey Moreland touched his forearm lightly as she spoke, then casually withdrew her hand.

"Not much," said Remo, sticking to the script.

"I've read your work on New World vipers," Stockwell said. "It was a fascinating piece of research."

"This will be a change from South America," said Remo, putting on a small, self-deprecating smile.

"No end of bloody snakes, though, if that's what you care for," Chalmers said.

"Some of them must be dangerous," said Audrey, sounding more like a B-movie damsel in distress than a professor on the verge of making history.

"There is some risk, of course," said Remo. "Kraits and cobras are the greatest hazard where we're going, though I doubt we'll be fortunate enough to glimpse a king cobra."

"Lord, I hope not." Audrey shuddered at the

very notion, her round breasts wobbling slightly underneath the clinging fabric of her blouse.

"Most of the Malaysian vipers, by contrast, tend to be smaller and less aggressive. The genus *Trimeresurus* is widely represented, with both terrestrial and arboreal species, but they seldom trouble man unless directly threatened."

"What about the big ones?" This time, Audrey let her fingers come to rest on Remo's knee.

"Reticulated pythons are the ones to watch," he told her, turning up the wattage on his smile. "Officially, the record is just over thirty-two feet."

"They must be dangerous, as well," said Audrey.

"Not unless you go out of your way to tackle one," he answered. "Of course, there is one documented case in which a fourteen-year-old Malay boy was eaten by a seventeen-foot python. As it happens, that's the only case on record of a human being swallowed whole."

"Can you imagine?" Audrey shivered. "Being eaten up alive."

"I wouldn't worry," Remo said. "You're much more likely to be eaten by mosquitoes.

"Or the bloody crocs," said Chalmers, scowling as he lit up an unfiltered cigarette.

"We can't rule out a few stray crocodiles, of course," acknowledged Remo, "but the fact is, none are native to the area we'll be exploring."

"Is that right?" The big ex-soldier's tone was challenging.

"Afraid so, Mr. Chambers."

"Chalmers."

"Sorry, my mistake." He turned back toward Audrey, all smiles. "*Crocodylus siamensis* is the most common species in Southeast Asia, but its normal range cuts off about two hundred miles due north of here. Now, *Crocodylus porosus* is larger, a certified man-eater, but its typical habitat runs toward coastal waters—hence the popular nickname of 'saltwater crocodile.' It's possible that one might swim upstream along the Rompin, here—" he pointed to the map, his elbow nudging Audrey's thigh in the process "—but it's not too likely."

"Well, it's good to have an expert on the team," sneered Chalmers.

"We can all learn something, I imagine," Remo told him.

"If we're lucky," Stockwell interjected, "we'll have bigger specimens to deal with than a crocodile, in any case."

"Now, Safford…" Audrey's tone was almost chiding.

"Yes, I know," said Stockwell. "Mustn't get my hopes up. Even so, you won't mind if I keep my fingers crossed."

"You think it's really possible," Sibu Sandakan

spoke up, "to find a prehistoric creature in the Tasek Bera?"

"Prehistoric specimens are not uncommon, if truth be told," said Stockwell. "Why, the lowly cockroach is a prime example, and the crocodiles described by Dr. Ward have survived, more or less unchanged, from *Protosuchus* in the late Triassic period, more than two hundred million years ago."

"Incredible!" The little Malay's eyes were sparkling with enthusiasm. "There is hope, then."

"For a startling find?" The expedition's leader glanced at Audrey Moreland, smiled, restraining his enthusiasm with an effort. "I believe that in a region like the Tasek Bera, anything is possible."

"We must be dazzling Dr. Ward," said Audrey.

"I can use a little dazzling from time to time," Remo replied.

"You've brought the necessary gear, I trust?" asked Dr. Stockwell.

"Hiking clothes, insect repellent, all that sort of thing," said Remo. "Back at my hotel, that is. I'll need a chance to pack."

"We all have work to do in that regard," said Stockwell. "I propose that we adjourn and meet again for breakfast, in the restaurant downstairs. Is 6:00 a.m. too early?"

"Not for me," said Remo, while the others shook their heads in unison.

"Till six o'clock, then."

Stockwell rose, a gesture of dismissal from the dean, and Remo made his way in the direction of the exit. He was only halfway there when Audrey Moreland overtook him and stopped him with a warm hand on his arm.

"I'm glad you've joined our little party, Dr. Ward."

"Please, call me Renton."

"Very well. I'm glad you're coming with us, Renton."

"So am I."

"I'll see you in the morning?"

"Bright and early," Remo said.

Her smile spoke volumes on the benefits of adolescent orthodontia.

"I'll be looking forward to it, Renton."

Remo rode the elevator down to give himself a change of pace, still wondering which one of them had tried to kill him in the marketplace and when the next attempt would come.

5

"What did you think of him?"

"Of whom?" asked Audrey Moreland.

Safford Stockwell smiled indulgently. "Our Dr. Ward. He caught your fancy, didn't he?"

"Oh, Safford, don't be silly. Just professional interest."

They were still in Stockwell's suite—alone at last, but Stockwell didn't feel relaxed somehow. A part of that was natural anticipation and anxiety, he realized. They were embarking, almost at the crack of dawn, on what would either be the crowning highlight or the most embarrassing fiasco of his long career.

But there was something else on Stockwell's mind besides the hunt. A twinge of something the professor was reluctant to identify.

"It's not a problem if you like him, Audrey," Stockwell said.

"I've barely met the man, for heaven's sake." There was a hint of irritation in her tone now, recognizable at once to anyone who knew her moods.

"I'm simply saying—"

"What? What are you saying, Safford?"

And the question stopped him cold.

It was an article of faith at Georgetown, where they taught and frequently took meals together, that there must be something "going on" between himself and Audrey Moreland. Stockwell didn't circulate the rumors, but he didn't bust his hump to contradict them, either. If the rest of Georgetown's staff—composed primarily of men and women Stockwell's age or older—chose to think that he had won the heart of Audrey Moreland, who was he to run around the campus bursting their balloons?

In truth, he had been startled when the first such rumor came to his attention, overheard in passing. Surprise had quickly given way to irritation, but before he got around to setting anybody straight, Professor Stockwell—then a sprightly lad of fifty-six—had felt a new emotion horning in.

He had been flattered.

It was something at his age for men who knew him well—several of them younger men, at that—to think he had the looks, charm and stamina to woo and hold a thirty-something female with traffic-stopping looks and a vivacious personality. The ego strokes were even more rewarding when he learned that many women staffers also took the story at face value.

They believed in him somehow.

He had been driven to a confrontation with his bathroom mirror, normally a prospect he avoided like the plague. The past few years, his mirror had become the enemy, a living *Picture of Dorian Gray* that emphasized the ravages of time up close and personal. The spreading rumors of his prowess as a Casanova forced him to look deeper, though, to see what others saw.

In fact, he never found it, but it didn't matter in the end. The lovely, ego-stroking rumors kept on circulating, pumping up his self-esteem, and while he never made a move on Audrey Moreland—pride was one thing, but courage another—Stockwell had begun to think of them as…well, a couple. There was nothing to it, and he took himself to task on more than one occasion, but it felt good just pretending and it did no harm.

Except when he felt pangs of jealousy.

That was the height of foolishness, he realized, and Stockwell had the common sense to keep those feelings secret, hidden from the world at large.

Until tonight.

"I'm sorry, Audrey." It wasn't an answer to her question, but he had no answer that would get him off the hook. "I didn't mean to come off sounding like your father."

"I'm a big girl, Safford." Telling him the obvious, as if he hadn't noticed, each and every day since they were introduced. "And I can take care of myself."

"Of course."

"It's sweet of you to worry, but I didn't fly half-way around the world to fall in love."

"That wasn't what I meant," he said, casting about to try to salvage something from the conversation. "I was curious to find out what you thought of Dr. Ward as an addition to our little family."

"Some family," she answered, and surprised him with her tone. "At least he's not like Chalmers. God, that man disgusts me with his swaggering and all that talk about the animals he's killed for fun."

"We need a man like Chalmers, Audrey. Just in case, you understand?"

"He's still a bully, Safford. And I hate the way he looks at me, like he was ordering a piece of meat."

"Has he done anything?"

The question slipped through Stockwell's teeth before he had a chance to catch it. What did he propose to do if Chalmers had made some improper overtures to Audrey? Challenge him to fight? The very notion was ridiculous.

"Not yet," she said, and let him off the hook. "I just don't like him. I don't trust him."

"He comes highly recommended, Audrey."

"By the old-boy network, I've no doubt. They stick together, just like any other clique."

"What is it that you think he's up to?" Stockwell asked her.

"How should I know? If we find this creature—if there is a creature to be found—what would prevent his killing it on sight to make another trophy?"

Stockwell longed to assume the role of noble hero, but knew how it would sound. Pathetic boasting. "We will, Audrey. All of us. Remember Sandakan. He represents the state. Our Mr. Chalmers may be callous, but I don't believe he's up to challenging the whole Malaysian government, do you?"

"This animal we're looking for would be worth millions, Safford, money in the bank. Of course..."

She didn't have to finish the remark. He recognized her skepticism and tried to mirror it, in fact, to keep himself from looking like a fool. A search for living dinosaurs was probably quixotic, possibly insane, but he had still leaped at the chance to head the expedition. Whether it was simple boredom with his teaching post and part-time work at the Smithsonian, or longing for a greater glory that would soon be hopelessly beyond his reach, Professor Stockwell had signed on despite the giggle factor, offering his solid reputation as a sacrifice. If they returned to Georgetown empty-handed...well, his job would still be waiting for him, thanks to tenure, and in the meantime there was no need to think about the personal humiliation he would have to face. A couple of the wags on campus were already calling him Professor Challenger, and they would have a roaring field day if he failed.

"I'm confident that the authorities can deal with any problems of that nature," he told Audrey. "All we have to do is find the creature, yes?"

"You're right, of course," she said. "But I don't have to like him."

"No, my dear, you certainly do not." Emboldened by the moment, Stockwell took a shot. "How would you like a glass of wine?"

"I'd better not," she told him, softening rejection with a smile. "We've got an early start tomorrow, and I still have things to do."

"I understand." Too well, he understood. "I'll see you in the morning, then. Sleep well."

"You, too."

She left him, headed back to her adjoining room, and Stockwell double-locked the door behind her. You could never be too careful.

"DO YOU BELIEVE their story?"

Sibu Sandakan faced his superior across a massive teakwood desk, his bearing ramrod straight. He had to stop and think about the question, even now, though it had been a frequent topic of discussion at the office for the past few weeks.

"I think their leader is sincere," he said at last.

"I'm not sure even he believes, but there is hope. He yearns for immortality."

"And what about the others?" asked Germuk Sayur, first deputy to Jantan Separuh, the minister of the interior.

"The Englishman loves money. He will go wherever he is paid to go. As for the new American, I think his curiosity is piqued, but he is skeptical."

He offered no opinion on the woman, nor was it requested. Sibu Sandakan and his immediate superior were of a single mind where females were concerned. This blond American might be a full professor back in Washington, but it was still impossible for them to take her seriously as a guiding force behind the expedition. Women followed men. So it had always been; so it would always be.

"And you, Sibu? What do you think about their chances?"

"Of returning with a dinosaur?" He frowned, considering the problem, desperate not to come off sounding like a superstitious peasant. "You have heard the Tasek Bera stories, sir. You know of the reports from our own soldiers and police."

"Indeed. I'm asking what you think."

"I don't believe in fairy stories," Sibu Sandakan replied, "but who can say about such things?"

"The minister has some concern about this dead man, Hopper."

"Oh?"

"He was prospecting for uranium, as you're aware. You also know the circumstances of his death."

"Yes, sir."

"There is suspicion at the ministry," Germuk Sayur continued. "Some believe this party may be more concerned with mining than with monsters."

"Customs has examined their equipment, I assume."

"Within their limits, Sibu. It would not require much effort to conceal a simple Geiger counter—or to purchase one from sources in the country, if it came to that."

"There are no mining experts in the party," Sandakan reminded his superior.

"None that we know of."

"Sir?"

"Who knows if anyone is what he claims to be these days? A passport can be forged, biographies concocted out of nothing. The Americans are skilled at fabrication."

"You believe their government may be involved?" The very notion boggled Sibu's mind.

"I am suggesting only possibilities," Germuk Sayur replied. "But then again, why not?"

"They would be risking much embarrassment."

"With much to gain, Sibu. A fortune for the taking."

"Surely we would not permit them to invade our sovereignty?"

"Americans are devious," the deputy reminded him. "They have been known to bribe officials, threaten economic sanctions when their will is thwarted, even sponsor revolutions to unseat a government if all else fails."

"I will be vigilant," said Sibu Sandakan.

"Is vigilance enough, I wonder?"

"Sir?"

"We must be ready to respond at the first sign of treachery, Sibu. You understand?"

He nodded, more from force of habit than real understanding. Sibu Sandakan was troubled by the turn this little chat had taken. He was no spy, much less a soldier or policeman. Nothing in his background had prepared him for the kind of cloak-and-dagger games Germuk Sayur was evidently planning.

"You will carry this." The deputy retrieved a plastic box, no larger than a cigarette pack, from an inside pocket of his coat and slid it toward Sibu across the desk. "It is a radio transmitter, specially designed for an emergency. You cannot send a message in the normal sense, by speaking into it, nor is it able to receive. Simplicity dictates a single button that, when pressed, transmits a nonstop signal for the next eight hours, on a special frequency. From noon tomorrow, until you return, the ministry will have an armed security detachment standing by with helicopters, waiting for your signal."

Sibu Sandakan was even more uneasy now. "What sort of an emergency?" he asked.

"You'll be the judge of that, Sibu. If the Americans should find uranium instead of dinosaurs, for instance, they will need immediate protection."

House arrest would be more like it, Sandakan imagined. Someone in the capital could always sort the matter out with an apology, by which time the uranium would be secure in native hands. That much was only fair, but he resented being drafted into work for which he wasn't trained or temperamentally inclined. Still, he couldn't refuse an order from the ministry.

The plastic box felt almost weightless in his hand. He stroked his thumb across the button, trying to imagine the reaction that a pound or two of pressure would evoke.

"You will, of course, be circumspect about its use." It was an order, plain and simple.

"Yes, sir. Certainly." Another thought was nagging at him now. "What if...?"

"Go on, Sibu."

"What if the expedition is successful, sir?"

"What if they find a prehistoric animal, you mean?"

"Yes, sir."

Germuk Sayur could only smile. "In that case, they will also need protection, Sibu, will they not?"

"The Englishman—"

"Must pose no threat to an endangered species. Not when its survival could prove beneficial to the state."

"I'm not sure—"

"Think of it, Sibu. The tourist trade we could attract. You've seen *Jurassic Park?*"

"No, sir."

"I recommend it highly. If museums can turn a profit from display of dusty bones, think what a modern and well-managed game preserve could do with living animals."

It was beyond imagination, and Sibu let it go.

"Yes, sir," he said.

"You're clear on your instructions, then? A signal in the case of an emergency, but no hysterics. If the party finds uranium or giant lizards, you must let us know immediately. Otherwise..."

"I understand."

"In that case, you should get some rest. You have a great adventure waiting for you in the morning."

"Yes, sir."

As he closed the office door behind him, pocketing the little radio transmitter, Sibu Sandakan was wishing he could pass the whole assignment off to someone else. A city boy at heart, he had no wish to camp out in the jungle, sleep beneath mosquito nets and watch each step he took for fear of deadly snakes. The rest of it—the dinosaurs, uranium and geopolitics—was all too much to cope with. He would simply have to watch and wait, be ready with the panic button at the first sight of a monster or duplicity from the Americans, whichever surfaced first.

With any luck at all, he told himself, the whole excursion would turn out to be a waste of time. He could endure the laughter of his friends around the office for a week or two, until they found some new amusement for themselves.

But the alternative was frightening.

Sibu Bintulu Sandakan was worried that he might turn out to be one more endangered species in the trackless jungle, and a flying squad of soldiers would be precious little good to him if they arrived too late.

PIKE CHALMERS LIT his last unfiltered cigarette and crumpled up the empty pack, discarding it with no attempt to find a litter can. The Malays lived like rodents in his estimation, crowded cheek by jowl, the best of them perhaps two generations from the bush. Surrendering the colony had been one of Her Majesty's mistakes—like India, Jamaica, Kenya and the rest—but it was no good crying over spilled milk now. That train had left the station, thank you very much, and it was never coming back.

Pike Chalmers missed the glory days of empire, even though the bulk of it had been before his time. He had been eight years old the year his father died, a victim of the Mau Mau uprising in Kenya. There were lean times after that, in Manchester, despite a soldier's pension for the widow and her son. It had been only natural for Chalmers to enlist when he was seventeen, but there were no great wars remaining to be fought. Three tours in Northern Ireland were enough, and he had briefly gone the mercenary route in Africa, before discovering that he could make more money killing helpless animals than stalking men with guns who might shoot back. Safari guides were always in demand, and when the namby-pamby "greens" began to flex their legislative muscles, curbing the majority of classic hunts, the flabby tourists with their cameras still required a man of courage and experience to take them out and bring them safely back again.

But it was killing Chalmers loved. You could forget about the "metaphysics of the hunt," conserving nature with a harvest of the weak, all that manure sportsmen ladled on their game to make it more politically correct. Back in the old days, you went out to shoot a rhino or a tiger for the fun of it, a stylish trophy all the validation any man required. White hunters were admired for their abundant courage, knowledge of the wilderness, the number of their kills.

It was a new world now, and Chalmers didn't like it much. Besides the hunting question, strident activists had poked their noses into everything from sex to smoking. A majority of Yanks had voted for a President who dodged the draft and promised higher taxes to protect them from themselves in any given situation, while at home the royals had fallen into scandal and disgrace.

Pike Chalmers often thought that he was born too late, a man whose time had come and gone before he made his way onto the stage. It would have pleased him to reverse the flow of time, skip thirty-five or forty years back into history and take his rightful place among the men who built an empire girdling the globe.

But why stop there?

If he could work a miracle, why not go back a century, get in at the beginning of the action, killing Zulus, Boers, Afghans. It had been open season in those days. Britannia ruled the waves, and it was easier to pack the white man's burden in a simple hearse than listen to the wogs and kaffirs whine about their "rights."

Of course, there were no time machines, no miracles, but men of daring still got lucky now and then, despite the odds against them. Chalmers reckoned he was overdue for some good luck, the way things had been going in his life of late, and if a handful of his colleagues thought that he was balmy, signing on to join a dinosaur hunt, he knew that most of their remarks sprang out of envy. They were jealous bastards, seeing Chalmers land an easy job of work while they were left out in the cold.

And what if it paid off?

Suppose there was a bloody dinosaur waiting for them out there in the bush. Pike Chalmers couldn't keep from smiling as he thought about the possibilities. He could retire on profits from the book and movie rights, pick up a ghost to hammer out the manuscript for pocket change and relocate to Ireland, where the writers lived tax free. Do all the talk shows like a bloody rock-and-roll star. He could well afford to let the Yank professors write their textbooks filled with charts and diagrams, all kinds of Latin jawbreakers that only another scientist would ever read. The real loot came from exploitation in the media.

Pike Chalmers thought he might be forced to hire an agent if the money started pouring in too fast for him to handle. Life was hard, but he would do his best to cope.

And if he felt like keeping all the glory for himself, then he could see his way to being the expedition's sole survivor. There were a hundred easy ways to die in the Malaysian jungle, even when you didn't have a handy dinosaur around to gobble the remains. This lot were amateurs, babes in the woods. He could dispose of them as if they were nothing, never even break a sweat. Without the profs around, there would be no one to dispute Pike's version of events, whatever that turned out to be. Something heroic, certainly, to keep himself at center stage.

He had begun to shop around for leading men to play his part in the inevitable movie when he caught himself. It was a grave mistake to count your eggs before they hatched, especially if they were dinosaur eggs. Pike Chalmers was no scholar, but he knew the odds were stacked against survival of a species thought to be extinct for umpteen billion years. Simple deductive thinking said the trip would be another paying job and nothing more.

Or maybe not.

They didn't have to find a bloody dinosaur for Chalmers to get something extra from the trip. That Audrey Moreland was a tasty dish, and no mistake. Oh, she was giving him the brush right now, the way her kind so often did, but that was in a posh hotel, when she could call downstairs for room service to fetch her up a glass of bubbly any time she chose.

It was a different story in the jungle, when you said goodbye to feather beds, dry clothes and decent food. The only running water in the Tasek Bera would be rain and jungle streams; her next-door neighbors would be snakes and scorpions and hungry tigers.

Not to mention Chalmers, most dangerous of all.

Before their little trek was finished, Audrey Moreland would acquire a new appreciation of his talents, not just on the trail, but in the sleeping bag, as well. She might protest at first, but who was there to take her part against a real man when the chips were down?

That brought his thoughts back to the new bloke, Dr. Renton Ward. A strange duck, that one. Didn't look like he could tear a piece of paper if he used both hands, but he had turned Pike's crushing grip around, and no mistake. The knuckles of his right hand still felt sore, as if he'd punched a concrete wall. Some kind of trick, no doubt, but Chalmers would be ready for him next time. Keep an eye on that one all the way, damned right, and fix a nasty accident first chance he got.

Pike Chalmers thought of Audrey flirting with the little bastard when she'd only just been introduced a moment earlier. There was no accounting for taste, of course, but she would find her choices strictly limited in two or three days' time. The old fart she was traveling with would never cut the mustard, and their native chaperon...well, he was just another bloody wog.

It was an article of faith with Chalmers that all women wanted sex from men who showed them who was boss. Some needed more persuasion, but he never missed…except, of course, with lesbians. And he had shown a few of those what they were missing, too.

A real man had the right—make that the duty—to extend himself where women were concerned, and Chalmers was a man who always tried to do his duty.

Yes, indeed, there would be some surprises waiting for his snooty clients on the trail. And it would be a pleasure watching as they tried to cope.

Pike Chalmers found that he could hardly wait. In fact, why should he wait?

The night was young, and he was feeling lucky.

First, a stop to buy more cigarettes, then he would take a chance and roll the bloody dice.

6

"None of your fellow travelers were startled to behold you in the flesh?" asked Chiun.

"I couldn't tell. It didn't seem that way."

The Master of Sinanju made a clucking noise. "White men neglect the art of observation," he suggested.

"I observed them well enough," said Remo. "Maybe one of them was covering."

"Then you did not observe," Chiun informed him. "There are always signals to betray a liar. Deviations in the normal pattern of respiration. Beads of perspiration at the hairline. Possibly a twitching of the eyebrows."

"Nothing," Remo answered, having checked for all the normal signs. "I got the bad eye from their pet gorilla, but he doesn't strike me as a mastermind."

"Did you reveal yourself to him?" asked Chiun.

"Not really."

"So you did."

"A little squeeze when we shook hands is all, to put him in his place."

"Put him on notice, you should say. He is a white man?"

"British, right."

"You may be fortunate in that case. White men, in their ignorance, are blinded by the perfect glory of Sinanju. He will probably suspect that you pump iron and do aerobics with the round-eyed girls on television."

Remo finished packing, double-checked the bathroom and the closet for forgotten items, finally zipped his duffel bag. "You know," he said, "it's always possible that I was burned by someone else, outside the team."

Chiun's shrug was lost inside the folds of his kimono. "Anything is possible," he said. "An ape may learn to sing someday. But is it logical?"

"You're right."

"Of course."

It made no sense, when Remo thought about it, for an outside force to want him dead. He was unknown outside of CURE, and his appointed cover was innocuous in the extreme. How many people outside academia had ever heard of Dr. Renton Ward, and how many of those would try to kill him in Malaysia of all places? Even if the herpetologist was eyebrow deep in debt to the most vicious of New Orleans loan sharks, they would deal with him at home, where they controlled the playing field. And CURE would certainly have run a background check on Dr. Ward before they cut a deal to borrow his identity.

No matter how he tried to skull it out, he kept returning to square one. The hit team in the central marketplace had been assigned to deal with Remo—or with "Renton Ward"—because someone was anxious to prevent his linking up with Dr. Stockwell's expedition. Motive was an unknown quantity, beyond deduction from the evidence in hand.

What evidence? he asked himself. The thugs who tried to kill him were beyond confessing now. The only way for them to finger their employer would be through an Ouija board. That left four individuals who might have motives for disposing of the new man on the team, with better than a dozen combinations possible if two or more of them were in cahoots. And so far, Remo didn't have a shred of proof connecting any one of them with the attempted hit.

He gave up trying to divine why someone he had never met before should want him dead. The possibilities seemed endless, anything from academic jealousy to common greed. CURE's background check had ruled out prior connection between Renton Ward and other members of the expedition. If there was an ancient grudge involved, one glimpse of Remo's face would be enough to tell the other party that they had a ringer on the team.

Which brought him back to wondering how anyone, much less a desk-bound academic, could have blown his cover off this early in the game.

"Where are you going?" asked Chiun.

And Remo had to smile at that. He had been standing by his bed, immobile, staring at his duffel bag, but Chiun could tell that he was on the verge of going out. The old Korean never failed to keep him on his toes.

"I thought I'd take a walk," said Remo.

"White man's logic," said the Master of Sinanju. "When confronted with a long trek through the jungle, you prepare by walking aimlessly around a city."

"It's a form of relaxation. As you know, I don't need lots of sleep."

"You need more training," said Chiun. "A student who has barely scratched the surface of Sinanju should devote his every waking hour to the work."

"First thing, when I get back from dinosaur hunting."

"I accede to this because Emperor Harold Smith demands it," said Chiun, "but you are not prepared."

"It's too bad you can't join us," Remo said.

"This frail old specter, tramping through the jungle like a savage?'' Chiun was visibly appalled by the idea.

"You wouldn't pass inspection anyway. No Ph.D.''

"True wisdom does not come from scrambling the letters of the alphabet behind your name," said Chiun.

"You got that right," said Remo.

"Was there any doubt?''

"I'll be home soon.''

"Home is Sinanju. This is but a place to sleep and hang your clothes.''

"Don't watch the tube too late. You need your beauty sleep.''

"More slander. The Korean countenance, illuminated by Sinanju, is perfection multiplied.''

Chiun would always have the last word, even if he had to whisper in Korean. Remo let it go and closed the door behind him. Never mind the dead bolt. Any hotel burglar who might try to loot this room was in for a surprise.

He took the stairs, ten flights, and practiced running down the banisters for exercise. It would have helped to take his shoes off, but he managed nicely just the same. A pause before he went out through the lobby, checking out his pulse and respiration. Normal on both counts, despite the moderate exertion.

Kuala Lumpur waited for him, light and darkness

intermingled with the smells of frangipani, curry and satay, the many Chinese-food stalls, here and there a hint of backed-up sewage. Remo drifted toward the smaller side streets, watching out behind him without seeming to. If he was being followed, the pursuers were too skillful for his senses to detect them. That was always possible, of course, and yet...

Within a quarter-hour, Remo satisfied himself that no one had been waiting for him outside the hotel. He had some freedom now, and it would give him time to think. Chiun was right about his need for exercise and practice, though. While he was thinking, he would also walk.

He turned toward Market Street, three-quarters of a mile away, and melded with the darkness like a shadow.

AUDREY MORELAND HAD no special destination when she left the Shangri-la Hotel. Her things were packed, and she didn't feel sleepy. Quite the opposite, in fact. She knew that it would be a waste of time to simply lie in bed, count sheep or some such nonsense, and she didn't feel like using chemicals to take the edge off her excitement.

Eight more hours till they all convened for breakfast, and the trip would start within an hour to ninety minutes after that. She thought about the jungle and its secrets, waiting for her just beyond the glare of city lights that made the stars invisible, and wished that she was out there now, this minute, getting started on the quest.

Calm down, she thought, it's coming. If you get yourself worked up, you'll never get to sleep.

Which brought her back to thoughts of Dr. Renton Ward.

He was a handsome man, not gorgeous in the standard movie-star tradition, but she wouldn't kick him out of bed. There was a certain air about him that she didn't often sense in fellow scientists—a hidden sensuality, she thought, that would require some digging on her part to realize its full potential. There was confidence, as well, beyond the sort that basked in the reflected glow of monographs and textbooks published. Renton Ward was not so much a man of science, she decided, as he was a man.

She thought of poor old Safford then, and had to smile. She was aware of the pathetic rumors circulating back at Georgetown, hinting at some great affair between herself and Dr. Stockwell. She encouraged the absurd belief as best she could, for reasons of her own. It kept the other campus Romeos at bay, for one thing, and it also seemed to satisfy her self-styled mentor, the illusion of a love affair relieving him from any need to stumble through the motions on his own.

Tonight, ironically, had been the first time Stockwell showed her any warning signs of jealousy. Perhaps their change of scene, to the exotic East, had goaded him to speak. In any case, she knew the situation would bear watching. There was no point leading Safford on, provoking some misguided confrontation he was sure to lose.

Try as she might to focus on the object of her visit to Malaysia, Audrey's thoughts strayed back to Renton Ward. Pike Chalmers didn't like him—that was obvious—but Chalmers had a major ego problem. God's gift to women, and a one-man mutual admiration society to boot. It made her skin crawl when he stared at her, undressed her with a gaze that felt like clammy hands on her flesh. She knew exactly what he wanted, from the moment they were introduced. He'd need to be watched on the trail, where true to type he might revert to original primitive man, though she wasn't certain those progenitors deserved such a comparison. The crunch would come if Chalmers tried to act on his desires, take what he fancied and to hell with her consent.

The nightclub looked like any other tourist trap in Southeast Asia, geckos clinging to the wall around a garish neon sign, but Audrey didn't mind. It was a change from the hotel and a diversion from the omnipresent native vendors with their handicrafts, who made the city seem like one huge marketplace.

Inside the smoky, strobe-lit club, a cut-rate stereo

was throbbing with the tones of Barry Manilow, advising anyone who cared that he had written songs to make the whole world sing. A smiling hostess looked around for Audrey's escort, finally grasped that she was on her own, and led her to a table near the bar.

"You are American?" the hostess asked.

"That's right. Is there a problem?"

Smiling at the very thought. *"Tudak sisah,"* she said. "No problem."

Coming back with Audrey's rum and Coke, the hostess also brought a tiny U.S. flag, its toothpick staff embedded in a piece of cork, and placed it on the table, near the scented candle that was Audrey's only source of light besides the flashing strobes.

Of course, thought Audrey with a smile. The flag would label her a tourist so that no man in the club mistook her for a prostitute on call. In some parts of the world, the little banner would have been a magnet for hostility, perhaps inviting physical attack, but there was said to be no great dislike for Yankees in Malaysia. If all went well, she could enjoy a drink or three in peace, unwind a bit and then walk back to the hotel in time to catch some sleep before her scheduled wake-up call at half-past four.

"We're both alone, I take it."

She recognized the voice with a sinking feeling before she saw Pike Chalmers, looming like a grizzly bear beside her table. What rotten luck for her to pick the very bar where he was killing time.

Or was it simply luck? Could he have followed her from the hotel?

"What a surprise," she said, no indication in her tone that she was thrilled by the coincidence.

"Mind if I join you, then?"

"The truth is—"

"Marvelous." He pulled the second chair out, carried it around the table to her left and settled in beside her. "There we are, all nice and cozy, then."

"I can't stay long," she said.

"No problem." Chalmers flagged the waitress as she passed and ordered a double whiskey, neat. "I couldn't sleep myself," he said. "Too much excitement, what?"

"I wouldn't think there's much about a trip like this you haven't seen before."

"You never know," said Chalmers, staring at her breasts. She felt the nipples pucker with embarrassment and knew that he was bound to misinterpret the reaction. If only she had worn a jacket, or at least a bra!

"I understand you have experience in the Malaysian jungle."

"Love, I've got experience around the world. You name it—Africa, the Amazon, New Guinea, India. One jungle's fairly like another when you're on the ground. New predators to watch out for, o' course, but that's my specialty."

"So I was told."

"One of my specialties, at least."

The wink made Audrey want to scream. This man was one great chauvinist cliché personified, an oinker in the first degree. She felt a sudden need to take him down a peg or two.

"I've never understood the thrill attached to killing helpless animals," she said, still smiling as an angry flush suffused his features.

"Helpless? Love, there's nothing helpless in the bush, except a man with no experience. The bloody ants and flies can kill you, never mind the tuskers, cats and buffalo. You ought to see the souvenirs I carry on my hide sometime," he told her with a yellow smile. "You might stop sympathizing with the beasts and have a bit of care for me."

"But surely, when you make a special trip to kill them with your traps and guns, whatever they do to you is self-defense."

The hunter's smile turned brittle. "Self-defense, you say? It may seem different to you on the trail, when you've got hungry jackals or a tiger sniffing at your tent flaps. You'll be bloody glad to have a man beside you then."

"Let's hope it never comes to that," she said. "If you'll excuse me—"

Audrey rose to leave, her drink untouched, but

Chalmers gulped his whiskey down and bolted to his feet.

"The streets aren't safe this time of night," he told her, peering down the V-neck of her blouse. "I'll walk you home, love. Tuck you in all safe and sound."

"If you insist," she said.

"I do, indeed."

THE CLUB ON MARKET STREET held no attraction for Remo, with its smoky atmosphere and reek of alcohol. He would have passed it by without a second thought, except that Audrey Moreland chose that very moment to emerge, with canned music trailing after her and Pike Chalmers almost treading on her heels.

They made an awkward couple, standing on the sidewalk for a moment as if neither one of them could find the proper words to end a dismal date. A second glance at Chalmers, though, and Remo knew he wasn't anxious for the night to end. As for the look on Audrey's face, it could be anything from boredom to an alcoholic daze. He didn't know her well enough to judge, beyond a vague impression that she seemed unhappy in the big man's company.

So much for aimless rambling.

Remo faded back into the shadows of a nearby alley, waited while the mismatched couple shared a few more words, then turned back in the general direction of the Shangri-la. He gave them half a block, then fell in step behind them, pleased that he could follow someone for a change, instead of watching out to see if he was being tailed.

They covered half a dozen blocks before Pike Chalmers made his move. The street was narrower than most, lights few and far between. From twenty yards behind, Remo saw Chalmers drape his arm across the woman's shoulders, Audrey flinching from his touch as if the arm had been electrified.

"Now, love, don't be that way."

Without the background noise of Market Street, the big man's words were clearly audible.

"Don't touch me!" Audrey took a quick step backward, wobbling on her heels.

"You don't mean that," said Chalmers. "Not deep down."

"I mean exactly that, you oaf!"

"Oaf, is it? Rhymes with 'loaf.' I've got a loaf just right to fit your oven, dearie, or I'm very much mistaken."

Remo moved up on silent feet with the speed of wind and was immediately behind them when he spoke.

"It's a small world, after all."

Pike Chalmers swung around to face him, squinting in the dark, then sneering as he recognized the face. "Too bloody small," he said. "You'll shove off if you know what's good for you."

"Is there a problem here?"

"No problem, Doctor."

"Yes!" As Audrey spoke, she moved to stand at Remo's side, warm fingers resting lightly on his biceps. "Would you walk me back to the hotel?"

"No problem," Remo said.

"You sure of that?" asked Chalmers. "I believe you'll find there is a problem when you start to meddle in another man's affairs."

"You're drunk, friend. Maybe you should hit the sheets so you don't miss the flight tomorrow, eh?"

"I'll hit your bloody sheets, you little faggot!"

Chalmers put his weight behind the swing, but it was nothing special. Remo pulled his punch to keep the hulk alive, but it was still enough to drop him in his tracks, out cold before he hit the pavement.

Audrey gaped at Chalmers, laid out in the street. "My God," she said, "what happened?"

"I suppose he slipped and hit his head," Remo answered. "We could try and carry him to the hotel."

"Forget about it. He can sleep it off right here, for all I care."

"Well, if you're sure—"

"I'm sure. If someone rips his wallet off, it serves him right."

She looped her arm through Remo's, and they

put the fallen hulk behind them, crossing over to Jalan Pudu and starting on the loop back to the Shangri-la.

"I'm glad you came along back there," she said. "It could have gotten ugly."

"You should be more careful choosing dates," said Remo.

"Bite your tongue! I wouldn't date that caveman on a bet. He saw me in the club and...oh, well, never mind. I wanted Safford—Dr. Stockwell—to get rid of him, but he's supposed to be the best at what he does."

"Which is?"

"Shoot animals," she said with thinly veiled contempt. "The great white hunter, don't you know?"

"I didn't understand this was a hunting expedition," Remo said.

"You're right, of course. It isn't. But we had to make some kind of gesture toward security and all that sort of thing. There was insurance to consider, and the truth is, I don't want to find a lion in my tent if I can help it."

"Lions live in Africa," said Remo.

"Anyway, I'm told the hired gun stays...unless he's cracked his skull and can't go on tomorrow. God, you don't suppose we'll have to push the trip back and look for a replacement?"

"I suspect he'll be all right," said Remo, "but I

wouldn't want the headache he'll find waiting for him in the morning.''

"Serves him right," said Audrey, "but enough about that creep. I understand you're from New Orleans."

"Not originally." Remo tapped into the file CURE had compiled on Renton Ward. "I've worked there for the past eight years, but I'm from Kansas, if you trace it back."

"What got you hooked on snakes?" she asked.

He smiled. "What got you hooked on plants that died a hundred million years ago?"

"Touché." She thought about it for a moment, then went on. "I guess it crept up on my blind side, Renton. I was into botany and horticulture as a freshman out in California, when I took a course on prehistoric life. It was supposed to fill a blank spot in my schedule, no big challenge, but it got me thinking. How can a species dominate the earth for several billion years, and then just fade away? I mean, if we can solve that riddle, there's a chance we still might save ourselves, you know?"

"Are we in danger of extinction?"

"Every day," she told him earnestly. "We've got pollution—air, sea and land—overpopulation and a lot of shaky fingers on the trigger that could blow us all away. So what if Russia fell apart? It's not like one regime was causing all the problems in the world. Hey, what's the joke?"

She caught him smiling, seemed about to take offense.

Remo moved to head her anger off. "No joke," he said. "It's just that you sound more like someone who should be out leading demonstrations than collecting fossils."

"I do both," said Audrey, "when I have the time. And what about yourself?"

"I mostly hang around the serpentarium and milk my snakes," said Remo.

Audrey giggled like a schoolgirl. "When you say it that way, it sounds positively lecherous."

"It gets to be a handful," he allowed.

"I can imagine. What's your favorite?"

"Snake? That has to be the king. Twelve feet of solid muscle. One dose of his venom is enough to kill a hundred men. We have a mated pair back in New Orleans."

"And you handle them?"

"I milk each of them once a month."

"You must be very brave."

"It keeps me on my toes," he said. "The other snakes are dangerous, of course—the rattlers, coral snakes, moccasins, the bushmaster—but if you mess up with the king, you're history."

"You must have magic hands."

"It's in the wrist," he said.

"You'll have to show me sometime. How you do it."

"Have you got a snake?"

"We'll improvise."

"That could be challenging," he said.

"You must keep busy in New Orleans," Audrey said. "I've read about the women there, in the French Quarter."

"Well—"

"Come on, now, Renton. Please don't tell me you're a monk."

"I don't have much free time," he said by way of explanation.

"It's a good thing that we got you, then, before you waste away. All work, no play, et cetera."

"I understood this was a working expedition, Dr.—"

"Audrey, please."

"All right.

"It is, of course, but there's no law that says we can't enjoy ourselves along the way, now, is there?"

Remo thought about it. "Not that I'm aware of."

"There you go."

They were a block south of the Shangri-la and gaining fast. When Audrey saw the progress they had made, she dropped her grip on Remo's arm and took his hand.

"You know," she said, "you saved my life tonight."

"I doubt that very much."

"My honor, then. The proverbial fate worse than death."

"Something tells me you make out all right on your own," Remo said.

"Oh, I do. But it's more fun with two."

"So I'm told."

"You deserve a reward from the damsel in distress."

"I'll have to take a rain check, Audrey. Gear to pack, that kind of thing."

"A rain check, eh?"

"If that's permissible."

"You *do* know where we're going, don't you?"

"Well—"

"Rain forest all the way," she told him, rising on her toes to kiss him lightly on the corner of his mouth. "You get some sleep, now. Save your strength."

"I'll see you in the morning."

"And don't forget to pack your rubbers," Audrey told him. "It gets wet here in the bush."

"I'll bet it does," said Remo, and he started back toward his hotel.

7

"The woman has desire for you?" asked Chiun.

"It looks that way to me," said Remo.

Chiun reached out and thumped him on the forehead with a bony index finger. "Think with this head, always," he demanded. "Sex is a temptation to be overcome, an instrument to be employed for higher purposes. It is the nature of the female to deceive."

"I hear you, Little Father."

"Yes, but do you listen?"

"Well, my ears are ringing at the moment."

"Always joking, like a monkey in the zoo."

"I have to go," said Remo, glancing at his watch. "It wouldn't do for me to miss the kickoff."

Chiun was seated in his customary place before the television, even though the set was not turned on. "If you can manage to retrieve a dragon's tooth," he said, "by all means bring it back with you. They make strong medicine and fortify virility."

"What difference does it make?" asked Remo.

"We're supposed to overcome temptation and employ our instruments for higher purposes."

"Nobody likes a smart wasoo."

"You'll have to tell me what that means someday."

"When you are old enough to understand."

"I'm going now," said Remo.

"Watch the big man," Chiun suggested as the door swung shut behind him. "It was negligent of you to let him live."

You may be right, thought Remo as he waited for the elevator, passing up the stairs this morning on a whim. But killing Chalmers on the street, in front of Audrey Moreland, would have caused innumerable problems off the top, including a police investigation and delay of their departure for the Tasek Bera. As it was, the hulking Brit had either learned a lesson or he hadn't. Either way, his clumsy fighting style would pose no major challenge.

Just remember not to let him get behind you with a gun.

Okay.

He taxied over to the Shangri-la and checked his gear in with the concierge. The others had assembled by the time he followed cooking smells into the restaurant. A Chinese waiter led him to the table, where an empty chair stood next to Audrey Moreland. At the far end of the table, Chalmers wore a wide strip of adhesive tape across his nose and glared with blackened eyes.

"Somebody had a restless night," said Remo. As he spoke, a warm hand came to rest upon his thigh and squeezed.

"I'm fit enough," said Chalmers.

"Shall we order?" Dr. Stockwell asked.

The menu advertised Traditional American Cuisine, which meant the eggs were runny and the bacon limp, with pancakes that resembled overweight tortillas. Remo settled for a rubber omelet and a side of rice, the latter more or less impossible to ruin, short of setting it on fire. The breakfast conversation centered on their travel plans, with Dr. Stockwell carrying the ball.

"We have an hour till we catch the flight to Temerloh," he said, negotiating soggy bacon as he spoke. "I hope you're all prepared."

A general murmur of assent appeared to satisfy, and Stockwell took the time to butter up a slice of whole-wheat toast before he spoke again.

"We should be in Dampar by four or five o'clock, from what I understand. Too late to meet our guide, in any case. Please don't expect accommodations on a par with these," he told them, waving vaguely with his knife and fork, "but it will be our last night with a roof above our heads until the job is done."

"And how long do you estimate the trip should take?" asked Remo.

"Why, that's difficult to answer, Dr. Ward. It may depend on the cooperation of our quarry."

"If the bloody thing exists," Pike Chalmers groused.

"We mustn't dwell on negativity," said Stockwell. "While a possibility remains, we shall pursue it in the spirit of a scientific inquiry."

"Of course," said Remo, turning toward the Malay deputy. "And what is the official posture on collecting dinosaurs these days?"

The little man put on a smile. "My government is very much concerned with preservation of endangered species," he replied.

"As are we all," said Dr. Stockwell. "I assure you, Mr. Deputy."

"There is, of course, no legislation on the subject of surviving species from a prehistoric age, but our prime minister and Sultan Azlan Shah agree that any living dinosaurs should logically be covered by the statutes dealing with antiquities."

"We have to find the bloody thing before you brand it," Chalmers said.

"I must remind you, Mr. Chalmers, that Malaysian wildlife is protected both by federal statute and conventions ratified by the United Nations, under Rule—"

"We really should be going," Stockwell interrupted, heading off the argument. "If everyone is finished? Shall we?"

Fifteen minutes later, they were packed into a Dodge Ram Wagon with their field gear, rolling toward the airport, fifteen miles outside the city. Remo wound up seated next to Sibu Sandakan, with Audrey and their leader in the front, Pike Chalmers just behind him. He could feel the hunter staring at him, cold eyes drilling holes in Remo's skull, but Chalmers kept his mouth shut, made no hostile moves.

He'll save it for the trail, thought Remo, when he figures no one's looking. Maybe try to stage an accident if he can pull it off.

Okay.

If one round didn't drive the message home, he would forget to pull his punch next time.

Their pilot was a slender Aussie with a long face and a patch of unkempt hair, his plane an old de Havilland Twin Otter with some rugged miles behind it. Even so, the aircraft had been fairly well maintained, and with its seating for eighteen, the passengers had ample room to stretch their legs. A pair of Malays dressed in denim jumpsuits stowed the gear before they went on board, and Audrey Moreland took the time to have a word with Remo while they stood around on deck.

"I have to be with Safford now," she said. "You understand?"

"Sure thing." His tone was perfectly disinterested, and something flickered in her eyes before she turned away. Annoyance or excitement, Remo couldn't tell with any certainty.

He watched the loading process from a distance, saw a heavy-duty Koplin Gun Boot go aboard with P.C. painted on the jet black polyethylene. A smaller, padlocked metal case was large enough to hold a pistol and a decent quantity of ammunition. Remo didn't know what Chalmers had in mind just yet or whom he might be working for behind the scenes, but he was dressed to kill.

When they were all aboard and buckled in, the Aussie pilot gunned his engines, aimed the old air taxi down the runway set aside for private charter flights and left the ground behind. They circled once around the airport, leveled out and locked on to a northeast heading bound for Temerloh, some fifty miles away.

It was a relatively short hop, twenty minutes at the Otter's standard cruising speed, but rugged mountains cloaked in steaming jungle lay below them by the time they found their course. The landscape was a stark reminder of the sharp dividing line between the city and the bush in Southeast Asia, treating Remo to a host of memories that took him back to active duty as a young Marine, when he had served his country in a war most modern college students viewed as ancient history.

The jungle had been deadly then, and it was deadly now—but he had changed. There was no trigger-happy leatherneck, still wet behind the ears and spoiling for a fight, a chance to prove himself. Those days were far behind him now.

The young Marine was gone—and well, there was no comparison, Remo thought, with the new dimension he moved in now, thanks to the Sinanju training. There were also scarier aspects, when Chiun claimed to see him become the avatar of Shiva the Destroyer, but Remo wanted to forget that.

Temerloh was to K.L. what Victorville is to Los Angeles...without the desert. The humidity was waiting for them when they stepped down from the plane, the jungle pressing close enough to let them know who was in charge. A matching pair of Nissan Pathfinders was waiting for them on the tarmac, one for passengers, the other for their gear. Chalmers made a point of breaking off to ride with the equipment as they drove directly to the river docks.

Their boat was something else.

"How quaint," said Audrey, staring at it from the safety of the dock while Malay crewmen took their gear aboard. "It looks like something from that movie—what's the name of it? Where they go up that river in the jungle?"

"*Creature from the Black Lagoon?*" suggested Remo.

"No, the other one. With Bogart and Bacall."

"Bogart and Hepburn," Dr. Stockwell said, correcting her. "*The African Queen.*"

"Of course, that's it."

"Could be the same," said Remo, edging close to Audrey as he spoke. "As I recall, they sank it in the final reel."

"It's not that bad."

"It's floating, anyway. How long until we reach Dampar?"

"A little over forty miles downstream," said Stockwell, joining them. "I understand we have to make some stops along the way."

And so they did. Their boat, the *Babi Kali,* was apparently on tap for everything from mail delivery to grocery drops, with better than a dozen ports of call along the route from Temerloh to Dampar, to the south. Some of the cargo squawked and cackled, trailing feathers on the deck, but most of it was bagged or crated, everything from fruit and vegetables to canned goods, medicine and a replacement motor for an ailing generator.

There were tiny sleeping cabins down below, next to the head, with bunks stacked one atop the other like a parody of summer camp, but Remo chose a spot on deck, along the starboard rail, from which to watch the jungle pass. It brought back memories, of course, but there were also things that he had never noticed in his other life, when he was focused on a kill-or-be-killed game to the exclusion of all else. A flock of brightly colored birds exploding from the treetops like a sentient rainbow. Fish that broke the surface, leaping up to snag a flying insect from the air. Small groups of natives peering from the reeds along the riverbank, believing they were perfectly concealed.

Sinanju went beyond the normal scope of martial arts, beyond the kind of David Carradine philosophy you got from watching whites portraying Asian mystics on TV. It was a way of life that harmonized the human form with Nature, giving up resistance and accepting what could be when body, heart and mind were one. It was not a religion, in the sense that any holy man or book dictated moral dos and don'ts to sheeplike followers, with promises of pain or pleasure based upon their willingness to grovel in the dirt. Instead, the Master of Sinanju taught his chosen students how to maximize potential, with a vengeance. Sloth, negligence, bad diet could hold them back, and proper breathing was the portal that opened up that other realm.

"It takes my breath away," said Audrey Moreland, stepping up to join Remo at the railing.

Remo glanced around. "Where's Dr. Stockwell?"

"Down below." She flashed a rueful smile. "He gets a trifle seasick, I'm afraid."

"We're on a river."

"All the same."

"And Chalmers?"

"Playing with his guns, I should imagine. Would you like me to go find him?"

"Not on my account."

She faced back toward the jungle, moved a half step closer, leaning on the rail beside him, with her shoulder touching his. "My fieldwork in the past has all been digs in the United States," she told him, lowering her voice to something like a confidential tone. "I can't believe I'm really here. It's like..."

"A fantasy?"

"Exactly."

"I could pinch you if you like."

"Why, Dr. Ward, is that a proposition?"

"Well..."

"You know, I really think I owe you something. For last night."

"Last night?"

"With Chalmers."

"That was nothing," Remo told her.

"Oh, I understand he slipped and hit his head. A funny thing about his nose, though, don't you think? I could have sworn he'd fallen on his back."

"It was dark," he said. "I didn't pay that much attention."

"Anyway, the point is you were willing to defend me, standing up to someone twice your size. If you hadn't come along...I mean, I'm sure he meant to...well, you know."

"It's done."

"I wish he wasn't coming with us, Renton. Anything can happen in a place like this," she said. "It would mean so much to me if I had someone to depend on."

Audrey turned toward Remo as she spoke, and edged a little closer so that one firm breast was pressed against his arm. She wore a bra today, but there was no ignoring the insistent pressure of her nipple, even masked by several layers of fabric.

"You've got Dr. Stockwell," Remo said.

Her laughter startled him—spontaneous, explosive. There was nothing shy or juvenile about it.

"Safford? Please!" Her nipple prodded Remo's arm for emphasis. "If we run into a *Tyrannosaurus rex*, he'll quote you all the vital stats before the damned thing swallows him alive. When it comes down to people in the real world, though, away from academia...well, let's just say he's no Clint Eastwood."

"Even in defense of someone special?"

Audrey blinked at Remo, with a hint of color rising in her cheeks, then laughed again. "My

God," she said, "don't tell me that nonsense has traveled all the way from Georgetown to New Orleans."

"What nonsense is that?"

"About my 'hot affair' with Safford. Christ, I'd like to get my hands on the pathetic creep who started that one circulating."

"So you're not...involved?"

She struck a pose, with one hand on her hip, the other on the rail. "Do I look like a fossil, Renton?"

"Hardly."

"There you go. We work together, and we're friends. The past three years, we've gone to dinner maybe half a dozen times. He's nice, you understand? And safe."

"But you get tired of nice and safe."

"Who doesn't?" Audrey moved in again, her body heat washing over Remo.

"Well, there's always Chalmers."

"I refuse to mate outside my species, thank you very much." She hesitated, staring into Remo's eyes. "Oh, hey...you're not...I mean..."

"Not what?"

She raised a hand, limp-wristed. "You know."

His turn to laugh. "Not lately."

"No, I didn't think so." Audrey's hip was rubbing his now, just in case the rigid nipple didn't make her point. "A woman knows."

"The intuition thing," he said.

"That, too."

"Does Dr. Stockwell know you're just good friends?"

"He should. I mean, we haven't done it, anything like that."

"Sometimes a man sees what he wants to see."

"I don't know what he's seeing, Renton, but I haven't shown him anything. I'm not responsible for anyone's imagination."

"So you're up for grabs, then."

"I've been known to do some grabbing of my own."

"Empirical research?"

"The finest kind."

"I hate to change the subject—"

"Don't."

"A brief detour."

Audrey almost pouted. "If you must."

"About this dinosaur…"

"Oh, Renton. This is where you ask me whether I believe we'll find a world that time forgot?" She smiled and shook her head. "The truth is, I don't have a clue."

"But here you are."

"Damned right. When was the last time you were in a classroom, Renton?"

"Oh, it's been a while."

"I teach four days a week," she said. "That doesn't sound like much, I know. The pay's all right—it's not some godforsaken high school where the students carry guns. I'm not complaining, really...well, I am, but it's a small complaint, okay? It's boring, Renton. Every twelve to eighteen months, I write another monograph on ancient spoors, whatever, and I play the game with office politics. But this...I mean, we're having an adventure, right? And if we do find something, think of it!''

"Like prospecting," he offered, dangling the bait.

"I never thought of it that way," said Audrey, "but I guess that's right. You go out looking, maybe strike it rich, or maybe come back empty-handed. But at least you did something."

"You're awfully young to be stuck in a rut," he said.

"I'm not that young, but thanks for noticing."

"I couldn't miss."

"It's hard to understand, I guess, unless you've been there, from a woman's point of view. I mean, if you want some excitement, all you have to do is milk your cobra."

Remo smiled at that. "You need a hobby," he suggested.

"Oh, I have one," Audrey told him, "but it needs discretion. Fraternizing with the students is a no-no, and I wouldn't touch most of my colleagues with a ten-inch pole, assuming I could find one."

"That's a problem, if you set your sights too high."

"I'm flexible," she said. "You'd be surprised."

"I might, at that."

A splash drew their attention to the riverbank, where a long reptilian tail was vanishing from sight.

"No crocodiles?"

"That's one thing, when you deal with living species," Remo said. "They don't play by the rules."

"Makes life more interesting," said Audrey. "What are your rules, Renton?"

"Live and let live," Remo said. "What goes around—"

"Is there a Mrs. Dr. Ward?" she interrupted him.

"Well, there's a candidate of sorts..."

"Sounds to me as if you still have...options."

"Those we have...until we die."

"I'm surprised."

"How so?"

"You seem the type a woman who would want to tie down for good."

"Most, or many women would. It's a certain instinct with them."

"I'm not most women," Audrey said.

"I'm picking up on that."

"I like perceptive men. They know what makes a woman tick."

"Is that so difficult?"

"You'd be surprised. I've had my share of 'wham, bam, thank you ma'am.'"

"Disgraceful."

"Which is not to say I'm out of touch with urgency."

"It never crossed my mind," said Remo.

"I mean, quickies have their place," she said. "In public, for example."

Remo smiled and shook his head. "I really couldn't say."

"You've missed a lot," said Audrey. "What you need is an accomplished tutor."

"I get wrapped up in my work," he said.

"You know the rule—all work..."

"You've got a point."

Her left hand dropped below the rail and out of sight, warm fingers lightly grazing Remo's fly.

"You, too."

A whistle sounded, and the *Babi Kali* swung toward shore. A sagging wooden dock thrust outward from the bank. On shore, a white nun in her fifties waited, flanked by half a dozen Malays.

"I should go and check on Safford," Audrey remarked.

"Sounds like a plan."

"I'll see you later, to continue our discussion."

"Looking forward to it," Remo said.

DAMPAR MADE Temerloh look like Times Square on New Year's Eve. The swaybacked pier groaned underfoot, as if it might collapse at any moment. There were about a dozen buildings visible, with jungle pressing close around them. The humidity had nourished jungle rot on anything that wasn't cleaned or painted frequently. The local "inn" consisted of eight cabins drawn up in a line to face the river, fifty yards back from the shore. The furnishings included steel-frame cots and camp chairs, folding tables, propane lamps and plenty of mosquito netting. The electric generator ran on diesel fuel and conked out periodically, without apparent reason. In addition to the cabins, there was a ramshackle trading post, a small infirmary, a one-room school and a communal dining hall.

Their host was a short, chunky Malay in his forties, squeezed into a well-worn polyester suit. His oily smile reminded Remo of a used-car salesman, but it turned out that he owned Dampar lock, stock and pesthole. He was generous with compliments when they arrived, and favored Audrey with a leer that would have had a hooker quoting prices. While a team of natives set about unloading their equipment from the *Babi Kali,* he conveyed them to their cabins.

One apiece, no roommates.

They were more or less on time, as punctuality is judged in Southeast Asia, and it was indeed too late for them to think of moving on. Night falls with startling swiftness in the jungle, great trees blotting out the better part of sunlight so that dusk is virtually nonexistent; dark and daylight are separated by a razor's edge.

Their evening meal was stew of some kind, served in plastic bowls, with home-baked bread and lukewarm coffee. Remo made the best of it, resisting a temptation to inquire about the meat. He would have gone for rice and vegetables instead, but there was no room service in Dampar, no special orders from the chef.

His fellow expedition members kept the conversation going for an hour after supper. Stockwell brought out his map and supplemented it with hand-drawn sketches, while Chalmers put in his two cents where he could. The Brit had obviously never hunted in the Tasek Bera, and he spoke in generalities, relating stories of ferocious tigers, quagmires baited with the rarest orchids and assorted other jungle horrors. Remo kept his mouth shut, met the big man's gaze when it was unavoidable and smiled at Audrey when her foot snaked out to toy with his beneath the table.

They broke up a little after 9:00 p.m., presumably to sleep, but Remo walked down to the dock. The *Babi Kali* had continued southward, toward Bahau and Segamat. Their expedition would be long gone by the time the old rust bucket turned around and started north again, the day after tomorrow.

Audrey found him by the water. Remo smelled her coming, bug repellent standing in for her traditional perfume. Instead of speaking first, though, he allowed her to "surprise" him.

"Penny for your thoughts," she said.

"You wouldn't get your money's worth."

"It can't be that bad. Here we are, one step away from the adventure of a lifetime. Man and woman in the wilderness."

"It's not exactly Eden where we're going," Remo told her.

"No. I'm glad we've got a man along who knows his serpents."

"Rule of thumb," he told her. "If it moves and breathes out here, don't touch it."

"That's no fun."

"Survival calls for self-control."

"Too bad. I had myself all primed for handling a big one."

"Be careful what you wish for," Remo said.

"I always am."

"You've heard the story of the turtle and the scorpion?" he asked.

"It doesn't ring a bell," she said.

"A turtle was about to cross the river, when he met a scorpion who asked him for a ride. 'I can't take you across,' the turtle said. 'You'll sting me, and I'll die.'"

"Smart turtle," Audrey said.

"The scorpion was thinking, though. He said, 'I will not sting you, Mr. Turtle, for I cannot swim, and I would surely drown.'"

"Makes sense."

"The turtle thought so, too. He let the scorpion get on his back and paddled out into the water. Halfway to the other side, he felt a sudden, burning pain, then numbness spreading through his limbs. 'Why did you sting me, Mr. Scorpion?' he cried. 'Now both of us will surely die.' The scorpion just shrugged and said, 'I couldn't help myself. It's in my nature.'"

"That's a lovely bedtime story. What's the moral?"

"I just tell the stories," Remo said, "I don't evaluate."

"Am I supposed to be the turtle?" Audrey asked. "That isn't very flattering."

"I could have said a swan. It all comes out the same."

"Are you the scorpion?"

"Could be."

"I don't think so."

"You haven't seen my stinger," Remo said.

"I'm looking forward to it, though. In fact, why don't we slip back to my cabin and—?"

"I wouldn't want to keep the neighbors up," said Remo.

"Never fear. I'm not a screamer."

"Maybe I am."

"Naughty boy." She hesitated, looking deeper into Remo's eyes. "Are you rejecting me?"

"Not even close," he said. "I'll have to take a rain check, though."

"Anticipation doesn't hurt unless you drag it out to long," she told him, turning back in the direction of the cabins. "This is a rain forest, you know."

"I'm counting on it," Remo said.

"In that case, pleasant dreams."

He stood beside the river for another twenty minutes, humming softly, keeping the mosquitoes at a distance, while he thought about the days ahead. One at a time, he told himself, and watch your back. Pike Chalmers would not be his only hazard on the trail, nor was he necessarily the worst.

There were at least a thousand ways to die out here, and none of them especially pleasant. Remo's presence in the jungle merely added one more to the list.

8

Remo literally woke up with the chickens. Someone had imported ten or fifteen brood hens, plus a scrawny rooster, and their racket in the yard outside his cabin roused him from bed near dawn. He didn't exercise, per se, but there was a routine he practiced every morning, briefly, to maintain his edge. More breathing than established calisthenics, with a bare hint of t'ai chi—which, as Chiun would never tire of pointing out, had stolen all its secrets from Sinanju.

Dressed and ready for another day of travel, Remo was outside by six o'clock, when daylight brought the forest back to life. Not that the nights were quiet, he reflected. There were predators abroad, and eerie cries that would ensure a sleepless night for novices, but now the day shift was arriving, and the darker shadows would be tucked away until the sun went down again.

Though Remo was the first one up, from all appearances, Pike Chalmers ran second by a good ten minutes. He had changed his bandage overnight, stark white against the deep-tanned leather of his face. The blotchy bruising underneath his eyes had started changing color, fading from deep purple into mauve, which would in turn become unsightly green and yellow in another day or two.

The hunter kept his distance, glared at Remo for a while, then turned his back and sauntered off in the direction of the dining hall. Aromas led the way, and in another fifteen minutes, all five members of the expedition were together, seated at a common table while the Malay waiters served fried eggs, fried fish and fried plantains. Whatever else these jungle dwellers dreaded, they were clearly not afraid of saturated fats.

"Is all this fried in lard?" asked Audrey, sounding horrified. "I mean, it can't be, can it?"

Remo frowned. "I didn't notice any Crisco on the dock when they were landing the supplies."

"Terrific. I'll be breaking out like I was back in junior high school."

"Please remember where we are," said Dr. Stockwell, gently chiding her. "These people do the best with what they have."

"Of course. I'm sorry, Safford."

"No apology required, my dear."

"I didn't see the bloody guide about," Pike Chalmers said, as if he would have known the man on sight.

"I'm certain he will be here," Sibu Sandakan

informed the group at large, his fleeting glance at Chalmers sharply critical.

Whatever talents he possessed in terms of wood-craft and the massacre of animals, the hulking Brit had obviously never gone to charm school. Only Dr. Stockwell seemed oblivious to his abrasive personality, a fact that Remo credited to Stockwell's single-minded focus on the object of their hunt.

"How long is it before we reach the Tasek Bera proper?" Audrey asked.

"Two days should see us there with any luck," said Stockwell in reply.

"That's if we don't run into trouble with the bloody natives," Chalmers said.

The Malay deputy pinned Chalmers with a glare. "I can assure you, there is no hostility between my people and your party," he declared.

"Your people live back in the city," Chalmers answered, fairly sneering. "I was thinking of the damned bush monkeys waiting for us up ahead."

"I find your attitude insulting, sir!"

"Is that a fact? Well, I—"

"Please, gentlemen!" The flush of agitated color in his cheeks made Dr. Stockwell look more lifelike than he had since Remo met him. "We are all together in this project, I believe. Discord can only damage us and jeopardize our efforts."

Chalmers scowled at Stockwell for a moment, then he dropped his napkin on the table and retreated, muttering an oath that sounded very much like "Bloody wogs."

"I must apologize for Chalmers, Mr. Sandakan. Whatever problems he may have, I can assure you that his outlook is not representative of ours." As Stockwell spoke, he waved a hand around the table, indicating Remo and the woman at his side.

"Perhaps you should have chosen someone else," suggested Sibu Sandakan.

"Now, there's a thought," said Audrey.

"We were short of time, you understand, and he came highly recommended. By your government, in fact," said Stockwell, speaking now in a defensive tone. "Replacing him at this late date is tantamount to canceling the expedition."

"Even so..." The Malay deputy was clearly not convinced.

"I promise you that he will cause no difficulty in the bush. You have my word," said Stockwell.

Sandakan was frowning thoughtfully. "In that case, Doctor, if you take responsibility for Mr. Chalmers and his actions..."

Uh-oh. Remo saw the trap but could do nothing to prevent their leader's walking into it with both eyes open.

"Certainly," said Stockwell. "Done. Let's try to make the best of it."

"Indeed." The Malay's tone lacked all conviction, but he let the matter drop.

Their guide was waiting when they left the dining hall. He was a young man, in his early thirties, with a shock of coal black hair that hung to shoulder length and seldom met a comb. The left side of his face was deeply scarred, with four long furrows running from his cheekbone to below the jawline. When he smiled, the scarred half of his face appeared to crinkle, folding in upon itself, reminding Remo of a crumpled photograph.

Their host came out and introduced the stranger as Kuching Kangar, one of the region's premier guides and trackers. "No one find the tigers like Kuching," he said, and pointed to the young man's face. "One time, I think he get too close."

"That's bloody reassuring," Chalmers muttered, talking to himself.

"We take canoe first part of journey," said their guide. "Walk later if you truly wish to find Nagaq."

"Indeed we do," said Dr. Stockwell, smiling big enough for all of them.

"Bring many guns to kill Nagaq?" the guide inquired.

"I've got the hardware covered," Chalmers said. "A Weatherby .460 Magnum ought to do the trick."

"We haven't come to kill Nagaq," said Dr. Stockwell, speaking more to Chalmers than to the

Malay guide. "We're hoping to observe and study it, perhaps obtain some photographs."

Kuching Kangar seemed suddenly confused. "Not shoot?"

"With cameras only," Stockwell said to an approving nod from Sibu Sandakan. "We're truly not a hunting party."

"Tell Nagaq," the young man said with an indifferent shrug. "He not like visitors so much."

They spent the next half hour storing packs and other gear in two canoes, tied up against the sagging wooden dock. Pike Chalmers came back from his cabin with a heavy rifle slung across his shoulder, shiny cartridges the size of human fingers slotted into bandoliers that crossed his chest. The bandit look was complemented by a pistol belt with a revolver on his right hip and a long knife on the left. His hat took Remo back to childhood Tarzan movies, with its wide brim folded Aussie style on one side and sporting a band of leopard skin.

They split up into two groups of three for the canoes. Kuching Kangar was up front, with Dr. Stockwell and their Malay chaperon behind him, while Remo joined Audrey and their troubleshooter in the second boat. He took the rear seat, leaving Chalmers to the bow, with Audrey in between them.

"We need muscle on that oar in back," said Chalmers, with a trademark sneer.

"I pull my weight," said Remo, "or have you forgotten?"

Chalmers scowled. "I'm not forgetting anything, old son."

"That's good to know."

The first half mile was easy, running downstream with the current, but it would have been too simple for their destination to be situated on the main course of the river. Thirty minutes out of Dampar, Remo saw the lead canoe veer left, or eastward, as Kuching Kangar proceeded up a winding tributary where the trees closed overhead and nearly blotted out the sun.

Their course was hard against the current now, but Remo had no difficulty with the wooden paddle, stroking first to one side, then the other, driving the canoe along. In front of him, Pike Chalmers had begun to sweat before they put the main stream out of sight, dark blotches spreading on his khaki shirt. He didn't glance around at Remo, but the woman did, her smile flirtatious in the artificial dusk.

Too many complications, Remo thought, but there was nothing he could do about it now. The best and only course would be for him to watch his back around the clock, while keeping both eyes open for a sign that any member of the party was more interested in traces of uranium than dino spoor.

And what if all of them turned out to be exactly

what they seemed? How should he handle it if the excursion proved to be a total waste of time?

It's not my problem, Remo told himself. Selection of his missions fell to Dr. Smith, and there was no way he could second-guess the head of CURE. If Smith was wrong this time, and Stockwell's expedition was revealed as nothing but a prehistoric wild-goose chase, so be it. Remo would have done his job, and he wouldn't complain about the fact that no one had to die. Consider it a paid vacation, then, with Audrey Moreland as a sweet fringe benefit.

But not just yet.

It was more difficult to prove a negative, sometimes, than to detect an enemy. Until he knew for sure that Dr. Smith was off the beam, he would proceed on the assumption that at least one member of the party—maybe more—had treachery in mind.

And he would deal with any enemies as they revealed themselves.

THE STOCKWELL EXPEDITION had been gone for ninety minutes when a chartered speedboat nosed in to the sagging Dampar dock. Its solitary passenger was short, frail in appearance, dressed in black from head to foot. The color of his garment was a small surprise, as were the style and choice of fabric. No one in Dampar had previously seen a silk kimono, and it further startled them to note the stranger's footwear: modest sandals, woven out of reeds, when most who passed that way wore heavy hiking boots.

But if the new arrival's garb was startling, it became as nothing when the Dampar residents beheld his age. The man was old—some later said that *ancient* would have been a better term—with long wisps of white hair that fell around his ears, and almost none at all on top. He also wore a wispy mustache, which was less surprising on an obviously Asian face. The locals would debate his nationality for days to come. Had the old man been Japanese? Chinese? Vietnamese?

None guessed Korean, proving they were less observant than they thought.

The wizened stranger had no luggage with him, but he wore a simple drawstring pouch around his waist. At that, he seemed to want for nothing but a decent meal. So slender was he that the women of Dampar took bets on whether he would fly away or simply topple over in a breeze.

It was a good thing for the locals that they had experience with strangers and were wise enough to keep their comments to themselves. A foolish bully might have tried to have some fun and entertain his friends at the old man's expense. Ill-mannered children might have laughed at him or even pelted him with stones. The fact that Dampar and its people still survive today is evidence enough that none of these unfortunate events took place.

The old man didn't introduce himself by name when he sat down to haggle with the landlord of Dampar. Nor did he state his business, and the headman of the river village didn't ask, since it would only be inviting trouble later on if anything went wrong.

The stranger had a look about him that discouraged questions. Rather, it seemed prudent to discuss his needs in simple terms, agree on price and send him on his way.

The old man needed a canoe, some rice—and that was all. He had no use for maps or guides, required no hiking clothes or other jungle gear. He made it clear that while he hoped to bring the boat back, it might not be possible to do so. Therefore, he would purchase a canoe instead of renting one. The headman named his price, then reconsidered when he glimpsed the stranger's frown. It was a small thing, one canoe. His sons could make a hundred in the time that it would take his bones to mend.

His second offer was acceptable. The old man nodded, smiling, and produced three coins of varied sizes from his pouch. The coins were like none other in the headman's limited experience, each bearing profiles of a different man he didn't recognize, but they were plainly solid gold. He tested them discreetly, with his teeth, then shook the stranger's hand to seal their bargain.

Afterward, in a reflective moment, he would rub his fingers and remark upon the curiosity of how a frail old man retained such power in his grip.

The stranger waited briefly while a pair of teen-age boys was sent to fetch his boat and paddle, plus the gunny sack of rice. He watched the two boys laboring beneath the weight of the canoe, and took it from them, holding it above his head without apparent effort as he walked down to the riverbank. The old man had an audience by that time, but the people of Dampar knew how to hold their tongues. Instead of pestering him with questions or remarks that might have caused offense, they stood and watched in silence, saw him paddle out into the middle of the stream and vanish to the south.

It had been, everyone agreed, one of the strangest days they could remember in Dampar. First came the round-eyes and their Malay chaperon, bound for the Tasek Bera, where they meant to stalk Nagaq. Now they were followed by an ancient little man who should have been at home in Tokyo or somewhere, rather than exploring the Malaysian jungle in his silk kimono, totally unarmed. At that, some said the old man seemed to have a better chance of coming out alive than the Americans, with all their fine equipment.

The old man, at least, wouldn't go looking for a

monster who ate men alive and used their bones to pick its teeth.

IT WAS APPROACHING 1:00 p.m. before Kuching Kangar beached his canoe and signaled for the second boat to follow his example. When the two canoes were high and dry, they shouldered packs and Remo volunteered to carry some of Dr. Stockwell's video equipment. It wouldn't add much to Remo's burden, and he would have a chance to check the gear, find out if there was anything resembling a Geiger counter in the pack.

"The main stream turning south from here," Kuching Kangar explained. "We going east more, to the Tasek Bera. That way."

He was pointing as he spoke, into a wall of trees that seemed to offer little hope of passage. At a closer look, though, Remo saw a narrow trail of sorts, no doubt worn down by animals who chose the path of least resistance when they came down to the river for a drink. If it was anything like Vietnam, he realized, the jungle would be crosshatched with a thousand secret trails, some of them leading nowhere, long abandoned by those early men who'd blazed them, others bustling with life around the clock.

A well-used trail meant predators and prey, the food chain in its basic, elemental form. From this point on, they would be forced to watch for everything from snakes to prowling tigers, careful not to wind up on the menu of some forest hunter who had never learned the fear of man.

Pike Chalmers had the rifle off his shoulder now, and while he didn't work the bolt, he could as easily have taken care of that before he left his cabin. Put a live round in the chamber, leave the weapon's safety off and you were primed for anything—an accident included, if it came to that. How easy it would be for him to stumble, yank the trigger as he fell...and who could blame him if the bullet wound up taking Remo's head off?

"After you," said Chalmers, smiling as they fell into a rough formation.

"I'll be fine," said Remo. "They could use the big artillery up front, in case we meet an elephant or something."

"Yes, please, come with me," the guide instructed Chalmers, waiting while the hulk moved up to take his place in line. With Dr. Stockwell in third place and Sibu Sandakan behind him, that left Audrey fifth, with Remo bringing up the rear.

So far so good, he thought. As last in line, he had a chance to watch them all, react to any challenge from the head of the procession as might be appropriate. And while the others had no way of knowing it, his placement at the rear provided more protection, from that quarter, than the big guns did up front—unless, of course, they wound up being ambushed by a dinosaur.

Get real.

For Remo's money, they were just as likely to encounter Elvis, or do lunch with Sasquatch on a UFO from Graceland. It didn't surprise him in the least that ivory-tower scientists would grab themselves a free vacation in the Far East, chasing pipe dreams, but it would amaze him if their quest bore fruit.

But then again, thought Remo, he'd been amazed before.

He had to give the storytellers credit, anyway. If they were going to select a spot on earth where almost anything seemed possible, the dark heart of peninsular Malaysia was a perfect choice. He didn't need a lecture from the head of CURE to realize that few white men had passed this way before, and none of them had lingered long enough to leave their mark behind. As for the natives—if there was a local tribe—they would be well content to hide themselves from prying Western eyes and go about their business as they had for generations, prowling thunder lizards notwithstanding. Given any kind of choice, the natives would feel kindlier to jungle creatures—even monstrous ones—than to a group of white men dropping in with guns and cameras to disrupt the scheme of things.

He wondered idly what Chiun would have to say

about their quest, beyond his yen for magic dragon's teeth. Would it amuse him, or would he be irritated by the scientific arrogance of men and women pledged to strip the globe of every secret it possessed?

Even as the speculative thoughts ran through his mind, his body remained focused on the impressions conveyed by this hotbed of life around them. For they were not alone. His ears picked up the sounds of rodents scurrying in the underbrush, while birds and monkeys flitted in the branches overhead. He glimpsed a snake, just gliding out of sight as Audrey passed, but couldn't make a firm ID from what he saw.

And there was something else.

It was a feeling more than anything Remo could put his finger on. No scent or sound to back it up as yet, but something told him they were being followed. From a distance, cautiously, with skill and cunning. Whether the pursuer was a man or animal, he couldn't say.

Snap out of it, he thought. You're dreaming.

Except he knew he wasn't.

Pursuit of the discipline imparted by Chiun had entailed the opening of senses most men never realized that they possessed. It took some practice, granted, but the trick, once understood, was no more difficult than listening to spoken words or opening your eyes to see.

And they were being followed, definitely.

He could feel it in his gut.

But Remo kept the knowledge to himself. First off, he could not prove his feeling to the others, short of putting on a full-scale demonstration of Sinanju, backtracking to find whoever—or whatever—was pursuing them, and he didn't intend to tip his hand that way. Not yet. Without the proof, though, they would simply think he was a nervous Nellie, suffering from jitters in a strange environment. And while his ego could withstand the knocks, there was another, more compelling motive for withholding what he knew.

If Dr. Smith was right about the ringer on their team, it was entirely possible the guilty party would have outside help available, on call for assistance with chores like digging, transportation or disposal of unwanted witnesses. How many helpers? Remo couldn't even start to guess. It could be two or twenty, even more if some official agency was chipping in to help find the uranium.

He didn't fear the numbers, but uncertainty displeased him. Chiun had always made a point of stressing that a skilled assassin takes pains to identify his enemies and deal with them by any means available to minimize the risks and stress of life. A head of state would only be removed if proper payment was received, but troops or terrorists pursuing the assassin were fair game at any time.

Chill out.

It would have been a simple thing for Remo to fall back, leave the party for a while and backtrack, find out who or what was hanging on their trail, but Audrey might glance back and miss him, raise a hue and cry that would result in inconvenient questions, at the very least. For now, Remo decided, it would be enough for him to know that they were being followed, and stay alert in case the tracker moved up into striking range. If that happened, he would have to act, if only to defend himself.

Meanwhile, his first job was observing Dr. Stockwell and the others, trying to decide which one—if any of them—was most likely to be harboring a secret, personal agenda. Chalmers almost seemed too obvious a choice, the way he put his feelings on display, but even that could be a sly diversion.

Dr. Stockwell was the classic scientist, a one-trick pony dedicated to his chosen field…or was he? Had the tedium of teaching gotten on his nerves? Did the potential profits from uranium make Stockwell's Georgetown salary resemble an insulting pittance?

What of Audrey Moreland, then? Her academic face concealed a sly, seductive personality that some of her acquaintances, at least, would never see. Was there another face behind those two, with greedy eyes fixed on a payday that would leave her set for life?

And there was always Sibu Sandakan, official watchdog for the Malay government. It would be simple for the deputy or his superiors to summon troops and track the expedition, just in case they stumbled over something—dinosaurs, uranium, whatever—that the government might later wish to seize and milk for badly needed revenue. Suppose their chaperon got greedy, went in business for himself on the black market. What would stop a troop of soldiers from obeying him if they believed his orders issued from the top?

Too many suspects, Remo told himself. If nothing else, at least the thought of two or three collaborating on some kind of shady deal appeared remote. More reason, then, for the true ringer to have reinforcements standing by.

They marched for several hours, pausing every mile or two for brief rest stops, before they reached a clearing in the jungle, maybe twenty yards across and thirty long. Nearby, a short hike northward, Remo's ears picked up the sounds of running water from a stream.

"Camp here tonight," their guide announced, and dropped his heavy pack.

9

"What would produce a clearing in the woods like this?" asked Dr. Stockwell, shrugging off his pack as he addressed his question to the group at large.

Their guide was first to answer. "Some say giants rest here long ago," he said. "Kick over trees while sleeping."

"Giants," Chalmers muttered. "Bloody rubbish."

"It could easily be something in the soil," said Audrey Moreland, speaking as their botanist in residence. "A nutrient deficiency, perhaps, or deviation in the depth of topsoil."

"I almost prefer the giant story," Stockwell said. "It's more…romantic somehow."

"Bloody great oaf sleeping rough and knocking over trees," said Chalmers. "Where's the romance?"

"You misunderstand me, Mr. Chalmers. Romance needn't be a thing of lust and sweaty flesh. It can be attitude and atmosphere, as well."

"I'll take mine straight up, thank you very much."

The pup tents were assembled quickly, Remo helping Audrey out with hers when she got tangled up.

"There's not much room in here," she told him, frowning.

Remo said, "There's not supposed to be. It's one per customer."

"Suppose I wanted company?" she asked, wide-eyed.

"I guess you'd have to improvise."

"I'm good at that," she said, and let him feel her breasts again as she brushed past him, wriggling clear.

He followed, caught a parting glimpse of Audrey's swaying backside as she headed for the tree line.

"Audrey?" Dr. Stockwell called, sounding anxious.

"Call of nature, Safford. I'll be fine."

Pike Chalmers watched her go, felt Remo watching him and glared back in defiance, resting one hand on his Colt revolver. Like a frigging cowboy, Remo thought, and broke off the staring game himself this time, as if he didn't recognize the challenge.

Let it go, he told himself. For now.

The time might come when he would have to

deal more forcefully with Chalmers, but he saw no need to push it now. He would give the Brit some rope, enough to hang himself if he were so inclined.

As if by mutual consent, the five men waited until Audrey had returned from answering her call of nature, only then resuming the assorted tasks required to put their camp in shape.

"Need dry wood for the fire," Kuching Kangar announced, at which point Dr. Stockwell and the Malay deputy went off to lay in a supply.

"Be careful, Safford," Audrey cautioned, her tone almost admonishing him.

"We won't go far," said Stockwell, taking it as a sincere expression of concern.

"Is there a stream nearby?" asked Remo, playing greenhorn to the hilt.

"That way," the guide directed him, a bony finger pointing toward the trees, due north. "Not far."

"I'll fetch some water," Remo said, and found the coffeepot among their meager cooking gear.

"I'll help," Audrey volunteered, scooping up another pot and trailing Remo toward the trees.

It didn't take them long to lose sight of the camp, though Remo still picked up the sound of voices crystal clear. There was another trail of sorts, though smaller than the one they had been following throughout the afternoon, which led directly from the clearing to the stream.

"Is this your first time in the jungle?" Audrey asked.

"In Asia," Remo lied. "I've tramped around a fair bit in the Western Hemisphere."

"When you were chasing vipers?"

"More or less."

"That sounds like an exciting life."

"It has its moments."

"I can imagine."

No, you can't, he thought, but said, "I can't believe you're all that bored. You don't seem like the type who'd stick with something if it drove you up the wall."

"Oh, really? What type am I, Renton?"

"An adventuress at heart, I'd say. You like a bit of living on the edge."

"That doesn't mean I turn my nose up at security," she said.

"Of course not. Still..."

"Still, what?"

"I can't imagine you'd be satisfied to settle for a safe job in a rut."

"You may be right, at that."

They reached the stream, and Remo found it somewhat larger than he had expected. Twenty feet across, he guessed, from where they stood, and deep enough that he couldn't make out the bottom more than two feet from the shore.

"No crocodiles, you said." Her fingers were already toying with the buttons of her denim shirt.

"I wouldn't recommend a swim, regardless," Remo said.

"Why not?"

"Contaminants, for one thing."

"What, you mean pollution in a place like this? I don't believe it."

"I was thinking parasites," said Remo. "Anything from microbes up to flukes and leeches. We'll be boiling any water prior to drinking it. And just because you don't see crocs, it doesn't mean the fish are friendly."

Audrey made a sour face at Remo. "Thanks for spoiling Eden, Dr. Ward."

"You said you wanted someone to watch out for you."

"That's right, I did."

They filled their pots and walked back to the camp, found Sibu Sandakan and Dr. Stockwell there ahead of them, with ample wood to build a decent fire. They put the water on to boil, while Chalmers took his Weatherby and went to have a look around. It troubled Remo, thinking of the Brit beyond his sight line with the big scoped rifle, but he let it go. If Chalmers pulled a stunt like that in camp, it would mean killing all the witnesses, as well, and Remo didn't think he had the stones for that.

Unless, of course, he'd planned from the beginning to be coming back alone.

Their evening meal was simple. Freeze-dried stroganoff in plastic pouches that relaxed a bit when it was boiled, producing not-so-haute cuisine with the appeal of third-rate airline food. Still, it was filling, washed down with a good supply of strong black coffee. Remo drank and felt the caffeine tuning up his nerves, preparing him to stay alert as long as necessary through the night.

Through practice of Sinanju, he had learned to minimize the sleeping time his body needed, taking full advantage of whatever relaxation came his way. He could remain awake for days on end without apparent strain, or "sleep" while he was marching, paying just enough attention on the trail to keep from stumbling into traps and snares. In any case, he had caught up on sleeping in Kuala Lumpur and Dampar. If something happened in the middle of the night, he meant to know about it and respond effectively.

Among his five companions, there were mixed reactions to a long day in canoes and on the trail. Their guide displayed no symptoms of fatigue, but that was only natural for someone working on his own home ground. Pike Chalmers also seemed alert, a veteran in the bush, while Sibu Sandakan and Dr. Stockwell were already yawning over supper, winding down their conversation early, with remarks about an early start and long days yet to come. A glance at Audrey showed her dozing by the camp fire, but she came awake at once when Stockwell called her name and urged her to turn in.

"I think I will, at that." She barely glanced at Remo, turning toward her pup tent, but his mind was elsewhere, focused on the job at hand.

He had lost touch with their pursuers since they stopped to pitch the camp. It was as if the others had retreated, drawing back to some safe distance, minimizing any risk of contact in the dark. There would be no point moving on the camp tonight, he thought, before they even had a chance to start their search, but it was difficult to judge the plans of strangers he had never even seen. If one of his companions simply meant to use the expedition as a cover at the outset, jettison the deadwood early on and start pursuing the uranium in earnest on his or her own, one killing ground might serve as well as any other.

Still, he told himself, they hadn't even reached the Tasek Bera yet. Another day, without any mishaps, before they reached the jungle neighborhood where Terrence Hopper's party had come to grief. If it was me doing it, thought Remo, I'd put the ambush off until the targets brought me closer to the mark, perhaps did some of the attendant dirty work.

Don't count on total strangers to be rational.

With that in mind, he said good-night and crawled into his pup tent, feigning sleep and waiting while the others turned in, one by one. Pike Chalmers sat up for an hour after supper, polishing the Weatherby but never speaking to their Malay guide. Kuching Kangar, in turn, was last to crawl inside his tent, as if his job included seeing all his charges safely tucked in bed.

Another thirty minutes passed, with Remo listening to those around him through the thin walls of his tent. When he was reasonably sure that all of them were sleeping, Remo wormed his way outside, a silent shadow gliding past the fire and off into the trees.

He spent a moment standing on the border of the clearing, eyes closed, reaching out with other senses to the night. He paid no real attention to the sounds of birds and insects and nocturnal predators. It was indeed the absence of their noise that would alert him to potential danger. That, and the peculiar, artificial sounds most men are physically unable to avoid. The whisper of a shoe sole brushing over sand or stone, so much more sinister than snapping twigs. Metallic sounds of any kind that rang out loud and clear in nature's realm. A sneeze or whisper. Fabric kissing flesh.

But there was nothing, and he walked back to the stream, content to be alone. The bats were out and skimming low across the water, snatching insects from the air. A fish jumped somewhere off to Remo's left, and something larger was growling on the far side of the stream, put off by Remo's scent.

Good hunting.

He heard the footsteps coming moments later, turned to greet the new arrival, smelling Audrey well before his eyes picked out her silhouette in dappled moonlight. When he stepped out, right in front of her, she jumped and gave a little squeal.

"For God's sake, Renton!" Even startled, she was whispering, as if to keep their meeting secret from the others.

"Trouble sleeping?" Remo asked.

"It's all too much, you know? I mean, I'm tired, but there's too much to see and do. It won't last long enough."

"You may feel differently this time next week."

"I won't," she said. "It's the adventure of a lifetime, right?"

"You'll have to work your butt off in the next few days," he said.

"Not all of it, I hope."

A subtle movement in the tree beside her caught his eye, and Remo's hand flashed out, almost too fast for Audrey's eyes to follow.

"What—?"

He held the wriggling viper up in front of her, gripped close behind its spade-shaped head, the body twining fluidly around his forearm. Remo checked the coloration of its scales and smiled at Audrey.

"*Trimeresurus flavoviridis,*" he announced.

"It's poisonous?"

"Sharp local pain and hemorrhages of the internal organs," he replied. "Intensive bleeding from the bite itself is not uncommon."

As he spoke, he flung the snake away from him, out toward the middle of the stream. It splashed down, quickly surfaced, started swimming for the distant shore.

"You have quick hands," she said.

"Sometimes.

"I guess you saved my life."

"My pleasure," Remo said.

"How can I ever thank you?"

"Well…"

"I know," she said. "I'll improvise."

Remo watched as she began unbuttoning her shirt. "I warned you once about the swimming," he reminded her.

"Who says I'm going in the water?"

Sometime in between the pitching of her tent and trailing Remo to the stream, she had removed her bra. Not that she needs one, Remo thought. Her breasts were firm and round, defying gravity, with nipples that seemed tawny but would almost certainly be pink in daylight.

She dropped the blouse behind her, moving faster

as she started on the buckle of her belt. It stalled her for a moment, Audrey blushing, but she got it then, unsnapped her jeans and ran the zipper down. Paused long enough to work her shoes off, treating Remo to a bit of jiggle in the process. Rolled snug denim down across hips, buttocks, thighs.

No panties, either, he observed.

"Is this what they call dressing for success?"

"Depends on what your goal is," she replied. "Now, you."

"We hardly know each other," Remo said.

"That's about to change."

"You think so?"

Audrey moved against him, toasty velvet. "I insist on seeing what else you can do besides catch snakes," she said.

And Remo showed her, starting slowly, using only some of the specific skills Chiun had taught him in the early days. His fingers came together at the small of Audrey's back, the touch enough to make her squirm against him, yet so light he barely grazed her skin. A dip to trace the cleft between her buttocks, then his hands rose higher, following the sleek curve of her spine to tease the nape of Audrey's neck. She trembled, moaning softly as she clasped her hands behind his neck and leaned against him, almost going limp.

Sex is a combination of psychology and physiology—the former more anticipation than achievement, while the latter is controlled by pressure, friction, heat and cold. Sinanju recognized three distinct techniques for bringing women to the pinnacle of sexual fulfillment. One method used twenty-seven steps, another thirty-seven and the last mode fifty-two—although Chiun was adamant that only a Korean woman could survive the total treatment with her sanity intact.

Remo started teasing her, beginning with the insides of her ears, then down the side of Audrey's neck. He found her pulse and lingered there, tap-tapping until she sighed in rapture before he moved down to the hollow of her throat. Her legs would not support her now, and all her weight was on his shoulders until Remo marched her three steps backward and leaned her against the nearest tree. He guided Audrey's hands above her head and showed her how to grip a branch to keep from falling down.

"Hang on," he said.

"God, yes!"

He picked up where he had left off, and it was getting hard to hold her back.

"Please hurry!"

Another breathless gasp came from Audrey as he gave her what she wanted, and he protected the sensation until her spasms had subsided into small, involuntary tremors.

"Act Two is next," he told her, rising to his feet.

"I can't," she moaned.

"You will."

"Too much!"

But she could handle it all right, although she was a quivering mess until her release came again, followed by a long, slow drift into the afterglow.

They lay together on the mossy ground, and after several moments Audrey started giggling. She pressed her face against his chest to mute the sound, but couldn't seem to stop.

"What's funny?" Remo asked her.

"Nothing, Jesus! It was—" Audrey hesitated, speechless for a moment. "I just realized, you're not a screamer after all."

"I'm screaming on the inside," Remo said.

"Tell me about it. I believe I shorted something out."

"I'll check your wiring for you," Remo told her, reaching down between her thighs.

She caught his wrist. "Not on your life! My life, I mean. You think they have a Flight for Life out here in case of strokes or heart attacks?"

She was coherent, but her eyes were slightly glazed, and Remo thought perhaps it was a good thing that his demonstration hadn't gone beyond the thirteen basic steps. It would be awkward, carting Audrey through the jungle on a litter, and they didn't have a straitjacket.

"We should be getting back," she said a moment later, stirring feebly, reaching for her clothes.

"I'll help you."

"No," she said. "I still know how to dress myself."

It took her three attempts to put her jeans on, though, before she got her balance back. The rest of it was simple by comparison, and with her clothes on, she looked more or less composed.

"You ought to package that," she told him. "You could make a killing."

"It requires a certain inspiration," Remo lied.

"And sweet talk, too. The total package. Do they teach that in New Orleans?"

Remo smiled. "I pick up bits and pieces as I go along," he said.

"I'll bet you do. All kinds of pieces, with a touch like that."

"We aim to please."

"Your aim was perfect," Audrey told him. "I can't wait to try some more of that once I regain my strength."

"If we have time," he said.

"I'll make time," Audrey answered, moving in to kiss him lightly on the lips. "We'd better not go back together, just in case."

"All right."

He watched her go, took time to check his pulse and blood pressure. Both normal, well below the average. Remo let five minutes pass before he followed Audrey back in the direction of the sleeping camp.

And this time, he was unaware of being followed through the trees.

10

The morning summoned mixed reactions from his traveling companions, Remo noted as he moved about the camp. Stockwell and Sibu Sandakan were visibly fatigued and out of shape, but each seemed anxious to continue with the march. Pike Chalmers was the same as ever—surly, misanthropic, with a hard gleam in his eye that spoke to Remo of a personal agenda he was keeping hidden. As for Audrey, while the early-morning sun highlighted shadows underneath her eyes, as if from weariness, she seemed to have a new spring in her step.

"I haven't slept that well in years," she said to Remo, passing on her way to make a pit stop in the forest. "That's some bedside manner, Dr. Ward."

"I try to keep my hand in," Remo told her.

"So I noticed. Don't waste too much energy today," she said in parting. "You'll be needing it tonight."

"I'll make a note."

Their breakfast was another freeze-dried meal, some kind of lumpy scrambled-egg concoction laced with colorful but tasteless cubes of meat and vegetables. Someone's conception of an omelet, Remo guessed, though he couldn't have sworn to the ID if he were under oath.

The best thing about bad food, he decided, was its tendency to vanish quickly; no one lingered to savor the experience before they were scraping plates and trooping down to the stream for K.P. duty. They were packed, including tents, inside of forty minutes from the time they first sat down to eat.

The jungle had begun to subtly change, thought Remo as they struck another trail beyond the clearing and resumed their eastward march. Not so much in appearance—which was standard tropic rain forest, from what he could observe—but more in terms of atmosphere. There was a darker feel about the new terrain; Remo would have been hard-pressed to put it into words, except to say that it felt dangerous, if not precisely evil. There was less room to maneuver on the trail, the jungle pressing closer on each side than it had the day before, and the mosquitoes came in greater numbers, reinforced by swarms of biting gnats and flies.

And they were being followed, yes indeed. The tail was back there, keeping a respectful distance, but maintaining contact all the same.

He thought once more about surprising their pursuers, falling back to search them out and wreak a little havoc for the hell of it, find out exactly who or what was on their trail. But Audrey kept on glancing back at Remo, smiling even when the heat and insects started getting to her, and he knew that she would sound the first alarm if she looked back and found him gone. Tonight, perhaps, if there was time and he could get a fix on their prospective enemies. A visit to the other camp in darkness might be just what Dr. Renton ordered.

In the meantime, Remo concentrated on the trail and his companions. Audrey working up a sweat in front of him, the rich aroma of her body wafting back to Remo on a sluggish jungle breeze. He put the stirring mental images on hold and checked the others, starting with their guide and working backward down the line. The men demonstrated varied levels of endurance, Remo saw, but none showed any signs of dropping from exhaustion. Up in front, their Malay pointman set a steady pace without demanding any superhuman effort. He appeared to have the oldest member of the team in mind, and Remo caught him glancing back at Dr. Stockwell every hundred yards or so, as if to reassure himself that the professor still had energy enough to carry on.

So far so good.

Three hours later, they stopped to rest for fifteen minutes, and Audrey winked on the sly before she settled next to Stockwell.

"Tell me, Audrey," the professor said, "have you seen anything unusual about the native flora?"

Audrey thought about the question for a moment, finally shook her head. "Not really, Safford. Much of what we see is rather primitive, of course—the ferns and fungi, obviously—but there's nothing I'd call prehistoric on the face of it. No fossil species sprung to life, by any means."

"An ordinary jungle, then?"

"In essence," she replied. "But we're not looking for a plant, remember. If I had to guess, I'd say that isolation would be more important to survival of an ancient species than specific flora. Even herbivores are fairly versatile, unless you're dealing with koala bears."

Their guide, Kuching Kangar, had seemed to follow the exchange with interest, though it was impossible to say how much he understood until he spoke.

"Nagaq eats meat," he said to no one in particular.

Professor Stockwell blinked and frowned. "A carnivore?"

The little Malay shrugged. "Eats meat," he said again.

"You've heard this from your people, I suppose?"

"Nagaq ate my *datuk*," the guide responded, slipping into Malay.

"His grandfather," Sibu Sandakan translated.

"What?" Professor Stockwell was amazed. "He surely cannot mean—"

"We hear him screams," the guide said, interrupting Stockwell. "Run down to the river where he go for water. Find his arm, *kiri.*"

"The left one," Sandakan filled in, appearing shaken.

"Also, tracks left by Nagaq," the guide went on. "This big."

He held his hands apart, three feet or so, then let them fall into his lap. The story of his grandfather's annihilation seemed to conjure nothing in the way of strong emotion.

"When did all this happen?" Audrey asked.

"Two years gone, maybe three."

"What bloody rot," Pike Chalmers said. "It must have been a crocodile."

"No crocodile that big," the guide replied. If he was angered by the tall Brit's open skepticism, he concealed it well.

"My God, that's food for thought," Professor Stockwell said. "That is…I mean to say…"

"It's all right, Safford," Audrey told him, resting one hand on his sunburned arm. "I'm sure he didn't take offense."

"Nagaq eat meat," their guide repeated with a twitchy little smile, then scrambled to his feet and grabbed his pack.

"Rest over," he informed them. "We go now."

THE MASTER OF SINANJU had no difficulty following his quarry. Even on the river, it was child's play, watching for the point where they had landed their canoes and made a sad attempt at hiding them. The boats were tucked away behind some ferns, but no real effort had been made to sweep away the tracks where they were dragged ashore, and footprints from the several amateurs were everywhere.

The game was that much easier when they began the rough trek overland. Their clumsy boots left imprints that a blind man could have followed, tapping with his cane, and there were other signs, besides. A broken sapling. Scratches on a tree, where someone's gear had scraped the bark. A stone inverted, kicked aside to bare the worms beneath it. Fronds and branches cut with a machete where the trail was overgrown and they were forced to clear a path. Great imprints from their buttocks where they stopped to rest.

Remo was better than the others, granted, but he still left traces that the Master of Sinanju could detect with only minor concentration. In a contest, it wouldn't be good enough, but Remo surely would have chosen better footwear and equipment if the choice were his to make.

Chiun had started out a day behind the Stockwell expedition, giving them a night to sleep at Dampar, picking out a charter speedboat that would quickly shave their lead. He was an hour and a half behind them when he acquired the canoe, with no white men in the boat to hold him back once Chiun applied himself to paddling at speed. His quarry had no more than forty minutes' lead time when the Master beached his boat and took the time to hide it properly, where no man would discover it without a thorough, time-consuming search.

At that, Chiun was almost forced to view his tracking prowess as a handicap of sorts. He could have overtaken Remo and the others in an hour at the most, and shadowed them from killing distance, but he had no wish to baby-sit.

And after fifteen minutes on the jungle trail, he knew there was another problem that he must examine first, before he showed himself to Remo.

Stockwell's expedition had a tail.

He couldn't say another tail, because the faceless strangers had begun their hunt ahead of him. For all Chiun knew, they may have been in place before the expedition left K.L. They had made no effort to surprise the expedition yet, but they were armed and therefore dangerous—at least to whites with no appreciation of Sinanju.

Master Chiun had sensed the enemy before he covered half a mile on foot, then took time to sort the scents and general impressions that combined to let him know an adversary was at hand. He left the trail at once and moved wraithlike through the forest to pick up a second track that paralleled the first. The boots that trod this path were older, more run-down than those of Stockwell's expedition, and they were more numerous. He counted seventeen distinct and separate signatures along the way, including two men wearing sandals soled with rubber cut from blown-out tires. A smell of gun oil lingered on the air.

Chiun followed them that day, observed their progress, counted heads and weapons. They were Malay, with a couple of Chinese—the sandal-wearers—and their weapons, plus a motley sort of uniform patched up from camouflage fatigues and faded denim, readily identified them as guerrillas. Since he spoke no Malay, and the Chinese didn't use their native tongue, Chiun could only speculate upon their motive for pursuing Dr. Stockwell's party. Even so, their motive, while obscure, was clearly not benevolent.

Chiun considered falling on them from behind and winnowing the ranks, or traveling ahead to meet them on the trail, pretend to be an ancient, fragile pilgrim until they were close enough to strike, but he finally decided to do nothing for the moment. When in doubt, if there was no emergency at hand, a wise assassin limited his action to the gathering of information, all the better to react appropriately once his target was identified.

With that in mind, he broke off the surveillance and moved on to pick up Stockwell's trail. He shadowed Remo and the others on their first day's march and watched them from the overhanging branches of a great tree as they set up camp. Chiun considered stealing in to speak with Remo, when the others were asleep, but he had faith in Remo to detect the common enemy, and there was little he could add beyond a physical description of their foe.

And by that time, of course, the woman had begun distracting Remo from his task. She was a brazen hussy, little better than a common prostitute, the way she bared her flesh to Remo on such short acquaintance. Chiun couldn't decide if her seductive actions were deliberate, a piece of conscious strategy toward unknown ends, or whether she was simply what the white men called a slut, devoid of self-restraint and moral fiber.

Either way, Chiun had witnessed Remo's personal response with disapproval. The Master was prim, and he well remembered a recent attachment that had surprised him at the time...though he also knew that these days the young were promiscuous. Even then, it was not so much the fact that Remo chose to grant the hussy's wish—although Chiun had warned him more than once about the risks of sacrificing vital energy through sex, when he was on a mission for Emperor Harold Smith—as in his pupil's blatant disrespect for the time-honored methods of Sinanju.

Remo made no effort whatsoever to begin the mating properly, by seeking out the woman's pulse and forcing it to escalate. Maybe, Chiun thought, it was the memory of Jean Rice that hampered his style. He skipped some of the classic steps and duplicated others, stopping cold before he had completed even the most basic ritual for bringing female flesh to ecstasy. Chiun could not deny the woman's rapture even so, but he would have to speak with Remo later and remind him of the need to follow through in everything.

There was a moment when Chiun believed that Remo would detect him, watching from the darkness, but the woman managed to divert him with her supple body. She was handsome for a white, of course, but there was something in the pallid skin and too-abundant curves that put Chiun off.

Korean women were the best.

Next morning, after dining on a handful of cold rice, Chiun had checked on the guerrillas, found them breaking camp, before he hurried back to join the Stockwell expedition. If the enemy had plans to strike, he knew they would most likely wait for darkness, but it wouldn't hurt for him to scout the trail ahead. He would take care to leave the forest undisturbed and give the scientific party's Malay guide no reason to suspect another human being in the neighborhood.

When the attack came, if it came, Chiun would not be far away.

THE STINKING JUNGLE had begun to wear on Lai Man Yau. Two days he had been waiting with his soldiers for the Yankee expedition to arrive, and now he had to track them at a snail's pace while they trekked into the Tasek Bera no-man's-land. It would have pleased him to attack the party and destroy them all—except, perhaps, the woman, who could entertain his men for several days before she died. Still, this was war, and Lai Man Yau was under orders. He would have to wait a bit, until the round-eyes found what they were looking for.

Beijing had been explicit on that point. A premature attack would ruin everything, and it would be considered treachery, deserving of a traitor's fate.

He could live on fish and rice, dried beef and fruit, for weeks if necessary. Long before that time, his enemies would either make their find or give up in disgust, and he would get approval for their execution either way.

It would be better, though, if they could simply find what they were looking for, deliver it to Lai Man Yau before they died.

Yes, that was how it ought to be.

Lai Yau was one of some six million ethnic Chinese living in Malaysia. He could trace his roots back thirteen generations, but he never saw himself as Malay. He would always be Chinese, and as a faithful son of China, he took orders from Beijing.

Six years ago, those orders had commanded him to organize a small guerrilla cadre, granting native Malays equal partnership, and to inaugurate a people's war of liberation that would ultimately doom the nation's constitutional monarchy, paving the way for a socialist regime patterned on the Chinese model. Everywhere throughout Malaysia, there were cadres much like his, intent on toppling the corrupt, outdated government in favor of a Beijing-type replacement. Communism might be dead in Russia and the mongrel states of Eastern Europe, but it was alive and well in Asia, with a program that demanded suitable respect.

The job at hand, as with so many missions ordered from Beijing, was long on orders, short on explanations. Lai Man Yau had been instructed to await the Yankee expedition, follow it and safeguard certain information that a spy within the party would provide when it was time. The information would be furnished to Beijing, the round-eyes executed. No provision had been made to spare the mercenary agent, once his work was done. Expecting Chinese gold, he would be paid in lead.

The ruthless plan appealed to Lai Man Yau. He

only wished that it were possible to get the waiting over with, put it behind him and get on with killing round-eyes. That was still, would always be, his favorite sport.

It would have been so easy to surround their camp last night, move in with AK-47s blazing, rip the pup tents and their occupants to shreds before the round-eyes woke to recognize their fate. Or he could just as easily have taken them alive, interrogated each of them in turn until he found out what they meant by tramping through the Tasek Bera with their pitiful safari.

The Americans were crazy; everyone knew that. But they were also clever, crafty. Lai Man Yau dismissed the media reports of living dinosaurs as a pathetic, simpleminded cover for the expedition's true pursuit—whatever that might be. His masters didn't share their knowledge with a simple soldier in the field. It was enough for them that he showed up on time and did the job he was assigned to do, without complaints or questions. If he failed, there would be punishment in store. If he succeeded, then success would be its own reward.

Sometimes, before he fell asleep at night, Lai Yau thought he could understand the Western profit motive, as corrupt as it might be. Material possessions were an opiate, much like religion, but he understood why they were so addictive. Money, houses, fancy cars and women would appeal to most men if they were not educated in the dialectic that explained how such things spoiled man's days on earth. Lai Yau knew all the arguments by heart, and even he wasn't immune to cravings of the flesh.

Suppose he managed to obtain the information that Beijing desired so urgently, then went in business for himself. What then? His masters would be furious, of course, but how much could they really do to punish him? Assassins could be sent from China, but they would be strangers in Pahang, while Lai Man Yau was perfectly at home. He could evade them or destroy them as he chose. With cash enough behind him, he could hold his enemies at bay forever if he so desired.

Of course, defying Beijing would be treason to the people's revolution. Lai Man Yau had spent the past six years, one-quarter of his life, attempting to advance the cause of communism in Malaysia. What would he be if he reversed himself, belatedly rejected Chairman Mao and his disciples?

Rich.

His troops would never have to know. They followed orders to the letter, trusted Lai Man Yau as he himself had always trusted his superiors. His men were peasants—broken farmers, onetime beggars off the streets—who saw themselves as soldiers now, content to take direction from the man who had supplied them with a second chance in life. They wouldn't question his commands or fail him short of death. To them, Lai Yau was nothing short of God on earth. The masters in Beijing, by contrast, were a group of men too far away to merit real concern.

At that, Lai Yau knew his superiors had solid reasons for the things they did. He might not understand why a particular Chinese or Malay was selected for assassination, why a certain public building should be bombed or burned, but reasons still existed. This time, when he got the information Beijing wanted, Lai Man Yau would have to find out what it meant and weigh the risk of going private, opening an auction for the highest bidders from around the world.

He had connections in K.L. who could arrange the details, businessmen unscrupulous enough to take a chance where money was concerned. The trick would be establishing a price that made him rich, while covering his necessary partners, but without discouraging potential customers. For that, he had to know exactly what the product was, its open-market cost and the black-market value that would double, maybe triple the established asking price.

His first step, obviously, was to get the information in his hands, eliminate the middleman and find a place to hide while Beijing went berserk. What happened to his men once they had done their job was of no concern to Lai Man Yau. If some of them fell prey to Chinese execution squads, so much the better. He might even find a way to stage his own death, throw pursuers off his track so that he wouldn't have to waste a moment of the good life glancing nervously over his shoulder.

Foresight. Patience. Courage. Lai Man Yau had all these attributes and more. He hadn't failed thus far in anything he'd set out to accomplish for himself or for his masters in Beijing.

And he wouldn't fail this time.

He would be rich, no matter what it cost. And if he had to come back from the dead to spend his money, he would find a way to do that, too.

BY NOON, the jungle atmosphere had thickened, grown more humid and oppressive than the day before. Was it a simple change of weather, Remo wondered, or some constant aspect of the territory they had entered, making it the worst uncharted wilderness Malaysia had to offer?

He had seen more snakes and lizards in the past five hours than on any single day before, outside a zoo. Most of them went unnoticed by the other members of his party, dangling from the branches overhead or wriggling out of sight amid the undergrowth beside the path. But there had been a brief, unscheduled interruption of their march an hour previously, when their guide came face-to-face with a reticulated python on the trail. Pike Chalmers had his rifle shouldered in a flash, but Dr. Stockwell and Kuching Kangar dissuaded him from firing at the snake. Instead, the little Malay cut a six-foot walking stick and prodded at the sleek, fat reptile, irritating it enough that it was driven to retreat and clear the way.

"Now, that's a snake," said Audrey Moreland as the python slid from view, a gliding monster all of twenty feet in length.

"With any luck," said Remo, "that's the biggest thing we'll see."

"Bad luck, you mean," said Audrey, putting on an impish smile for Remo. "Don't you want to take a baby brontosaurus home?"

"I'd never make it back through customs," Remo answered. "Anyway, no pets allowed in my apartment building."

"That's a shame. No little pussycats?"

"If I get lonely," Remo said, "I stop off at the petting zoo."

"You don't know what you're missing," Audrey said.

"You may be right."

Their trek resumed from there, the python pit stop being counted as a rest break by Kuching Kangar. By Remo's estimate, the heat had gone up twenty-two degrees since they broke camp, and coupled with the increased humidity, any physical activity was a challenge, bathing them in sweat,

while simply breathing called for conscious effort.
Remo took the necessary steps to regulate his body
temperature and respiration, let himself perspire
without becoming drained of vital energy. In front
of him, the others labored underneath their heavy
loads like beasts of burden, pack mules hauling
freight across a trackless wilderness.

Remo barely felt his own pack. He moved with
the weight instead of fighting it, one foot in front
of the other as he kept up with the expedition's
steady pace. They weren't breaking any land-speed
records, but there seemed to be no desperate hurry,
either. If their guide was equal to his billing in
Dampar, he knew exactly how much farther they
would have to travel in relation to supplies on hand
and the anticipated personal endurance of his team.
As for the dinosaur, thought Remo, it would either
be there waiting for them or it wouldn't. Either
way, the game that held his full attention was about
uranium, not prehistoric reptiles.

It would help, he realized, if he could find out
something about the people who were trailing them.
He had discounted the idea that they were being
followed by a jungle predator; no animal he knew
of would be interested enough in human beings to
pursue them for a second day, when it had passed
a chance to raid their sleeping camp last night. On
top of that, it *felt* like people, sticking with the sin-

gle-mindedness that indicated some specific purpose.

Waiting to find out if we get lucky, Remo thought.

In which regard? He tried to picture jealous dinosaur enthusiasts pursuing them for miles upriver, through the jungle, but it didn't play. A rival expedition would have gone out for the fanfare of publicity to scoop the competition.

No, he reckoned as he felt the earth grow softer, spongy, underneath his feet, they would be looking for uranium. And that, in turn, left him with either one of two distinct and inescapable conclusions. On the one hand, it was possible that their pursuers simply had suspicions that Professor Stockwell's team was looking for uranium. The flip side, much more ominous from Remo's point of view, would mean they knew the team—or part of it, at any rate—was searching for the mother lode and using Stockwell's dino hunt for camouflage.

And how could anyone be sure, unless he or she was associated with the ringer? Standing by as back up, perhaps, if something necessitated getting rid of pesky witnesses.

Remo could have checked the stalkers out last night, but Audrey had distracted him. A nice distraction, he admitted to himself, but Remo knew that he would have to keep his mind on business in the future.

Which was not to say that Audrey would be wholly out of luck. He might be forced to skip a few more steps in the Sinanju love technique, speed matters up a little and make time for prowling in the jungle after she was tucked in for the night.

An ugly job, he thought, half smiling to himself, but someone has to do it.

He would think of it as one more sacrifice for duty and Emperor Smith.

He checked his watch against the sun, deciding they could march for several hours yet before they had to pitch camp for the night. There was no way of knowing if their guide had picked another campsite in advance, or whether he was playing it by ear. In any case, the trackers would be somewhere fairly close at hand.

He knew their general direction—south and west of Stockwell's team right now—and had no doubt that he could find them in the dark. They might be smart enough to camp without a fire, but men still gave off a distinctive odor, still made conversation and a host of other noises that would serve as well as any beacon in the night.

The only question left in Remo's mind was what to do with them once he made contact, whether he should kill them on the spot or let the waiting game continue for a while, find out exactly what they had in mind.

With any luck, the faceless enemy might help

identify the ringer on his own team. He would have to ask around before he killed them if it came to that.

"Are you okay back there?" asked Audrey, sounding winded.

"Hanging on," said Remo, hoping that he sounded tired.

"Don't overtax yourself," she told him, winking on the sly. "You'll need your strength tonight."

"My thoughts exactly," the Destroyer said.

11

They pitched camp in another clearing, smaller than the first one, with the jungle pressing closer on all sides. The nearby stream was smaller, too, and somewhat farther from the camp than last night's stop. Their guide went out first thing, with his machete, and spent half an hour hacking out a narrow path between the clearing and their only source of water. By the time he finished, everyone but Audrey Moreland had their tents assembled. Remo helped her out again, despite his firm conviction that she could have managed this time on her own.

"I don't know what I'd do without you," Audrey whispered.

"Something tells me you'd survive," he said.

"Oh, I imagine so," she told him, smiling. "But it wouldn't be much fun."

Kuching Kangar went out to scout around before the sun went down, while the others settled in to rest a bit before they started on the evening meal. Pike Chalmers made a show of wiping down his big-game rifle with a chamois, maintaining a deliberate distance from the scientific members of the team.

"We should be close now," Dr. Stockwell said, considering his map. "A few more miles will bring us to the western finger of the lake."

"So, what about the Tasek Bera?" Audrey asked him.

"Technically, we're in the region now," said Stockwell, "but the sightings all originate from farther east. We'll look around the lake for tracks and so forth, but I don't expect the great Nagaq to make himself so readily available for photo opportunities."

"I shouldn't think so," Chalmers said with no real effort to conceal his mocking tone.

Professor Stockwell turned to face him. "You're the expert hunter, Mr. Chalmers. How would you proceed from this point on?"

"Depends on what I'm hunting," Chalmers said. "On normal hunts, you've got three options. If you're stalking a specific animal—a local man-eater, let's say—you may get lucky with a fresh spoor from the latest sighting, and go on from there to track the bugger down. Another way is bait, o' course. Fix up a blind or tree stand, stake your bait out in a clearing and be ready with your hardware when some hungry bastard comes along.

"If all else fails, you watch the nearest water

source around the clock. No matter what you're hunting for, it has to drink.''

"Which method would you recommend in this case?'' Stockwell asked.

The hunter thought about it, finally shrugged. ''There's been no recent sighting that we know of, and we can't track anything without finding its spoor to start from.''

"What if we could find the former expedition's camp?'' asked Stockwell.

Chalmers frowned. ''We'd have to be damned lucky. If we find the camp, and if there's any tracks remaining, they'd be old by now. As far as picking up a trail that old and making something of it...well, it's not impossible, you understand, but damned unlikely.''

"And the other methods you suggested?''

"What I understand,'' said Chalmers, ''you've got no clear fix on what this bloody creature is or might be, other than some kind of prehistoric honker. Am I right?''

"Well—''

"And you've no idea what sort of menu it prefers, except for ravings from a dead man and the disappearing-granddad story, eh?''

"The evidence would seem to indicate a carnivore,'' said Stockwell stiffly. A tinge of angry color marked his cheeks.

Chalmers snorted in controlled disdain. ''You've

got no bloody evidence. Native superstition and the last words of a crazy man don't tell me anything. If there's a monster waddling around this patch, I need to see it for myself."

"And that's precisely why we're here," Stockwell reminded him. "We're paying you—and rather handsomely, I think—for your advice on how to make that sighting a reality."

"All right, then, here it is. We can't use bait without knowing what our intended likes to snack on, see? In fact, if it's a bloody carnivore we're after, I'll remind you that the only bait I've seen the past two days is us."

"In which case…?"

"We can either get damned lucky with a set of tracks," said Chalmers, "or we find a likely place to sit and wait."

"Why can't we simply search the forest?" Stockwell asked.

"You mean go out and beat the bushes?"

"Well…in essence, yes."

"You're not a hunter, are you, Doctor?"

"Well, no, but in theory it should work…"

"I thought not," Chalmers said with thinly veiled contempt.

"Enlighten me, by all means, Mr. Chalmers."

"Beating works all right for birds and other small game," Chalmers said. "You scare 'em up and shoot 'em as they fly or run away. It sometimes works with larger game, as well, if you can place your quarry in a given area and pick your stand, have the beaters run him toward the guns. All clear so far?''

"I follow you."

"Then follow this," the hunter said. "We have no beaters, Doctor. There's the six of us, and no one else. Besides which, I'll remind you that we don't know where this bloody creature is—if he exists at all—and he's got several hundred square miles he can play in while we run around in circles, going nowhere.''

"You appear to think it's hopeless, Mr. Chalmers.''

"Bloody difficult, I'd say. You knew that going in.''

"And what is your advice, in that case?''

"We should check around the lake for tracks, just like you said. That's first. If we get lucky, fine. If not, my guess would be that something really big will make its way down to the nearest water once a day at least. Good pickings by a jungle lake, if you're a hunter. All the grazers come to drink and have a snack some time or other. Big cats watch the water when they're on a hunt. Hyenas, too. No reason why your lizard shouldn't do the same, I'd say.''

Their guide returned just then, with nothing to report. They spent the next half hour fetching wood and water, stoking up a fire and laying out the kitchen gear. The evening's fare was freeze-dried stew, complete with stringy shreds of beef and vegetables the consistency of rubber. Remo would have settled for a bowl of rice, and gladly, but he didn't have the choice.

The conversation lagged while they were eating, no one seeming anxious to prolong the meal. Their second day of marching through the jungle had exhausted Dr. Stockwell, and their Malay chaperon was equally fatigued. The trail had left its mark on Audrey Moreland, too, but from the hungry glances she gave Remo, it was evident that she retained a fair amount of restless energy. Pike Chalmers was his normal hulking self, apparently unfazed by roughing it, despite the sweat stains on his khaki shirt.

They finished cleaning up the supper pots and pans in record time, an easy round-trip to the stream, and left the gear to drip-dry on its own for breakfast. Dr. Stockwell couldn't stop himself from yawning as they finished up the chores and sat around the fire. It was full dark now in the jungle, with the night sounds closing in.

"We're getting closer," Stockwell said. "I know we are."

"I hope so," Audrey said, her eyes on Remo.

"If we reach the lake in decent time tomorrow,

there's no reason why we can't start searching straightaway.''

"We are agreed, I think," said Sibu Sandakan, "that no new species shall be harmed in any way?"

"Of course," Professor Stockwell said. "That's understood."

"You make allowances for self-defense, I take it?" Chalmers asked.

"Legitimate defense, of course," their Malay escort said.

"Because I tend to take a dim view of an animal that tries to eat me, if you get my drift."

"That shouldn't be a problem," Audrey told him, "since you don't believe there is a dinosaur."

"Nagaq is here," Kuching Kangar declared. "We find him soon, I think."

"Whatever name the bugger goes by," Chalmers told the group at large, "I'm not his bloody appetizer. If we're clear on that, we've got no problem."

"On that note," said Dr. Stockwell, "I believe it would be wise for us to get some sleep. We have another early day tomorrow, as you know."

It was a repeat of the night before, retiring to their tents. Remo waited while the others fell asleep, Pike Chalmers taking longer than the rest, their Malay guide the last of all to pack it in. Before Kuching Kangar was wrapped up in his bedroll, Remo had begun to plan ahead, imagining what Audrey would expect of him, deciding on the steps that he would take to satisfy her quickly and leave enough time for himself to make a night search for the men who were pursuing them.

He could avoid the scene with Audrey altogether, Remo knew, but slipping past her would create more problems than it solved. She would be wandering around the jungle, looking for him, maybe getting into trouble on her own, and she would almost surely check his tent if Remo stood her up. That would mean questions in the morning, and if she was pissed enough, the woman scorned, she might say something to the others.

No, he thought, don't risk it. There were clearly worse chores in the world, and he was confident that he could have her ready for a good night's sleep in thirty minutes, tops. Once she was safely tucked into her sleeping bag and dreaming, Remo would be free to go about his business, prowling in the deep, dark woods.

He gave it twenty minutes more, then slipped out of his tent and edged around the clearing, to the rough trail. Another moment brought him to the stream, where Remo waited in the shadows, dodging moonlight. He would wait ten minutes, give her ample time, and if she had not shown by then—

A sound of cautious footsteps on the trail brought Remo into focus. Audrey came in view a moment later, stepping to the water's edge, briefly hesitating, then glancing left and right.

"Renton?"

"Right here."

She turned to face him. "There you are. I didn't hear you leave the camp."

"You weren't supposed to," Remo said. "I hope the others didn't hear me, either."

"They're all sawing logs," she told him, moving closer. "Did you learn to move that way from hunting snakes?"

"I've found that there are times it doesn't pay to make a lot of noise."

"How right you are." She was unbuttoning her blouse, below the pastel scarf she wore. "I'll do my best to hold it down, if you can keep it up."

His suave reply was interrupted by a tiny sound that emanated from the general direction of the camp. It wasn't loud, but it came to Remo's ears with great distinctness.

A sharp, metallic sound, as of an automatic weapon being cocked.

"Stay here," he said to Audrey.

"What? Why?"

"We have some uninvited company. Do as you're told and keep out of the way."

"I—"

Remo never heard the rest of it. He was already moving back along the trail at full speed, a flitting shadow in the jungle night. Before he reached the clearing, Remo veered off to his right and circled

through the trees, his every sense alert to danger
now. It only took a moment for his nostrils to detect
the smell of unwashed human bodies, sweaty
clothes and gun oil. From the shifting, rustling
sounds, he estimated there were ten or fifteen men
positioned in a ring around the camp.

How had he missed them when he left the clearing? How had they missed Audrey Moreland?
Remo guessed that it came down to timing, possibly
a shifting breeze that had prevented him from picking up their scent, and his distraction at the thought
of meeting Audrey for another one on one.

Chiun would gleefully have kicked his ass for
screwing up a practice exercise through simple negligence, but this was even worse. A blunder in the
field put lives at risk, potentially endangered
Remo's mission. He would have to make it right,
and quickly, if he didn't want the whole damned
game to fall apart.

He reached out for the nearest prowler with his
senses, found a target twenty feet away and closed
the gap between them with long, silent strides. The
gunman was a Malay, carrying an AK-47, with a
pistol on his hip. He watched the sleeping camp and
waited for the order that would send him forward
into battle.

Were they here to kill or merely watch?

No matter. Remo couldn't take the chance.

He came up on the gunner's blind side, snapped

his neck before the dead man realized that he was not alone and caught the body as it sagged, collapsing toward the forest floor. He laid the corpse out carefully, as one might put a drowsy child to bed, and left the automatic rifle propped across its owner's chest.

One down, and Remo went in search of number two. The second man he found was taller, slightly older, similarly armed. Because he huddled with his back against a tree, it was impossible for Remo to approach him from behind. He came in from the left instead, and used a floater strike to crush the gunman's skull, his free hand clutching fabric to prevent a noisy fall.

How many left exactly? There was no way to be sure except—

All hell broke loose. Someone was shouting from the far side of the clearing, and bodies crashed through the jungle. Remo didn't speak the language, but he recognized a signal to attack.

No shots were fired until Pike Chalmers bolted from his tent and saw a gunman charging toward him from the west. The Weatherby .460 Magnum roared, his target crumpling like a rag doll by the fire, and Chalmers whooped in satisfaction at the kill.

A scattering of automatic weapons opened up at that, and while it seemed to Remo that at least one Malay voice was calling for a cease-fire, those with itchy trigger fingers were in no mood to restrain themselves. Whatever their original intent, some members of the raiding party were content to kill these round-eyes on the spot.

He met a third guerrilla coming through the trees and dropped him with a short jab that ruptured heart, lung, spleen. The dead man wriggled for a moment on the ground, and then lay still. Behind him, in the clearing, the staccato sounds of gunfire tore the night apart.

Remo moved in that direction, caught a glimpse of Chalmers firing off into the trees. Professor Stockwell called out Audrey's name and got no answer as he peered briefly from his tent before a bullet kicked up dust mere inches from his face and drove him back to cover. Sibu Sandakan remained inside his tent, as if he thought the flimsy canvas could protect him from an armor-piercing round, but Remo couldn't spot their guide.

Halfway back home by now, he thought, and wondered whether they would ever see Kuching Kangar again—or if there would be anyone alive to guide should he return.

The sound of rapid firing close at hand led Remo to a Malay gunman who was pumping rounds into the camp without regard for where they went or who got hit. The surest, quickest way to stop him was a simple twist that left him facing backward while his lifeless body toppled forward, spinal column neatly severed at its juncture with the skull.

And that made five, including one for Chalmers. Remo calculated that the hostile force had been reduced by thirty-odd percent in something like a minute, but the odds were still against his comrades coming out unscathed.

He recognized the scream immediately, knew that it could only come from Audrey Moreland. In his mind's eye, Remo saw her waiting by the stream until the shooting started, drawn back toward the camp by curiosity and some part of the same fear that repelled her. Audrey on the narrow trail, advancing toward the sounds of battle, when a Malay gunman stepped across her path and—

Remo made his choice and bolted through the trees, directly toward the clearing that had turned into a shooting gallery. It was the path of least resistance if he kept his wits about him and remembered not to zig when he should zag. If it was not too late for Audrey, he could get there.

Pike Chalmers saw him coming, either failed to recognize him on the run or simply did not care whom he was firing at. The rifle swung around to cover Remo, Chalmers closing one eye as his other found the telescopic sight. It only took a gentle squeeze now, and the bullet that could drop a charging elephant would tear through Remo's chest.

Or maybe not.

In fact, he dodged the slug as he had done a hundred times before, anticipating Chalmers with a sidestep that did nothing to reduce forward momentum. By the time Pike understood that he had missed, began to work the rifle's heavy bolt, Remo was past him, reaching out to flick the weapon's muzzle with a fingertip and spin the Brit around, unceremoniously dumping him on his ass.

At that, he saved the hunter's life, though it had not been part of Remo's plan. Another member of the hit team, rising from the undergrowth beyond the clearing, had been set to riddle Chalmers where he stood, but now his spray of bullets cut through empty air, the big man sprawled just below the line of fire.

Another heartbeat put Remo in the startled gunner's face, an elbow rising at the speed of thought, connecting with the Malay's forehead, flesh and bone imploding into brain. The sweaty man went down without another sound, his useless weapon lost from lifeless fingers.

Back in camp, the Weatherby boomed again, but Remo didn't hear the bullet pass his way. Perhaps the trigger-happy hulk had been disoriented by his fall, or maybe he had simply found another target in the firelight, going where the action was.

Another scream came from Audrey, somewhere off the trail and to his right. Before he could correct and change directions, Remo was confronted with another gunman, this one a grim-faced Chinese. His AK-47 had been fitted with a bayonet, and now he made the critical mistake of thrusting with the blade instead of leaping back and firing from the hip. The man couldn't have saved himself in either case, but as it was, he made things easier.

A simple grab and twist disarmed him, putting the Kalashnikov in Remo's hands, where it became a deadly bludgeon. Only one stroke was required to shatter the guerrilla's skull, but Remo spared another second as he passed. He turned the gun around and hurled it like a javelin, impaling his late adversary with the bayonet and pinning him against the nearest tree before he had a chance to fall.

No sound from Audrey now, but Remo had fixed the general direction of her last outcry. Another ten or fifteen yards brought Remo to the place—he was convinced of it—but he had come too late.

The ground beneath his feet was moist and spongy here, like peat, and it gave way to quicksand several paces farther on. A shallow film of stagnant water overlay the quagmire, insects flitting here and there across the scummy surface, and a flash of color in the moonlight caught his eye.

A pale pastel.

The scarf that she had worn around her neck.

He grabbed a trailing vine and waded in, his free arm plunging deep into the mire, but he felt nothing underfoot, quicksand slithering around him like a vat of lukewarm oatmeal. There was no firm bottom to it, and suction dragged at his legs and buttocks, threatening to pull him down.

He gave it up before the stagnant water reached his chin, clung to the vine and dragged himself hand over hand until he cleared the quicksand, settling back on solid ground.

Sweet Jesus!

She was gone.

It took a moment for him to recover from the shock. He was accustomed to all forms of violent death, but Remo wasn't made of stone. Whatever he had felt for Audrey Moreland, simple lust or something more, it would demand a decent grieving period.

Okay, time's up.

He scrambled to his feet and turned back toward the clearing, suddenly aware that the Kalashnikovs had fallen silent. One more shot from Chalmers split the night, an exclamation point for the proceedings, telling Remo that at least one member of the party was alive.

In fact, they all were.

When he reached the clearing, Dr. Stockwell stood beside Pike Chalmers near the fire, and Sibu Sandakan was crawling from his tent. It took another moment for their guide to reappear from his concealment in the jungle, but he seemed to be unharmed.

"Is everyone...?"

The question died on Stockwell's lips as he saw Audrey's pup tent, torn by bullets. Dropping to his hands and knees, he peered inside and found it empty.

"Audrey? Audrey!" he called out to her but got no response. "Where is she?"

"Where's the lizard man?" asked Chalmers, peering briefly into Remo's empty tent.

"Who? Dr. Ward? You mean he's gone, as well?"

"Seems so."

"For God's sake, where? Will someone tell me what is happening?"

Instead of stepping forward with an answer, Remo faded back into the darkness, silent as a falling leaf. A hasty body count informed him that a number of the enemy had managed to escape unharmed, and he wasn't content to let them go. It would be relatively simple to pick up their trail, despite the darkness, and pursue them till they stopped for rest.

And then he would have answers—or at least a taste of vengeance. Either way, this gaggle of guerrillas had performed their last night ambush in the Tasek Bera.

Remo left his traveling companions huddled near the fire, with Chalmers standing guard. As far as he could tell, from scouting out the area, they were at no risk of a new attack. The enemy had fled, perhaps to lick his wounds, but he would never get the chance.

12

Lai Man Yau was physically exhausted when he called a halt for his surviving troops to rest. A forced march in the jungle could be difficult, but running through the jungle in the dark was something else entirely. When he counted heads by moonlight, Yau discovered he had lost eight men. Precisely half his fighting force.

The worst part of it was, he still had no clear fix on what had happened, why his plan had come apart like tissue paper in a weeping woman's hands.

The plan itself was simple and direct, foolproof from all appearances. He had examined it from every angle he could think of in advance, deciding that it didn't matter if a couple of the Malays missed their cue or moved in prematurely. There were only four round-eyes to deal with, after all, and only one of them was armed with anything besides a knife. If he resisted, it would be no challenge for a force of seventeen trained soldiers to subdue him with a minimum of force.

Yau sat and thought about the raid in detail, try-

ing to pinpoint the moment when it fell apart, un-
raveling before his very eyes. It was impossible to
say, of course, because he couldn't be with each
one of his men every moment. Still, there had been
no alarm before he gave the signal to attack, move
in and seize the round-eyes while their minds were
fogged with sleep.

The big one with the gun had been a rude surprise; Yau could admit that to himself. The round-
eyed bastard came out shooting, not at all the
groggy fool they hoped for. Yau had seen him drop
one member of the strike force, and he had fired
several other rounds before the raiders turned and
ran. With eight men missing, who could say how
many he had killed or wounded in the brief engagement?

Wounded?

Lai Man Yau felt tension coiling in his stomach
like a viper poised to strike. Suppose that one or
more of his commandos had been captured, still
alive? If they began to spill their guts—

No, he wouldn't give in to that line of thought.
They had all been trained, albeit briefly, to resist
interrogation, and anyways, it really didn't matter
if they cracked or not. Yau had been careful not to
share the substance of their mission with the troops,
withholding all the major details for himself and
Sun Leo Ma, his second-in-command.

Sun Ma was lost now, almost certainly among

the dead, and Yau felt his loss most acutely. He couldn't relate to Malays in the same way that he did a fellow countryman. They were all right as cannon fodder, handling the dirty work, but when the revolution came at last, a Chinaman—perhaps Lai Yau himself—would lead it, marshaling the people's army for a rousing victory.

Before that happened, though, he had to try to do a "simple" job with the survivors he had left, attempt to salvage something from the rubble of his master plan.

Beijing would not be understanding or forgiving if he failed. His contact had been crystal clear on the importance of this mission, and a disappointment could have painful—even fatal—consequences. Lai Man Yau had pledged himself to die, if necessary, to promote the people's revolution, but he didn't plan to be rubbed out because he'd let that revolution down.

Yau sat and thought some more, remembering a sound that had briefly distracted him in the midst of the battle, when everyone was firing. He recalled a scream. A woman's scream that emanated from outside the camp.

It had to be the round-eyed woman, screaming from the jungle. Why? What was she doing out there in the dark? Yau took the simplest answer and decided she was probably responding to a call of nature. Westerners liked privacy when they relieved themselves, as if their shit were something sacred, to be envied by the world. Perhaps this round-eyed bitch had left the camp before his troops took their positions, and no one saw her go.

But why was she screaming?

She had started only after shots were fired, Yau thought. Perhaps the sound had frightened her. And she had stopped almost immediately after that. Did she have sense enough to know the screams would give away her hiding place? Or had some member of his strike team found the woman, silenced her forever with a bullet or a blade?

Yau hissed for quiet in the ranks and waited till he had their full attention, asked the question to their faces. None of them admitted contact with a woman, and judging by their blank expressions, he had no reason to believe that they were lying. Furtive glances would be one thing, pointing to a guilty conscience, knowledge of a critical mistake, but Yau saw nothing of the kind.

If she was dead, then, it meant one of Lai Yau's missing troops had done the job. It would hardly matter, except he still had no idea which member of the expedition was supposed to be his contact, and it suddenly occurred to him that he might never know. If he was forced to stalk and kill the others, it would be a total failure, and Beijing's reaction would be inescapable.

The raid had sprung from an impulsive notion.

Yau was tired of tramping through the jungle on a mission that could last for weeks without result, if the round-eyes found nothing. On his own, he had decided it was better to corral the foreigners, interrogate them and discover which one was supposed to be his ally. Once that information was obtained, the round-eyes could continue with their expedition, more or less—but under guard and with a very different goal in mind. Forget about the fairy tales of giant lizards tramping through the forest. Yau would let them hunt uranium instead, and he would also let them dig for it, relieve his troops of one unpleasant task.

Before he sent them on to meet their round-eyed god.

Now he had botched it, and the fault was his alone. He had considered laying off the blame on Sun Leo Ma, but that was unacceptable. Friendship aside, Beijing would never understand why Yau, the officer in charge, had delegated such authority to a subordinate, with such disastrous results.

The only way to save himself, he realized, was to retrieve the situation somehow. He would have to do it soon, and he couldn't be subtle, given the present circumstances. There could be no question of negotiating with the round-eyes, making friends or ''burying the hatchet,'' as they liked to say in the United States. It would be force or nothing, and his troop had already been cut in half. Their three-to-one advantage had been whittled down to something closer to two to one, and the Americans had shown a startling talent when it came to self-defense.

Surprise was critical, he understood, but it wouldn't be easy to achieve a second time.

"Be quiet," Yau snapped at his men, "and listen while I tell you what we have to do."

THE TRACKING PART WAS easy. In their haste, his enemies had made no effort to disguise their trail. He could have followed them on nothing but the fear smell in a pinch, but they had also left him footprints, trampled ferns and broken tree limbs—someone in the raiding party even dropped an empty AK-47 magazine and left it on the trail as he reloaded on the run.

It was no challenge, hunting clumsy amateurs.

The raiders had a six-or seven-minute lead when Remo started after them. Although they knew the territory better, they weren't all that adept at running for their lives in almost total darkness. Pushing it, with all the skills Chiun had taught him, Remo started picking up their panicked scurry-noises after just two minutes on the trail. Then he had to slow down to keep from overtaking them while they were on the move, and forcing a chaotic confrontation in the dark.

There was no question in Remo's mind of the

outcome, but he wanted information first. He had no qualms about a battle on the trail, but Remo knew that it might be impossible for him to single out the leader, spare his life and save him for interrogation once the others were eliminated. He decided to follow them until they stopped to rest, as they were sure to do within the next half hour or so, and then to pursue the matter with a more coherent strategy.

Think first, Chiun had told him countless times, then act. The thinking didn't have to be prolonged in every case, no great excursion through the labyrinth of military tactics or philosophy, but it was never wise to strike in anger, blindly, without weighing the potential risks against rewards.

The hunt was twenty minutes old when Remo's quarry took a break, the early rush of panic fading as they picked up no immediate suggestions of a hot pursuit. They fanned out in a small glade overgrown with ferns, three gunmen keeping watch while the remaining six were huddled in a group, their heads together.

Remo studied them, moved past the guards as if he were invisible. The leader of the party was Chinese, but he spoke Malay to the others. Remo didn't understand a word, but no translation was required for him to know they must be hashing over what had gone wrong with the raid on Stockwell's camp. The leader started out with questions, but the answers clearly failed to satisfy him, and he had progressed to curt instructions by the time Remo began to make his move.

He started with the sentries, closing on the nearest one and striking from the shadows, catching man and weapon easily before they hit the ground. No noise. He didn't think of Audrey or of anything beyond the fine points of the stroke he knew by heart.

Imagine every move before you make it. See it in your mind and let your muscles feel it.

Done.

He moved on to the second guard, had no more trouble there. The target was not perfectly aligned, so Remo let the sentry hear him coming, just a scuffling in the dirt to bring the soldier's head around. He pulled the punch enough to keep from shattering his adversary's skull—too much potential for the sound to carry—but it did the trick, regardless. Blood was leaking from the dead man's nose and ears as Remo eased him down onto the turf.

The third lookout appeared to have no clue of what it meant to stand a ready watch. He had his back turned toward the forest, busy listening to every word his leader said, when Remo took him from behind and snapped his neck without breaking a sweat. Three up, three down—but now he had a problem on his hands.

The other six all carried automatic weapons,

most of them Kalashnikovs, and while the distance was not great, their huddle almost perfect for his purposes, he didn't want to simply fling himself among them, striking left and right as if it were a barroom brawl. For one thing, he couldn't be sure the leader would survive that way. And for another, he wasn't convinced that the Chinese would be of any use to him, alone.

Which meant that he would have to use a gun.

It ran against the grain. Those days were long behind him now, the teachings of Sinanju having lifted Remo to another plane, where firearms were both awkward and unnecessary. He could snatch life from his adversaries in a hundred different ways, bare-handed, and if that failed, he had learned the secrets of converting household objects into deadly weapons as the need arose. With guns, you had the noise and smell, ballistics tests, the problem of disposal—but the rules were all on hold tonight. Whatever happened in the next few moments, the authorities could search for months and come up empty.

On the flip side, if he made his next move empty-handed, Remo could be forced to kill all six of the guerrillas, and come out of the experience no wiser than when it began.

The choice was made. He held the third dead sentry's rifle cocked and ready as he stepped into the glade.

"Does anyone speak English here?"

The sound of Remo's voice brought six men scrambling to their feet, a couple of them aiming guns in his direction. They were startled, but they also saw the AK-47 in his hands, and when their leader barked an order to the rank and file, they held their fire.

"I said, does anyone speak English?"

There was a momentary hesitation. Several of the Malays glanced back and forth at one another. Finally, the leader made things easy, holding up one hand as if he were a schoolboy asking for a bathroom pass.

"I do," he said.

"That's fine. Now, tell your boys to lay their weapons down—no tricks—and line up over there." As Remo spoke, he pointed with the AK-47's muzzle to a clear spot in the glade, some ten or twelve feet to the left of the Chinese.

The would-be soldiers did as they were told, reluctantly at first, but when the leader started snapping at them, they got motivated in a hurry. Remo had them covered as they stacked their weapons in a pile and lined up touching shoulders, as if waiting for a uniform inspection.

Remo could have shot them where they stood, one burst to knock them down like bowling pins, but he had something else in mind. Six pairs of eyes were focused on him as he crossed the glade in dappled moonlight, thick ferns swishing feather soft around his legs.

"You sit down on that log," he told the Chinaman, and pointed to a spot that placed the leader six or seven strides from the collected hardware.

It would have to be enough.

"All comfy?"

Remo waited for the leader's curt, resentful nod before he went to work. He used the AK-47 as a cudgel, spinning it around, first striking with the butt and then the barrel, crushing skulls, ribs, Adam's apples, breastbones, vertebrae. He caught the first two absolutely by surprise, and nailed the other three as they tried to break and run. The rifle wasn't balanced for such work, but it served well enough until he broke the stock on number four and had to kill the fifth by hand.

Their leader sat and watched them die, a stunned expression on his face. He didn't have to ask what had become of his three sentries when he saw the bodies strewed at Remo's feet. A sharp flick of the wrist, and Remo sent the broken AK-47 spinning out of sight.

"Okay," he said, not even winded by the massacre, "let's talk."

"Who are you?" asked the Chinese leader when he could find his voice.

"I'll ask the questions," Remo told him, stepping closer just to emphasize the point. "All right?"

"All right."

"You made a move on Dr. Stockwell's expedition, and I need to find out why."

"Stockwell?"

He closed the gap, reached out and grabbed his adversary by the throat. It was a simple thing, no trick at all, to hoist him off the ground and let him dangle, choking as a steely grip cut off his flow of oxygen.

"I guess I wasn't clear about the rules," said Remo. "When I ask a question, you're supposed to answer it, not pick a word and give it back like I was talking to a parrot. Do we understand each other?"

Remo shook the man a bit, then dropped him in a heap. Stepped back and gave his prisoner enough room to get up on hands and knees.

"We don't know Stockwell," the Chinese informed him, holding one hand to his throat and speaking in a raspy tone. "No names. I'm told a group of round-eyes will be coming, one of them a comrade. He has information I must send back to...send back."

He let the fancy footwork go for now. "Which round-eye?"

"We don't know. He will reveal himself when it is time."

"You took a chance back there," said Remo, "shooting up the camp. How did you know you wouldn't kill him?"

"My men get excited," the Chinese replied. "I try to stop them. They are not much good."

"Not anymore. You want to join them?"

Blinking rapidly, the Chinese shook his head. "No, please."

"Okay. What kind of information were you looking for?"

"Don't know. The round-eye would deliver. We would pass it on."

"On, where?"

The kneeling soldier hesitated, finally shook his head. Remo's hand moved to his neck and at a certain spot applied pressure. The soldier's eyes bulged as he was overtaken by a universe of pain he never even knew existed.

"That was just a love memento," Remo told him when he let go. "I don't think you really want to piss me off."

The Chinese stared at Remo. Silent tears of pain left bright tracks on his sallow cheeks.

"Once more, then," Remo said. "Who's waiting for the information? Where's it going?"

Silence, and he was about to try a different strike, had one arm poised and ready, when his hostage blurted out a single word.

"Beijing!"

And it made sense, of course. The Chinese had uranium at home, but there was no such thing as too much weapons-grade material these days. If they could strike a bargain in Malaysia—or promote a revolution that would sweep the present government away, put friendly Reds in charge—then Chairman Mao's disciples would be points ahead. The value of an ore strike would depend on size and easy access, the expense of mining and a dozen other factors Remo had no time to ponder at the moment.

He had managed to identify one set of players in the game, and that would have to do. The placement of at least one ringer on the U.S. team had also been confirmed, but he was short on evidence in that department.

"You've been a great help," Remo said, and chilled the rebel leader with a kick he never saw.

The forest glade was silent, still as death. He knew that when he left, within an hour at the most, a troop of scavengers would home in on the first faint smell of carrion and start to feed.

"Bon appétit," he told the night, and started back toward camp.

"I CAN'T BELIEVE they both just disappeared," said Safford Stockwell, staring hard into the fire.

"Under the circumstances," Sibu Sandakan reminded him, "it's possible they are unable to respond."

"But both of them? What were they doing out of camp?"

"That's what I'd like to know," said Chalmers, standing well back from the camp fire, with a captured automatic rifle braced against one hip.

"I thought..." Professor Stockwell hesitated, shook his head. "No, it's ridiculous."

"What is it, Doctor?"

"Well, there was a moment," he told Sandakan, "right in the thick of things, when I was almost certain I saw Dr. Ward. He seemed to come out of the jungle over there and run across the camp and out the other side. I must have been mistaken, though. You surely would have seen him, Chalmers."

"I'd have seen him right enough," the hulking Brit replied. "And all I saw were bloody wogs with Rooshian weapons, like this here." He brandished the Kalashnikov for emphasis. "I dropped one of them over there," he boasted, "and may have hit a couple more, besides."

"Of course you did your best," said Stockwell, "but I still can't fathom why they ran away. One gun against so many, and they simply vanished."

"All depends on who's behind the gun," said Chalmers, puffing out his chest. "I'd say they understood they'd met their match."

"But where is Audrey, then?" asked Stockwell in a woeful voice. "I could swear I heard her voice."

"A scream," said Sibu Sandakan. "I heard it, too."

"Outside the camp, it was, just like you said," Pike Chalmers told them. "She had no good reason to go traipsing through the woods that way. The neither of them did."

"My God, what if she was abducted by those men?" Professor Stockwell blurted out.

"Then you can kiss her pretty arse goodbye," said Chalmers.

"We must try to get her back!"

"And follow them, the three of us? Don't make me laugh." The big man caught himself and rushed to qualify the comment. "I could track 'em down, o' course, and try to take 'em by myself, but that's a sucker's game. The two of you would only slow me down, and as for fighting, well..."

His sneer left no doubt as to Pike's assessment of the value his companions would contribute in a killing situation. Neither Sibu Sandakan nor Dr. Stockwell rushed to contradict him, each man conscious of his limitations when it came to playing soldier in the wild.

"But if she's still alive—"

Their guide returned as Dr. Stockwell groped for something more to say. Kuching Kangar had gone to make a rapid circuit of the area, find out if he could pick up any trace of Audrey or the missing herpetologist. A tattered, muddy scarf was dangling from his left hand as he stepped into the firelight, moving closer to the fire.

"That's Audrey's!" Stockwell blurted, pointing with a shaking hand. "Where did you find it?"

"I find in quicksand, that way." As he spoke, Kuching Kangar inclined his head back to the north and east, the general direction of the nearby stream.

"Quicksand?" On Stockwell's lips, the word came close to sounding like a curse.

"No bottom," said the guide. "Sink down, too late."

"Dear God!"

"And what about the other one?" asked Chalmers.

"Nothing," said the guide. "Too many footprints. Dead men all around. Count seven, plus the one you shoot."

"God's truth! I must've hit more than I thought," said Chalmers.

"Only one more shot," Kuching Kangar replied. "The others killed by hand. Find one, back there, up on a tree, with his own rifle sticking through."

"What does it mean?" asked Sibu Sandakan.

"It's rubbish," Chalmers said. "If they were killed that way, it means the bloody wogs were killing one another. Can you make sense out of that?"

"But if he says they were not shot—"

"So, what the hell does he know, looking at a lot of bodies in the dark? He's not a bloody coroner, for Christ's sake."

"Well, there can't be much mistake about a rifle sticking through a man," said Dr. Stockwell.

"I'll believe it when I see it for myself."

"Eight dead men altogether," the professor said. "How many bullets does your rifle hold?"

Chalmers scowled as he said, "I have the Colt, as well."

"Did you fire it?"

Angry color rushed into the big man's cheeks. "All right by me, if you prefer to take this bloody wog's word over mine," he said. "But don't come asking my advice on anything, while you've got Mr. Answers over there."

"Now, see here, Chalmers—"

"We must certainly turn back," said Sibu Sandakan, his firm voice breaking Stockwell's train of thought.

"Turn back?" The very notion seemed to boggle Stockwell's mind. "But why? We're almost there!"

"We've been attacked by rebels, Doctor, and they may come back at any time. Two of our group are missing, one of them apparently without hope of return. It is enough."

"For you, perhaps!" It was the first time Stockwell's tone had risen to this pitch or taken on such grim determination. "I, for one, have not come to this godforsaken place and sacrificed so much to simply turn around and slink home with my tail between my legs. If there is something to be found here, I intend to find it. Audrey would expect no less."

"But surely, Doctor—"

"Mr. Chalmers, if you will continue with the expedition, I can promise you a fee of half again what we agreed."

"You'll double it, or there's no deal," said Chalmers.

Stockwell didn't even have to think about it. "Done," he said, and turned to face Kuching Kangar. "Will you continue as our guide?"

"I paid to find Nagaq," the little Malay said. "Not finished yet, unless you say go back."

"It's settled, then. We're pressing on."

"I really can't allow—"

"Excuse me, Mr. Deputy," Professor Stockwell said, "but if you feel like turning back, it seems you'll have to go alone. You're free to take a fair share of the food, of course. We're not barbarians."

"My duty is to stay with you and guarantee your safety."

"I suppose you'd better get some sleep, then," Stockwell told him, hollow eyed and grim. "It's morning now, and we'll be moving out at dawn."

13

Remo was in no great hurry to rejoin the expedition once he reached the clearing where the tents were pitched. Pike Chalmers was pulling sentry duty with his growing stash of weapons. Like Tom Sawyer at his funeral, in the Mark Twain novel, Remo understood that there were certain definite advantages to being dead.

The first time he had "died," in the New Jersey State electric chair, it opened up a whole new life for Remo. There was Dr. Harold Smith. His work with CURE. Chiun, of course, and the endless hours of his instruction in Sinanju. There had been understandable resistance on Remo's part in the beginning, but today, all things considered, Remo knew that he wouldn't have turned the clock back and resumed his first life for a million dollars in cold, hard cash.

This time across the River Styx, he calculated that the gains would be more modest. Still, it never hurt to learn what people said about you when you left the room, especially when they reckoned you were gone forever. Failing a disclosure from loose lips, he was content to watch and wait, convinced the ringer would be revealed before much longer, now that they had voted to proceed with the expedition despite the apparent losses sustained.

The vote surprised him in a way. He understood that Dr. Stockwell was a focused man, where old bones were concerned, but Remo had suspected that his grief for Audrey Moreland and the lurking threat of danger in the jungle would persuade him to retreat. Instead, he showed amazing—even foolish—courage, seasoned, Remo told himself, with just a dash of stubborn pride. The way he found the key to Chalmers's heart with cash, then silenced Sibu Sandakan, had been impressive for a man of Stockwell's seeming Milquetoast disposition. There was still the guide, though, and his bland acceptance of continued danger troubled Remo most of all.

"I paid to find Nagaq," Kuching Kangar had said, as if that answered everything. In fact, from Remo's personal experience, the hired help was the first to bail when things got dicey—locals in particular, because they knew the countryside, its dangers and the glaring limitations of the men they had been paid to chaperon. This guide, however, was not only willing to resume the hunt, despite a band of armed guerrillas breathing down his neck, but Remo would have almost called him anxious to proceed.

It didn't fit the profile, but he couldn't get a handle on the problem. Was their guide the ringer? That made even less sense, when he could have gone out searching on his own, made better time without a bunch of round-eyes straggling out behind him.

No. It made no sense at all. Whatever drove Kuching Kangar, hard logic said that it wasn't uranium—perhaps not even cash. The little Malay needed watching, then, but so did Chalmers, Stockwell, even Sibu Sandakan.

Four suspects, Remo thought. And while he hoped that it was Chalmers—anything to give him one more crack at the conceited Brit—it struck him that the odds were fairly level, all around.

He sat and watched their small camp as the night wore on and dawn's first light broke in the sky. Pike Chalmers nodded twice, but caught himself before he dropped the captured AK-47. With the sunrise, Chalmers roused the others from their tents, and they began the desultory task of boiling breakfast in a plastic bag.

It smelled like shit and looked a bit like corned-beef hash.

The long night watch had given Remo time to think. He had already come to terms with Audrey Moreland's death, accepting it as one of those events no man can truly guard against, and none can change. He had been fond of Audrey, in a piggy sort of way, but there had been no prospect for an ongoing relationship, once Remo's mission was completed. And although Jean Rice and he clicked in a nice way, deep down he knew that a settled life was not for him—especially given his role in life that the fates threw his way. When he thought about it, Remo realized that he was something of a hermit, but he liked it that way.

It was better than his first life, by a country mile.

He would miss Audrey Moreland, in the sense that he had taken pleasure from her luscious body, giving pleasure in return, but that was transitory, like an itch, a sneeze. Their conversation had been limited, confined primarily to subjects that meant nothing to him outside the parameters of his assignment. Once the job was finished, Remo knew that it would be a rare occasion when he thought of her at all.

That sounded cold, and so it was. It wasn't just because he was a professional assassin, part of a highly focused breed. As a matter of fact, Remo had his problems with that fact, problems that were ameliorated somewhat by the very cause CURE served—his native country, the home of the free. Beyond this, he knew his past life was gone, never to be resumed again. Then there was Sinanju, a way of life that had become his recipe for life, not something he could abandon for the comforts of a hearth—and the unthinkable, an ordinary job.

Sinanju was the work, the work was all, and God help the idiot who tried to take that work away.

He watched the shrunken team break camp, and noticed that they left two tents behind. His own and Audrey's.

"We can pick them up on the way back," Pike Chalmers said. "Enough to carry as it is."

"You're right, of course," Professor Stockwell said, despite a wistful parting glance at Audrey's pup tent.

They were on the trail by half-past seven, pushing hard. Kuching Kangar was still on point, with Chalmers next in line. The Brit had slung his Weatherby and kept the AK-47 in his hands, a liberated bandolier of extra magazines contributing more weight to his selected gear. Professor Stockwell was the third in line, and Sibu Sandakan had landed Remo's tail position by default. He seemed unhappy with the ranking, glancing frequently and fearfully over his shoulder, but he held a steady pace and didn't slow the party down.

They had been marching for an hour, Remo hanging back some twenty yards, when he discovered they were being followed once again.

He stopped dead in his tracks and closed his eyes, the other senses reaching out for any information they could gather. It was nil on the aroma, but his ears picked up a sound of someone moving through the jungle thirty-five or forty yards to

Remo's right, due south. One person, by the sound
of it, and he was taking care to limit the unnecessary noise.

The stranger's path ran parallel to Stockwell's,
eastbound, and there could be no coincidence in
that. With all the jungle territory of Malaysia to go
hiking in, the odds against an honest chance encounter in the Tasek Bera had to be immense. No,
make that astronomical.

He tried to guess who it might be—a lone guerrilla he had missed last night, perhaps, or someone
who had picked up rumors of their mission in Dampar and trailed them out of curiosity…or greed. In
fact, he knew that there was only one way to find
out.

He homed in on the sounds, still meager and sporadic but enough to put him on the stranger's track.
Five minutes later, he was standing on another
game trail, where his quarry must have been just
seconds earlier.

The man was gone.

A tiny rustling in the undergrowth ahead, and
Remo braced himself, prepared to spring. The momentary tension drained out through his feet, as
something like a giant guinea pig broke cover and
ran squeaking down the trail, away from him.

The blow came out of nowhere, struck him
square between the shoulder blades, and slammed
him to the earth, facedown.

Somewhere behind him, to his left, a dry voice said, "You must not let your guard down, even for a moment, if you wish to stay alive."

IT TROUBLED Sibu Sandakan, the way that everything had suddenly gone wrong. He hadn't taken to this job from the beginning, didn't feel himself cut out for slogging through the jungle, but the past few hours had been a waking nightmare. The guerrillas bent on killing them, apparently succeeding with two members of the team, were bad enough. And now the old American, this "doctor" of old bones, insisted that they must go on with the charade. Pursuing dinosaurs, of all things, when their lives were certainly at risk!

The others had predictably agreed with Dr. Stockwell, since he held the purse strings for the expedition and could seemingly increase their salaries at will. Pike Chalmers was a racist mercenary who, in Sandakan's opinion, would do anything for money, while the guide was just a simple peasant. He might earn a whole year's salary for this one expedition if he went along with Dr. Stockwell and pretended to believe in giant prehistoric lizards plodding through the jungle.

Sibu Sandakan considered pulling rank and ordering the guide to turn around. He was a representative of the Ministry of the Interior, second deputy to the appointed minister, and as such he deserved respect. Unfortunately, peasants in the countryside were known for their indifference to authority. They failed to pay their taxes promptly—sometimes altogether—and were prone to settle arguments with violence. The last thing Sandakan desired, right now, was for an unwashed peasant to defy him while the Brit and the American looked on, amused by his discomfiture.

In fact, he had already tried to summon help and scrub the expedition, last night when the bullets started flying. Huddled in his pup tent, braced for death at any moment, Sibu Sandakan had searched his pockets for the small transmitter that First Deputy Germuk Sayur had provided on the night before their party left K.L.—but it was gone.

In panic, he had dumped the contents of his backpack, fingered each in turn and came up empty. There was simply no sign of the plastic box that was supposed to summon troops to his defense in an emergency.

Where had it gone? He thought about the past three days, couldn't remember any single incident where he had fallen, dropped his gear or anything of that sort. Still, the small transmitter had been in the pocket of his trousers, close at hand. It could have fallen out when he withdrew a handkerchief to mop his sweaty face or wriggled free when they sat down to rest at some point on the trail. Its bulk and weight were insubstantial; he had barely no-

ticed it five minutes after they were on the plane to
Temerloh.

The damned thing could be anywhere by now.

Which meant that he was trapped with Stockwell,
Chalmers and the guide. He could start back alone,
as the professor mockingly suggested, but it would
be suicide for him to strike off through the jungle
on his own. He had no compass, and it would have
made no difference if he did. A city boy at heart,
he looked for landmarks in the form of street signs
and familiar buildings. Sibu Sandakan could no
more chart a safe course through the wilderness
than he could build a rocket ship from scratch and
fly it to the moon.

Thus far, he thought he had concealed his mounting panic from the others fairly well. The argument
in camp had been a test for him, and Sandakan had
passed, not shouting once, and swallowing the
tremor in his voice before the others could detect
it. They already thought of him as weak, but if they
knew that he was terrified, it could become a different game entirely. Chalmers was a bully, and
Sandakan would have no peace for the remainder
of their journey.

Which, if the guerrillas struck again, would not
be long.

He didn't grieve for the dead Americans, although the news would be embarrassing when it got
back to the United States. His first consideration

was potential damage to his own career resulting from his loss of the transmitter and whatever followed as a proximate result. Germuk Sayur and the men above him were expecting an alert if any member of the party found uranium, a dinosaur or any other object that the sitting government could seize and turn to profit for the state. Sandakan's own negligence had let them down—or would if there was anything to find in this forsaken hell on earth—and he couldn't expect the lapse to go unpunished.

He would be disciplined, of course, but there were varying degrees of punishment in civil service. Flat dismissal was among the worst, accompanied by the humiliation of explaining to his friends and family why he was fired. Sandakan knew men who had committed suicide with lesser provocation, but he wouldn't feel like dying for a job already lost. With any luck, he might get off with a demotion, possibly a reprimand. It would depend on what came next, the expedition's course from that point on, and whether they actually found anything of interest.

Before Germuk Sayur had a chance to punish him, however, Sandakan would have to make it back alive. And at the moment, he had no great confidence in his ability to manage that. No confidence at all.

He knew that he must watch the others—Chalmers in particular—and be prepared to save himself at any cost. Guerrillas might turn out to be the least of it where they were going. Sibu Sandakan didn't believe the legends of Nagaq, but there were hungry predators aplenty in the wilderness, and any one of them might prize a second deputy for dinner.

It would be different, he considered, if he were armed. Pike Chalmers held their only firearms, though, and he wasn't the sort to share his toys with "bloody wogs."

If I get out of this alive, thought Sibu Sandakan, I'll see the bastard's visa canceled. Yes, indeed.

But getting out alive would have to be the first priority.

And it would take up every bit of concentration he could muster in the next few days.

"YOU DIDN'T have to hit me," Remo told Chiun as he was dusting off his clothes.

"A simple touch," the Master of Sinanju said. "If you were properly alert, I could not have surprised you."

"Some surprise," said Remo, blustering. "I heard you tramping through the forest like a water buffalo. You must be getting old."

"I let you hear me," Chiun responded, "and your impudence is unbecoming, even for a white man."

"Impudence? You knocked me on my ass."

"You fell upon your face," Chiun corrected him,

"although I must admit the two are easily confused."

"Oh, that's hilarious. I see you're doing stand-up comedy these days."

"At least I manage to stand up."

"So, what's the story? Did you travel all this way to get a few digs in?"

"I am the Master of Sinanju, not a common miner. Is there something precious here that I should dig for it?"

"Could be," said Remo, frowning as he flexed his shoulders, working out the pain that lingered from Chiun's "simple touch."

"It is appropriate for an instructor to observe his student," Chiun remarked. "Your style leaves much to be desired."

"You ought to see the other guys."

"I have," Chiun replied. "Did you have difficulty killing them?"

"Get real."

"Then you have set yourself no challenge. In the early days of training, students learn from repetition of the simplest moves. A more advanced practitioner must test himself, seek new plateaus of knowledge and achievement, always learning."

"You've been watching Sally Struthers."

"Who?"

"You want to learn a new trade? Sure, we all do."

"You speak gibberish."

"Forget it," Remo said. "What brings you all this way?

"A wish to supervise your mission. It occurred to me that you might not be totally prepared."

"I couldn't have a better teacher than the Master of Sinanju," Remo said.

"That much is obvious. The doubts lie not in my ability, but yours."

"Oh, thank you very much."

"Don't mention it. A master is expected to correct his pupil as the situation merits."

"Besides, I already earned the right to be a future Reigning Master, remember? So what exactly have I done to make you doubt me, Little Father?"

"Aside from simple negligence, there's nothing—yet." Chiun considered what he had to say for several seconds more before continuing. "I'm not convinced that you are ready to confront a dragon."

"What?"

"The challenge may be more than you can handle. It was not appropriate of me to send you on a job that needs a Reigning Master's touch."

"That's it?"

"Disposing of a dragon calls for special knowledge. We have not addressed it in your lessons up to now. I do not doubt your courage, Remo, but it may not be enough."

"You can relax," he told Chiun. "We haven't seen a footprint or a dragon turd so far, much less the Big Kahuna."

"'Big Kahuna' is no fit name for a dragon."

"Little Father—"

"It is settled," said the Master of Sinanju. "I cannot allow you to proceed without the proper supervision."

"This is all about uranium," said Remo with a smile. "The dragon's just a smoke screen."

"Are you certain?"

"Well—"

"The white man often scoffs at things he has not seen or does not understand."

"The fact is, no one on the team apparently believes there is a dinosaur, except for Dr. Stockwell and the guide. He says it ate his grandfather."

"The doctor's grandfather was eaten by a dragon?"

"No, the guide's."

"Do not be quick in denigrating native tales," said Chiun. "I grant you, these are not Koreans, and their understanding of the world is therefore minimal at best, but they are not completely ignorant of their surroundings."

"*Superstitious* is the word that comes to mind."

"Even superstition may be based on fact. A legend stretches truth, but it does not begin without some circumstance to prompt its telling in the first place.''

"What I'm thinking," Remo said, "is that the story makes a handy cover. Now, I know they've got a ringer on the team, who works for the Chinese. I got it straight from the guerrilla leader."

"He was Chinese?" asked Chiun.

"That's right."

"And you believed him?"

"In the circumstances, yes."

"You tortured him," said Chiun with satisfaction.

"I persuaded him."

"The Chinese want uranium?"

"He wasn't told, but that's what Dr. Smith believes. I can't see Beijing wasting agents on a dinosaur hunt."

"The Chinese are a mystifying race," Chiun replied. "They want to be Korean in their hearts, but since perfection has eluded them, they scheme like Japanese and try to make up, through intrigue, what nature has denied them."

"An unbiased view, of course," said Remo.

"When the truth is biased, should we lie? I had no hand in the creation of mankind, thus I gain nothing from a simple statement of the facts. All Asians envy the Korean people."

"What about the rest of us?" asked Remo.

Chiun responded with a gesture of dismissal.

"Black men envy whites," he said, "and white men are the most pathetic of the lot. They envy one another. It is too absurd," the Master of Sinanju finished, chuckling dryly to himself.

"Well, this has been a slice," said Remo, "but I really ought to catch up with the others now."

"And how will you explain your absence?"

"Oh, they think I'm dead."

"So your appearance may surprise them."

"I don't plan on dropping in," said Remo. "I've been following their trail since dawn and watching from a distance."

"In the hope this 'ringer' may reveal himself?"

"It's all I've got to go on at the moment."

"And your dalliance?"

"Say what?"

"The woman. What is she expected to reveal, beyond what you have seen already?"

"You were watching?"

"It is my responsibility," Chiun said.

"Well, you can scratch her off your worry list. We lost her in the raid last night."

"I never worry. Was she shot?"

"Quicksand."

"Another clumsy white."

"You shouldn't talk that way about the dead."

"Who better to discuss, without a fear of contradiction?" asked Chiun. "I trust that you did not become attached to this one."

"No," said Remo.

"It would be a grave mistake."

"I know that."

"Very well. You may wish to consider a revision of your plan."

"Which plan is that?"

"Your plan of hiding from the others."

"Why?"

"Consider the effect a ghost may have upon a guilty conscience."

"That's a thought."

"You are perceptive," said Chiun.

"I'm also out of here. You coming?"

"In my own time," said the Master of Sinanju. "These frail limbs—"

Remo grinned. "Just try to keep the noise down, will you? The Big Kahuna may show up and use you for an appetizer."

"Whelp."

"I'll see you, Little Father."

"Only if I want you to."

14

Dr. Stockwell's dwindling group had gained a quarter of a mile since Remo left them, but he had no trouble catching up. Their progress was sluggish, with Stockwell plodding like a man whose hope was gone, continuing the march on stubbornness alone. Pike Chalmers didn't seem to care how fast they traveled, pausing every thirty yards or so to scan the jungle, listening, his AK-47 leveled from the hip. Their guide had slowed to the professor's slogging pace, and Sibu Sandakan resembled nothing quite so much as an exhausted marathoner suddenly confronted with the prospect of a twenty-seventh mile.

Remo was still debating Chiun's suggestion when he overtook the party, coming up behind them through the trees. He understood the logic of surprising them and watching for the kind of odd reaction that would point a ringer out, but he had tried that once before without results. Besides, he had no reason to believe the raid had been coordinated with his quarry, much less aimed at him. It seemed to

Remo that the rebels had been jumpy. Looking for a way to speed things up, they had exercised poor judgment, acting on their own initiative. In that case, every member of the team would be surprised to see him still alive, but none had any special cause for disappointment at the fact.

Except, perhaps, for Chalmers.

He had definitely drawn a bead on Remo in the clearing last night, no excuses based on the excitement or confusion of the moment. He had also killed at least one of the rebels, though, and that appeared to mitigate against him as their contact on the team. More likely, Chalmers simply wanted Remo dead as payback for their brief encounter in K.L.

But who else on the team would fit the profile of a turncoat? Remo had examined each of them before, and none would be his own first choice for a clandestine operation. Only Chalmers, with his mercenary background, seemed to have the requisite credentials for the job, but his contempt for Asians and a certain lack of finesse made Remo yearn for more-persuasive evidence.

At least today he knew there was a ringer on the team. He trusted the guerrilla leader that far, even if the man had initially lied about his knowledge of the mission's goal. One member of the party was in league with the Chinese, had sold himself, and eighteen lives had already been lost as a result.

How many yet to go?

The question had no relevance for Remo. He wasn't concerned with numbers, unless they prevented him from finishing his job. What Remo needed at the moment was a suspect he could focus on and deal with one-on-one.

If he rejoined the others now, there would be calls for an explanation of his disappearance. He could always claim that he was knocked unconscious, maybe got disoriented in the dark and only found the group again by pure dumb luck, but would they buy it? And if not, what then?

He had about decided to maintain his distance, watching from concealment, when Kuching Kangar stopped short and raised a warning hand to halt the others. Remo froze in place, his senses reaching out in search of danger signals.

He almost missed it, but a subtle movement in the undergrowth before him marked the presence of another human being. Make that several human beings, crouched beside the trail. He hadn't seen or heard them going in, because they made no sound or movement to betray themselves. As for the human smell, once Remo saw the nearest of them, it appeared the almost-naked men were daubed with mud, like body paint, that covered them from head to foot.

Pike Chalmers almost cut loose with his AK-47 when the natives showed themselves, but he was concentrating on the new arrivals, and he over-looked Kuching Kangar. Before the Brit could aim and fire, their guide had turned on him and swung the heavy bolo knife he carried, knocking the Ka-lashnikov from Chalmers's hands.

Chalmers cursed, reached for his pistol, but the Malay guide was faster, leaping forward with a snarl to press the bolo blade against his adversary's throat.

"No guns," he warned, and Chalmers spent a moment glowering before he gave it up and raised his hands.

The tribesmen carried spears, some bows and ar-rows, with a hand-carved war club here and there. It was not their equipment, though, that held Remo's attention. He was looking at their faces, bodies, frowning as he checked them out.

Of twenty natives he could see, their guide in-cluded, only six were normal in appearance under-neath the layers of mud. The rest displayed a wide range of bizarre deformities that made them look like something from a circus sideshow. Three were pygmy sized, but with heads out of proportion to their bodies, clutching six-foot spears in tiny hands. Another held his fighting club in hands like lobster claws. A fifth had short, bowed legs beneath a mas-sive torso, with a dwarfish, pointed head on top. The man beside him only had one eye, but it was planted squarely in the middle of his forehead. Yet another stood on cloven feet, resembling fleshy hooves. Webbed fingers, crooked spines, diminished and distorted limbs—as Remo glanced around the group, he saw it all.

The expedition was surrounded by a tribe of pissed-off freaks. Professor Stockwell glanced around at the distorted limbs and bodies, frightmask faces that surrounded him, and felt his last reserves of courage drain away. It was too much: first the guerrillas, then losing Audrey in a quicksand bog, and now this, surrounded by a band of nightmare creatures armed and seemingly intent on mayhem. And Kuching Kangar was clearly part of it—a friend of their assailants, possibly a member of their tribe. There were a few among the native band with normal faces, well-formed bodies, and he guessed their trusted guide was one of those, at liberty to move in the society of men without provoking undue curiosity.

When Stockwell found his voice, he spoke directly to Kangar. "What is the meaning of this outrage?" he demanded. "Are you mad?"

The guide faced Stockwell, smiling, while he kept his bolo pressed against the tall Brit's throat. "Some of us," he replied in English notably improved, "are surely mad, but it is no great handicap. As for the meaning of this outrage, you are needed, Doctor."

"Needed?"

"For Nagaq."

Professor Stockwell failed to catch his drift. "Of course," he said. "It's what we've wanted all along. We chose you as the man to help us find Nagaq."

"That's where you are mistaken, Doctor. I chose you," Kuching Kangar replied. "And you will not be searching for Nagaq. We have arranged for him to visit you."

"So much the better," Stockwell said, but he was frowning as he spoke. There was an undercurrent to the guide's voice, he belatedly decided, that did not bode well for the surviving members of his party. "I hope we can conclude our business promptly, then," he said.

"Your business is concluded, Doctor," said the Malay guide. "You have a very different role to play in what must happen next."

"You bloody wogs won't get away with this," Pike Chalmers snarled.

"And who will stop us, sir?" Kangar was grinning as he spoke, the sharp blade of his bolo drawing blood from Chalmers as he pressed it close against the tall Brit's flesh.

"I must inform you," Sibu Sandakan announced, "that I am here to represent the government. It will go badly for you if you harm us."

Kangar flashed him a mocking grin. "Punishment, you mean?"

"Of course."

"Who will punish us? Not you, I think."

"The government has troops—"

"And you were told to signal them," the guide told Sandakan, interrupting him. He reached into a pocket of his trousers with his free hand and withdrew a smallish plastic box. "With this device, perhaps?"

"Where did you get that?" Sandakan demanded.

"Why, from you, of course." The guide's smile stretched almost from ear to ear. "You won't be needing it."

That said, he cocked his arm and pitched the small black box into the forest, out of sight.

Professor Stockwell didn't hear it fall. "You were prepared to summon troops?" he asked, now facing Sibu Sandakan.

"In the event of an emergency," the deputy replied. "We're in the middle of the wilderness, for heaven's sake. It was a simple safeguard—"

"Which has failed to save us, after all," said Stockwell, interrupting him. He turned back to their former guide and asked, "What do you want from us?"

"I've answered that. You have been chosen for Nagaq."

"And what does that mean, if you don't mind telling me?"

"In good time, Doctor. We have miles to travel

yet, before you meet the object of your heart's desire. It will not be an easy march, but that cannot be helped. We should arrive by nightfall if you do not slow us down too much.''

''I'll do my best,'' said Stockwell, not without a hint of sarcasm.

''I'm sure you will,'' Kangar replied. ''But if you lag along the way, my brothers will encourage you.''

The Malay snapped his fingers as he spoke, and two of his compatriots—a grinning cyclops and a dwarf with six toes on each foot—stepped forward, prodding Stockwell with their spears.

''That won't be necessary,'' the professor said.

''In that case,'' said the little Malay, ''shall we go?''

PIKE CHALMERS OFFERED no resistance as the mud-smeared natives stripped him of the Weatherby, his Colt and hunting knife. They didn't frisk him like policemen, but it made no difference; he was effectively disarmed.

But that was not the same as being helpless. No, indeed.

From under lowered eyebrows, Chalmers counted twenty adversaries, with their erstwhile guide, but most of those were what the bloody PC crowd back home called ''challenged'': stunted limbs and missing digits, crooked spines, misshapen skulls. One bugger seemed to have no lips to speak of, while another's nose was nothing but a perforated pimple in the middle of his face. It was a blessing, Chalmers thought, that they had sense enough to cover up their genitals with loincloths.

He imagined running wild among them, swinging left and right with massive, angry fists. One stiff poke in the eye would blind the frigging cyclops, and the dwarfs would be no problem; he could boot them down the trail like flabby soccer balls. Six normal-looking men could be a problem, true enough, but if Pike could grab the bolo knife—or better yet, one of the spears...

On second thought, however, there was something that he didn't like about the bowmen. They were small and stupid looking, Chalmers granted, but they also held their bows as proper archers might, with arrows nocked and ready, pointed in the general direction of their targets. Long, sharp arrows, he couldn't help noting, with the tips discolored, as by some vile potion used to make them twice as deadly in the flesh.

The more he considered things, the less he liked those six-foot lances, either. That was no way for a man to die, with spears stuck through him till he looked like some damned insect on a bug collector's mounting board. And from Kuching Kangar's expression, he would only be too happy for a chance to use his bolo on a proper Englishman. The

bloody wogs were all that way, ungrateful bastards
to the bitter end.

So he would bide his time, thought Chalmers.
Find out where the freaks were taking him—and
his companions, too, of course—before he tried to
break away. He didn't follow all this rot about
Nagaq, but what could anyone expect from savages
whose normal microintellect was cooked in a genetic soup that obviously left much to be desired?

He would find out where they were going, keep
a close eye on the local landmarks so that he could
make his way back out again. If there was profit to
be taken at the end of their forced march, he would
do everything within his power to secure the lion's
share of it—and failing that, he would by God remember the location of his captors' sanctuary, come
back later with a solid team of men who knew what
they were doing, men who took life seriously, not
a gang of bloody scientists who couldn't tell a pistol
from a piss pot when the chips were down.

The world would never miss a tribe of freaks like
this, he reckoned. It would be a public service to
the gene pool, wiping this abomination off the map.
If anyone found out and thought about complaining,
it would be a clear-cut case of self-defense. There
would be weapons to support Pike's claim...and
maybe the remains of several recent victims, too.

The more he thought about it, slogging down the
trail and sweating like a pig, the more Chalmers

came to realize that he should make his break alone, when it was time. He didn't give a damn for Sibu Sandakan, the bloody wog, and Dr. Stockwell was an old man who would slow him down, most likely get him killed if Chalmers tried to pack him out with natives howling on their heels. Looked at another way, the old bone doctor made a perfect sacrifice. His death at savage hands would raise a bloody hue and cry from K.L. to the States, and anything Pike Chalmers did to pay his killers back would likely get a rubber-stamp approval from the powers that be.

All right, then.

By the time the first mile was behind them, Chalmers had his mind made up. He would be careful, watch and await his chance.

A SMALL BLACK PLASTIC box came sailing at him through the trees, and Remo snatched it from the air, examined it and dropped it in his pocket. It was obviously a device for signaling. The brief exchange between their guide and Sibu Sandakan suggested it would summon army troops if Remo pressed the button, but he didn't want a mob of reinforcements rushing in.

Not yet.

The ambush had surprised him, an embarrassment that Remo swiftly overcame in his determination to pursue the natives and their hostages, find out where they were going and what bearing it might have on his mission to the jungle.

The deformities he saw among the natives meant no more to Remo at the moment than they seemed to mean among the tribesmen. He could think of several handy explanations for an isolated tribe where freakish traits had run amok. Inbreeding might explain it, some genetic taint passed down through generations, while new blood became increasingly uncommon. A pollutant in the air or water was another possibility, as with the plague of mercury-infected fish some years ago at Minamata, in Japan. Insecticides and toxic waste were out, considering the territory, but there were minerals and heavy metals found in nature that would have the same effect.

His train of thought was sidetracked as the party started moving. They kept on heading eastward, veering slightly to the south when they had covered half a mile or so. The trail was left behind, but it meant nothing to the natives, who guided their three prisoners by secret paths no white man had traversed in living memory.

Behind them, Remo was their shadow, hanging back enough to keep from being noticed but never falling far enough behind to lose their scent or sound. The natives were adept at forest travel, but they still left traces of themselves behind for anyone with eyes to see. If necessary, Remo could have let them lead him by a day, but he preferred to keep the hostages within his reach in case the end—whatever that turned out to be—came suddenly.

The hiking gave him time to think about what he had overheard while spying on the Malays and their prisoners. The captives were supposedly en route to meet Nagaq, whatever that meant. Remo didn't like the sound of it, but he was still inclined to wait and see what happened in the short run rather than attacking from the shadows and endangering his recent traveling companions. There was no fear on his own behalf, despite the heavy odds, but he couldn't prevent one of the natives spearing Stockwell, Sandakan or even Chalmers while he dealt with their associates. Whatever lay in store for the three hostages, Remo could be ready in a flash if someone tried to execute them on the trail, but otherwise, he thought it best to watch and wait.

The jungle felt more claustrophobic here, a combination of congested undergrowth and something less substantial—almost metaphysical—but Remo had no problem keeping up with the bizarre procession. Once, he traveled for a quarter mile above them, skipping through the treetops, feeling very much like Tarzan as he left the ground behind. It was a whole new world up in the canopy, some sixty feet above the forest floor, complete with creatures who were born, lived out their busy lives and died without a single visit to the ground below.

He thought of waiting for Chiun, but had no way of knowing where the elderly Korean was, when he would choose to reappear or what he had in mind. Right now, the more important task was keeping up with Dr. Stockwell and the others, making sure they didn't stray beyond his reach.

Some unknown ordeal lay ahead of them—that much was obvious. With luck, Remo thought it might just help him single out the ringer he was looking for and finalize his mission. Once the traitor was eliminated, Remo could decide what he should do about the freakish natives, the survivors of the expedition and the panic button nestled in his pocket.

Choices.

What was all this talk about Nagaq? It seemed that Stockwell's party had been captured by some kind of native cult, though Remo couldn't say for sure. Devotion to a mythic creature wouldn't be the strangest notion he'd ever heard of, and the setting clearly lent itself to legends, whether they revolved around a dragon or a tribe of forest trolls. In fact, it wouldn't have surprised him to discover that the freakish tribe itself had given rise to some peculiar stories in the neighborhood if he had time to ask around.

Mythology didn't concern him at the moment, though. His more immediate priorities were flesh and blood—the natives, their three hostages, the

man he had been ordered to identify and kill. The
jungle spooks and demons, meanwhile, would be
forced to watch out for themselves.

There was a brand-new predator advancing on
the Tasek Bera. Grim. Impervious to pity. Ruthless.
And he wouldn't stand down until his work was
done.

And old Nagaq would have to take a number if
he wanted Remo's prey.

15

Safford Stockwell slapped at his neck. The heat and the incessant hum of insects buzzing in his head was driving him mad. He'd come so far, risked everything, only to be stopped by these primitives before he reached his goal. It was just too much. It meant that Audrey's sacrifice had been for nothing, all their effort a pathetic waste of time. When he was gone, another white man swallowed by the jungle with no clue to what had happened, how his mocking colleagues back at Georgetown would amuse themselves at his expense!

Kuching Kangar had promised they were being taken to Nagaq. Of course, the comment was intended as a threat, but Stockwell took it as a hopeful sign. The natives obviously meant to kill their prisoners, but there was still a chance that he could change their minds. And if he failed, at least there was a possibility to see his curiosity assuaged.

Stockwell was not an anthropologist, but he was literate, well-read in many disciplines. He knew, for instance, that most cults—at least among the aborigines, where modern drugs and psychopathic "saviors" weren't an issue—had their roots in some concrete and tangible event. The Polynesian cargo cults were an example, sprung to life from Allied air drops during World War II. Some isolated tribes still worshiped mock-ups of the aircraft that had showered them with blessings fifty years ago, a whole new generation waiting for the sky gods to return.

Why should Nagaq be merely fantasy, a witch doctor's hallucination? Was there any reason to rule out that this group, at some point in the past, had encountered some forgotten creature thought to be extinct?

It need not mean Nagaq was still alive, or even that it had been sighted by living men within this century. However, since the last known dinosaur abruptly vanished more than sixty million years ago, which was some fifty million years before the first appearance of a protohuman ape, it stood to reason that no man had ever seen a dinosaur...unless a few stray specimens had somehow managed to survive.

There were alternative hypotheses, of course. Nagaq might not be an official dinosaur at all. Stockwell had seen enough, when he was younger and more heavily inclined toward working in the field, to realize that science still had far to go in terms of understanding life on earth. New species weren't found as quickly as the old ones disappeared, but each year still brought some remarkable discoveries. Most of the "new" arrivals were diminutive—insects, amphibians and reptiles, with a few stray birds and mammals, but a larger species surfaced every now and then. The great Komodo dragon was a "legend" until 1912, and the first specimen of the "mythical" Kellas cat had been bagged—in Scotland, no less—as recently as 1983. If the immense, uncharted Tasek Bera region did not hold some secrets of its own, then Dr. Stockwell would be very much surprised.

He only hoped that he would live to find an answer to the riddle, even if he never had the chance to share his information with the world at large. There would be satisfaction just in knowing for himself, a certain pride in realizing that his last great effort hadn't been a total waste.

They didn't stop for rest at all that day, and there were times when Stockwell thought he would collapse from sheer exhaustion on the trail. Each time he faltered, though, one of his captors would rush forward, jabbing at him with a spear or crude stone knife until he found fresh energy and struggled onward. Sparing sips from his canteen kept Stockwell going, that and fear, but he grew famished as the afternoon wore on, exertion burning up the calories with nothing to replace them. His stomach growled like a caged animal, but no one seemed to notice, and the feeling of embarrassment passed.

By late that afternoon, their path was winding

downward, losing altitude, although he reckoned
that must be a function of his own fatigue. According to the topographic maps he carried, this whole
region was a sort of swampy floodplain, nearly
level, with no striking highs or lows. There were
no mountains in the district, for example, and it
stood to reason there would be no valleys, either.
Still…

But as dusk approached, he realized there could
be no mistake. Their path was intersected by a gully
that led steeply downward for a hundred yards or
so, then leveled out again. Trees from each side of
the gully met overhead and blocked out the sunlight. More than once, he saw the disappearing tails
of serpents startled by their passage and half expected a king cobra to rear up and block the path
at any moment.

Watching out for snakes made Stockwell think
of Renton Ward, and that in turn brought painful
memories of Audrey Moreland back into the fore-
front of his mind. Such beauty, squandered in a
godforsaken wilderness, and she would be forgotten
almost overnight back home.

The trees cleared out in front of them, a sudden
break in the oppressive gloom, and in the few short
yards before they closed in overhead once more, he
saw it.

He stood rooted to the spot until his captors
shoved him on.

Stockwell thought he must have lost his mind. The heat had poached his brain; that must be it.

He blinked, then blinked again, but nothing changed. The scene in front of him was real, and his companions saw it, too. Pike Chalmers, too, had stopped dead in his tracks, dumbstruck, until a couple of the pygmies prodded him with spears. Stockwell now kept on moving, even though his legs had lost their feeling. He was giddy with excitement, close to passing out from the combined effects of hunger, heat, exhaustion and surprise.

But he kept moving.

Toward the ancient, hidden city that had risen from the ground in front of them, as if by magic.

COMING HOME WAS always a relief and pleasure for Kuching Kangar. He hated visiting the outside world, but he had no real choice. Cruel Fate had marked him with a face and body that were different from others in his clan—"normal" in the words of men who didn't know his people—and it meant that he was preordained to bridge the gap between his tribe and those Outside.

In every generation of his people, there were six or seven normal ones, enough to carry on their necessary commerce with the world of common men. It was a part of great Nagaq's own master plan, and while Kuching Kangar could recognize the genius of it, he was still uncomfortable with his special role. Raised from birth to be as those Outside, he always knew that he was strange, a fact the other children of his tribe wouldn't let him forget. They teased him constantly, threw pebbles at him when he tried to join them in their games and made it crystal clear that he would never be entirely welcome. The young women of the tribe had shunned him, too, as if his normal aspect was revolting, something to be feared. In time, he knew from adolescence, elders of the tribe would choose a normal female for him, to perpetuate the freakish bloodline, even if they had to snatch one from Outside.

The normal ones must never die out absolutely, after all. They were the only link between his people and the larger world that brought them special treasures: gold and silver, precious stones and sacrificial offerings for great Nagaq.

When he was sent away for education with the common men, Kuching Kangar had worried they would find him out, see something in his eyes or in his manner that would instantly betray him as a member of the tribe. He had been wrong, of course. The men Outside were idiots, for all their schooling. They knew nothing of his people or Nagaq. They even raised their children to believe that dragons were a figment of imagination.

Fools.

These days, he lived between two worlds, with one foot in the City and the other one Outside. With his diplomas duly registered and filed away, Ku-

ching Kangar took pains to hide his education,
building up a reputation as one of the foremost
hunting guides in all peninsular Malaysia. He was
famous, in his way, among the Outside men who
came with guns or cameras to stalk the native wildlife, study plants or mingle with the aborigines.
Some came in search of oil or other minerals, but
it was all the same to him. Each year, a number of
his clients vanished in the jungle, always under circumstances that would not reflect upon Kuching
Kangar or make him suspect in the eyes of the authorities.

Nagaq demanded periodic offerings, but there
were millions of unsuspecting fools Outside, and
each new season brought a crop of them, intent on
finding riches, romance or adventure in the wild.
Most made it back intact, but if a member of the
party should be lost occasionally, snatched by "tigers," "crocodiles" or "quicksand," who would
be the wiser? After ten years in the game, Kuching
Kangar had come to realize that strangers from Outside were fond of tragedy. It made their own lives
more exciting, satisfying somehow, if they knew
somebody who had died.

Perhaps it reassured them of their own invinci-
bility, when Death brushed shoulders with them and
selected someone else. The roots of their peculiar
mind-set held no fascination for Kuching Kangar.
It was enough for him, and for his people, that the
idiots still made themselves available—and paid

him very handsomely for leading them to meet their fate.

He'd never before snared an entire expedition, but Dr. Stockwell's group was special. They had come to find Nagaq, the first time in a generation that Outsiders had taken any interest in a "simple native legend." Last time, in the year before Kuching Kangar was born, a group of British soldiers had come hunting for the dragon, but their disbelief had blinded them, and they were too well armed for any member of the tribe to challenge them. Besides, they had been more concerned with pitching tents and practicing survival exercises than in hunting for Nagaq. A normal member of the tribe had been their guide, and he made sure they never passed within a day's march of the City.

There had never been another name for it, as far as he could tell. The tribe didn't possess a written history, of course, but the traditions were preserved in oral form, passed down among the normal ones and any others capable of holding long-term memories. It was "the City," plain and simple, built from massive blocks of jade, erected in the time before remembering. The site was chosen by an ancient father of the tribe who was the first to see Nagaq and worship him with offerings.

According to tradition, early members of the tribe had all been normal. It took a few years in the City, worshiping Nagaq, before the dragon god had started blessing them with special children. At first, in the beginning of the change, some members of the tribe were horrified, repulsed by "monster" children in their midst, but then a wise priest recognized the blessing of Nagaq and carefully explained it to the others.

They had chosen wisely in their god, and he rewarded them by setting them apart. He placed his mark on those who served him, leaving normal ones among the blessed to help deceive the world at large. Sometimes, he even favored normal ones with special children, so they wouldn't be discouraged by their lot in life or blame themselves for having failed to worship him with proper offerings.

Nagaq had placed his mark upon the City, too. A secret river from below ground fed a stone fountain in the spacious courtyard where the tribe conducted many of its rituals. And sometimes, in the dark of night, the very water seemed to come alive with eerie, dancing lights.

The blessing of Nagaq.

He stared ahead now, his heartbeat fast and joyous. His first glimpse of the City, after time Outside, inevitably caused his pulse to quicken. *Beautiful* was not a word that sprang to mind—the jade was ancient, weathered, faded, mostly overgrown with moss and creeping vines—but it was home. His heart was here, among the other members of the tribe. So would it always be.

The massive gates were fashioned out of square-cut timber, thirty-five feet tall, and flanked by sentries on the wall. At the appearance of the warriors and their captives, one of those on guard gave out a birdlike call to someone in the courtyard, an all clear for opening the gates. It took some time—each gate weighed tons, and only Small Ones were permitted, for some reason, to perform the opening—but Kangar felt no need to hurry. He had performed his mission, and he would receive his just reward.

Perhaps, he thought, already conscious of a restless stirring in his loins, he could request a night with Jelek, the three-breasted one.

"What is this place?" the old professor asked, yelping when one of the Small Ones jabbed him with a spear.

"The City," said Kuching Kangar, as if that answered everything. Which, in his own mind, was the truth.

"You live here?" There was amazement in the voice.

"The tribe lives here, white man. I am a member of the tribe. Where should I live?"

"I simply meant—"

The Small One used a bit more force this time, and Dr. Stockwell got the point. He shut his mouth and kept it shut, eyes focused on the double gates as they crept open, inch by groaning inch.

"I'll guess you don't have many visitors," Pike Chalmers said. "Be bloody tiresome, going through this nonsense every time somebody rings the bell."

The one-eyed member of their party stepped in close to Chalmers, lashed out with his spear as if it were a cudgel, using force enough to bruise the tall Brit's shin.

"Goddamn your eye!"

The next blow dropped him to all fours, a dazed expression on his face.

The gates stood open before Kuching Kangar now, his people gathered in the courtyard to behold the offerings he brought Nagaq.

He smiled and led the way inside.

HIS FIRST GLIMPSE of the hidden city startled Remo, made him double-check his map, but there was no mistake. He didn't have a fever, wasn't prone to fantasy and this was no mirage.

The maps were simply wrong—or rather, incomplete.

He watched and waited while the massive gates were opened, a laborious procedure that convinced him there must be some other means of access to the city, for emergencies. If fire broke out, if they were suddenly attacked, there would be some hidden exit, almost surely more than one.

The trick would be to find it, if he didn't want to scale the wall for starters. Not that it would be a challenge, since the weathered stone offered countless cracks and crevices, all kinds of creepers on the outside that could double as a ladder. Even so, the wall was guarded, and while Remo had the utmost confidence in his ability to take the sentries out, there would be hell to pay if one of them lived long enough to sound a general alarm.

In that case, Remo knew, the hostages would be in greater peril than himself. It was impossible to know exactly how the tribesmen would react, but at a glance, he didn't think they would be noted for their self-control.

It was ironic, when he thought about it, that he felt compelled to try to rescue these three men, when one of them was his enemy and Remo was pledged to kill another on behalf of CURE. The rub was that he didn't know which member of the party was the ringer, which one he should terminate.

No problem, Remo thought. Just let the natives have all three.

It was a way to go, of course, but there was more to it than that. If possible, he needed to find out what had become of Terrence Hopper's expedition—though he had a fair idea by now—and also dig up any leads he could discover on a new strike of uranium.

Which meant that he would have to make his way inside the ancient city, check it out and go from there.

He was just starting on a quick reconnaissance of the perimeter when Remo heard someone approaching through the jungle. Solo, by the sound of it, and trying hard to keep the noise down, even though it didn't help that much. He scanned the wall, saw nothing to suggest the living gargoyles stationed there heard anything to put them on alert and turned away to meet the new arrival.

He chose his spot, a tree limb fifteen feet above the ground, well out of sight from sentries on the wall, and settled in to wait. Short moments later, Remo focused on a figure moving through the jungle, drawing closer to the ancient city, seemingly oblivious to its existence.

Seconds later, Remo knew this was no tribesman. This one's clothes were torn and stained, but they would never be mistaken for a layer of mud. The face, turned up toward Remo once without detecting him, was neither Malay nor malformed.

He chose his moment, dropped to earth behind the solitary hiker, pinning both arms while he clapped his free hand over Audrey Moreland's mouth.

She struggled for a moment, with surprising strength, then ceased when Remo whispered in her ear. "Don't make me break your neck."

The woman nodded, faced him as he cautiously released her.

"You're alive!" she blurted, smart enough to whisper on the home turf of their enemies.

"You, too, I see."

"Of course. I mean, what made you think I wasn't?"

"Our esteemed guide found your scarf in quicksand," Remo told her, leaving out his own discovery. "You never made it back to camp. It was assumed—"

"That I was dead," she finished for him. "Wrong, as you can see. I'm right here, in the flesh."

"So why the disappearing act?" he asked.

"I was afraid, I heard all kinds of shooting and I got lost in the jungle. Spent the whole night up a tree, in fact, and never got a wink of sleep. What happened at the camp?"

He fought the urge to smile. It was a variation on the same lie he had planned to use on Stockwell and the others, and it had the hollow ring of fabrication to it.

"I got lucky," Remo said without elaborating.

"What about the rebels?"

Remo did smile then. He had a flash of Audrey as she stood by a jungle stream in moonlight, well beyond sight of their last night's camp. Where he had left her, moments prior to any gunfire or anything at all to give the enemy away. How could she know who the attackers were, their politics, unless...?

"Their leader asked about you," Remo said.

"Excuse me?" Audrey looked confused, fearful and angry all at once.

"Your contact," Remo said. "They must be disappointed in Beijing."

She stared at Remo for a moment, finally heaved a weary sigh. "What tipped you off?"

"It's not important. You were all right for a while, but in the long run, I'm afraid you don't have what it takes to pull it off."

"Which means?"

"The cloak-and-dagger business, Audrey. You're a lousy spy."

"I haven't had much practice," she informed him.

"That's apparent. Why the big career change?"

"Money, plain and simple, Renton. Is it Renton, by the way?"

"What difference does it make?"

"Not much, I guess. If you were really a professor, any kind of academic type, you'd know how boring it can be. Sometimes I feel like I'm the fossil. Can you understand that?"

"It's a lame excuse for treason," Remo said.

"There's no such thing in peacetime, Renton. Honestly, I looked it up. The laws on spying don't apply, since I've done nothing in the States."

"Except to meet with the Chinese."

"A business meeting," Audrey said. "One million dollars was the going rate, with half up front. A bonus when they make arrangements to deliver the uranium."

"You'll have to find it first."

"No problem." Audrey raised her left arm, turned it so that he could see the wristwatch, featuring the time zones of the world and phases of the moon. As Remo studied it, the second hand lurched drunkenly from left to right.

"A silent Geiger counter," Audrey said. "I'm getting closer."

"You'll need help," he told her. "Your connection isn't with us anymore."

"I'll manage, Renton. It's a seller's market."

"When did you become an expert?"

"I'm a damned quick study when I need to be."

"I've gathered that."

The pistol came from Audrey's pocket. Remo saw her telegraph the move but didn't try to stop her yet.

"I wouldn't use that now if I were you," he said.

"I'd rather not."

"In case you missed it," Remo said, "the others have been taken prisoner. They're being held back there."

He cocked a thumb in the direction of the ancient city, watching Audrey as her eyes and pistol wavered from the proper target.

"Taken prisoner? By whom? Held where?"

"You won't believe it till you see it," Remo told her. "Come with me."

He turned, pretending to ignore the weapon, kept on turning with a spinning kick that broke her wrist and sent the pistol flying. Audrey's shock gave Remo time to finish it, a tap behind one ear to put her down and out.

He tore the sleeves from Audrey's shirt, used one

to bind her hands behind her back, the other as a makeshift gag. With some determination, she could free herself, but she would still be out for a while, and Remo meant to get his work inside the city done as rapidly as possible.

It was a simple rescue mission now, except for pinning down the main lode of uranium. With Audrey's Geiger-counter watch around his own wrist, Remo felt as ready as he ever would.

It wasn't quite an emerald city, and the road in front of him was mud, not yellow bricks, but he was off to see the wizard, come what may.

16

It took ten minutes, searching in the dark, but Remo found his secret way inside. There was a small gate, overgrown with weeds, near the northeast corner of the city's high surrounding wall. It was unguarded at the moment, and the hinges had been fashioned out of wooden pegs that had long rotted through. They offered faint resistance, but couldn't prevent his entering.

He wondered how long it had been since anybody used this exit, then dismissed the thought; it was a waste of time to ponder things that had no bearing on his mission. Off to Remo's right, a hundred yards or so, there was a spacious courtyard with a fountain at its center, water burbling from the open maw of what appeared to be a dragon carved from stone.

The fountain caught his eye because it shimmered, almost seemed to glow, as if there was some phosphorescence in the water. It was curious enough to draw him from his hiding place, a slow creep in the shadow of the looming wall, aware of sentries walking on the parapet above him.

Remo was no scientist, but he knew water in its normal state was not a source of light. At sea, you might find phosphorescent plankton, maybe larger creatures from the depths who gave off light from chemical reactions to attract prey, summon mates or frighten off their enemies. The same phenomenon was seen in fireflies, and in some inhabitants of caverns underground.

What did it mean? Were microscopic organisms found in water down below somehow escaping through the fountain, flaring into sudden brilliance as they reached the world above? Could they be toxic? Did consumption of the water help explain some of the freakish defects he had seen?

He had halved his distance to the fountain when a pair of tribesmen suddenly came into view, approaching from the far side of the courtyard. Remo froze, merged with the shadows, watched them as they stood before the fountain, genuflected and reached out to cup their hands beneath the sparkling flow. He saw them drink and bathe their grim, misshapen faces, all the while intoning syllables that ran together, slow and rhythmic, like a chant.

When they were done, the tribesmen rose and kept on walking, straight toward Remo. Neither saw him as he huddled in the deeper darkness at a corner of the wall, but he saw them up close. One was a giant, fully seven feet in height, with wrinkled pits in place of ears and fleshy growths on each side of his neck that looked like gills. His sidekick was a man of average height, who had a tiny third arm sprouting from the center of his chest. It twitched and groped its way across his upper torso, as if someone trapped inside his chest—a midget or a child, perhaps—were trying to break out.

The needle on his silent Geiger counter gave a violent lurch, then fell back to a desultory twitching as the human monsters put more space between themselves and Remo. Staring at the fountain, he knew everything he had to know about the freaks, their hidden city and the new lode of uranium.

They had been drinking, eating, breathing it for centuries, and breeding mutants all the while. Somehow, as if by destiny, the ancient tribe had built its city at ground zero, with predictable results for generations yet unborn.

Don't drink the water, Remo thought, and almost laughed out loud.

For he was standing in the middle of their nightmare now, breathing the same polluted air. According to his Geiger counter, simple ambient exposure held no short-run danger, but he wouldn't like to hang around and test the proposition. Was it sheer, perverse psychology that made him thirsty now, when he couldn't afford to drink at any cost?

Okay. So find the others and get out of here, he told himself.

Somehow, the ancient city had acquired a throbbing pulse. At first, he thought it was the amplified reverberation of his own heart, thumping in his ears, but then he recognized the muffled sound of drums. Big drums, at that, their steady cadence amplified by the acoustics of a chamber somewhere close at hand.

He couldn't name that tune, but he could damned well track it down, and that would have to do. His instinct told him he would find the other members of the Stockwell expedition when he found the drummers.

It wasn't a tune that made him want to tap his foot and sing along. If anything, it put Remo in mind of war drums, or perhaps a funeral march.

Somebody's funeral coming up, for sure.

He let the darkness cover him as he went off to find the pulsing heartbeat of the city.

CHIUN WAS TIRED of walking through the jungle. He wasn't fatigued, but rather losing patience with the long trek through a landscape he had mastered in his first few hours on the trail. Where was the challenge for a Master of Sinanju? Where was the reward in tramping over muddy trails and following a group of men who made no effort to conceal their tracks?

Remo had shown imagination, taking to the trees, but Chiun wasn't inclined to follow his example. Not yet, anyway. For in addition to the tedium of following these clumsy savages and white men—

terms the Master of Sinanju viewed as more or less synonymous—he had another goal in mind.

Chiun was watching out for dragon spoor.

At one point, midway through the long day's march, he thought that he had found it. An aroma, strong and pungent in his nostrils, beckoned him away from the main trail, a little to the north, and he couldn't resist the detour. What he found was a surprise and disappointment all at once.

He stood in front of a steaming pile of excrement. Not small, by any means, but neither was it dragon size, if he accepted the dimensions spoken of in legend. Pausing, peering closely at the mound, Chiun wondered, Could it be a baby dragon?

No.

Another glance and sniff told him the composition of the pile was wrong. Whatever mighty beast had dropped this load was strictly vegetarian, and anyone with common sense knew dragons were carnivorous.

He walked around the reeking pile once more, examining the ground for tracks, and blinked at what he saw. They were not dragon tracks, but they would be no trick to follow, and the effort might pay off. Indeed, if Chiun applied himself, he might acquire a weapon and a means of transportation at a single stroke.

It was worth a try.

He struck off at a tangent from the course his human quarry had established, following the clear path that a massive, ambling body had prepared for him. He could not calculate the creature's speed with any accuracy, but the excrement was fresh, and Chiun knew he couldn't be far behind.

It was good luck, Chiun thought, that those he followed hadn't found the creature, or vice versa. They would certainly have tried to kill it, possibly succeeded, and the Master of Sinanju would have been deprived the pleasure of a jungle ride.

He marked a change in course as he saw that the jungle giant had veered off toward water, and began to jog. If he could overtake his quarry at the stream, it would be perfect.

Chiun ran for half a mile without the first signs of fatigue, when suddenly the trees began to clear a bit, and he could hear the rushing stream ahead of him. He slowed his pace, and moved without a sound as he approached the water, coming at his quarry from behind.

The elephant didn't belong there. It wasn't a native of Malaysia, and while India was not so far away in global terms, Chiun wasn't inclined to believe that the beast had wandered over by mistake.

In fact, he knew that elephants were often used as beasts of burden through the whole of Southeast Asia. Some were bred specifically for work, while others were imported, oftentimes illegally. This pachyderm still wore the riding harness—nearly rotted through, but plainly visible—which marked him as a runaway.

That meant he was familiar with the ways of men, but might despise them. Asian handlers were notoriously cruel, at least by Western standards, and it hardly rated mention in the newspapers when an occasional "rogue" elephant rebelled against its master, using trunk and tusks and crushing weight to take a measure of revenge.

Chiun wasn't afraid of being gored or trampled by the great, unwieldy beast. It would require some effort for him to destroy the elephant, but that wasn't his goal. The Master of Sinanju had a very different plan in mind.

He circled wide around the animal while it was drinking from the stream, approaching slowly from the downwind side. It wouldn't smell him coming that way, and the gamy reek that stung his nostrils was a small price to be paid for the advantage of surprise.

When he had closed the distance to a dozen paces, still outside the creature's striking range, Chiun halted, stood with hands clasped at his waist and watched the elephant. A low-pitched trilling sound began to issue from his throat, almost hypnotic in its tone.

The elephant froze where it stood, its trunk poised midway between the water and its small pink mouth. Another moment passed before the gray behemoth turned its head to stare at Chiun, the small eyes narrowed with suspicion.

Chiun stopped trilling and addressed the forest

giant in Korean. He had no illusion that the elephant could understand him, but a soothing tone was all-important as he made the first advances, opening communication between man and beast. The elephant, in Chiun's opinion, had an intellect on par with most white men he had encountered, and a memory superior to all of them. It would remember injuries inflicted by the hands of men, but he believed that it could also differentiate between one human and another, given half a chance.

Five minutes into the one-sided conversation, when the pachyderm had still made no aggressive moves, Chiun advanced one slow step at a time. He made no sudden moves, continued speaking in the same mild tone until the elephant was close enough for him to stroke its tough hide with his fingertips. The creature snorted at Chiun in warning, but he showed no fear and responded with the trilling sound that acted as a sedative upon the beast's nerves.

Five more minutes passed while Chiun allowed the elephant to test his scent and prod him with the soft tip of its trunk. He waited, knew when it was time to make his move. The handlers used commands to make an elephant kneel down, or hoist them with its trunk, but Chiun preferred another route. He stepped back from the beast four paces, got a running start and scrambled up the gray cliff of its side as if the hulking creature came complete with ladders. In another instant, he was seated on the giant's neck, his knees dug in behind the floppy ears.

There was a moment when the creature trembled, seemed about to spin and throw him off, but Chiun resumed his trilling, and the elephant relaxed. He let it finish drinking, then asserted his control, a nudge from his right heel that made the creature turn in that direction, facing eastward. Another nudge—both heels this time—and Chiun was on his way.

It would require some patient guidance for the elephant to pick up Dr. Stockwell's trail, but he had time. His days of plodding through the mud were over now.

Chiun was traveling in style.

THE FIRST THING Audrey Moreland noted, on regaining consciousness, was the ungodly throbbing in her skull. It felt as if a tribe of gremlins had moved in while she was dozing, and the little monsters were engaged in frenzied renovations, moving things around to suit themselves.

She knew that Renton Ward had punched her, even though she never saw the knockout coming. He was fast, that one, and she would have to be alert, tip-top, when she set out to pay him back. His hands were good for something more than milking snakes and foreplay that could drive a woman crazy.

Hands.

The second thing she noticed was that her hands were immobilized behind her back. A heartbeat later, she was conscious of the gag, a cool night breeze against her flesh that told her Ward had ripped her sleeves off and used them to bind and muzzle her.

Goddamn him!

Audrey's legs were free, however, and that marked his first mistake. It took ten minutes of intensive effort, straining till she thought her spine would snap, her shoulders pull completely out of joint and leave her crippled, helpless. She finally succeeded, worked around her aching legs to get her hands in front of her again.

And it was easy after that. She used her thumbs to pull the gag down, off her chin, and worried at the knotted shirtsleeve with her teeth until the knot gave way and she was free. Another moment, stretching stiffened muscles, working achy joints, and Audrey knew she was as ready as she'd ever be.

Another flare of anger burst inside her when she missed the Geiger counter, realizing instantly where it had gone. Ward knew her business now, what she was looking for, and it appeared that he was bent on getting there ahead of her.

But what did that make him? Forget about the serpentarium in old New Orleans. Renton might know snakes, but Audrey doubted whether any desk-bound herpetologist could move like he did, decking someone like Pike Chalmers with a single blow. Where had he come from, popping up behind her on the trail that way? Was he some kind of gymnast, in addition to the other talents he possessed?

Or could he be some kind of spy?

It hardly mattered at the moment. He had duped her for a while, and it had been a pleasure—some of it, at least—but she saw through him now. They had the same goal, more or less, and while she had no way of knowing who his sponsors were, she didn't really care. There was a million dollars riding on the line, half of it sitting in a special numbered bank account already, and she didn't plan on giving back one solitary cent.

Worst case, if Renton got to the uranium ahead of her, and she could find no way to rid herself of the intrusion, Audrey had a fallback plan that would allow her to escape with the half million she had already received. Of course, successful execution of the scheme required her to survive this foray in the jungle, but she still had confidence, despite her inexperience and the fact that she was now entirely on her own.

She was determined to track Safford's party and would willingly proceed on hands and knees if necessary. Renton said the others had been taken prisoner by natives, which would mean she had a larger group to follow, with a greater likelihood of clues along the way. The downside, Audrey realized, was that the tribesmen might be taking Safford and the others anywhere, perhaps away from the uranium, and in the absence of her Geiger counter, Audrey couldn't know for sure if she was getting warm or cold.

Damn Renton anyhow!

He had a swift kick coming when she caught up with him, and the delivery would be a pleasure. She would have to watch him, though. That one had more tricks up his sleeve than David Copperfield, and Audrey had the feeling he could just as easily have killed her instead of simply knocking her unconscious.

What had stopped him? Did she have a small edge where his feelings were concerned? If so, could she exploit it when they met again, to throw him off his guard?

She made herself slow down and take it one step at a time, or she risked losing everything, her life included. Even as a novice, Audrey knew the jungle was more dangerous at night, when predators came out to stalk the darkness, seeking prey. It would be bitterly ironic if she tangled with a panther, or whatever prowled this territory after nightfall, and wound up as so much raw protein on the big cat's menu.

Audrey found her way in moments, grinning as she realized that Renton had seen fit to leave her within several paces of the trail. She noted, too, that he had left her on the ground, where anything from ants to this Nagaq the natives raved about could come along and nibble on her flesh.

Some gentleman!

Make that two kicks where they would do the most good when she saw him. Nothing personal, old buddy, just a little message to your gonads from my foot!

Despite the darkness, Audrey found the trail wasn't as difficult as she had feared. The party—more than twenty strong now, from appearances—hadn't wasted time covering its tracks, as if the natives had no fear of being followed on their own home turf. So much the better, then, except that Renton Ward would have a decent lead by now. Without the Geiger counter, she couldn't tell exactly how long she had been unconscious, but she guessed at something like two hours, judging from the darkness and the drop in temperature.

Two hours was a lifetime in the wilderness, but she had managed to survive. And that was Renton's first mistake.

She took it easy on the trail, despite the sense of urgency that called for haste. The last thing Audrey needed at the moment was to blunder through the jungle in a rush, make noise enough to wake the dead and wind up drawing every predator and native in the neighborhood. At last she found her rhythm and moved along at a steady pace. She was just congratulating herself for her presence of mind when she realized her assessment might have been premature.

First she became aware of a muted throbbing in the foliage, then realized she must have been hearing the drums for a while. The natives seemed to come from nowhere, as if rising from the earth in front of her. She stopped short, biting off a scream, and turned to flee, but there were more behind her, blocking her escape. She stood her ground, willing herself not to panic as the shadow-shapes moved closer, spears in hand.

It was the moonlight that undid her, breaking through the canopy just then to pick her captors out. Two dwarfs, she saw, with queer, misshapen hands like crab claws, feet splayed out with webbed toes, like a scuba diver's fins. The other three were taller—normal size, in fact—but there was nothing else about them that would classify as normal. One appeared to have no nose, just shiny sockets in the middle of his moon-shaped face, below a pair of bulging eyes. Another had one normal arm, its withered mate the size she would have looked for on a five-year-old. The last one, their apparent leader, was a walking nightmare: earless, bald, with bright eyes glaring from beneath a caveman's brow, and crooked, fanglike teeth protruding from his thin slash of a mouth. Instead of a chin, there was something that appeared to be a second, half-formed face regarding Audrey from the middle of his chest.

She couldn't help it then.

Opening her mouth wide, she screamed and kept on screaming, helpless to resist them as the human monsters swept her up and carried her away.

THE CITY'S INNER WALLS were etched with vast, elaborate designs in bas-relief, depicting men and animals, some of them giant creatures that could pass for dinosaurs—or dragons. Remo didn't linger for a critical assessment, but followed the pulse of drumbeats toward their source, a winding trek that led him from the phosphorescent fountain to the ancient city's very heart.

He found guards posted on the way, avoided them whenever possible, but had to kill a pair who blocked his access to a giant, looming structure where the throbbing dirge originated. They died instantly and silently, still on their feet, before they even recognized their peril. Remo took the bodies with him as he crept inside what seemed to be a temple dedicated to the worship of a giant lizard-god.

Nagaq, he thought, and stashed the corpses in an alcove to his left, not far inside the temple, where he hoped they would go undiscovered long enough for him to scout the place and find out where the prisoners were being held. If an alarm was raised before he found the others, he would have to carry on and play the rest of it by ear.

So, Remo asked himself, what else is new?

The corridor in which he found himself was

dank, dark, musty, lit by torches in the distance, where it turned into another, wider corridor. The sound of drums was louder here, and behind the pulsing drumbeat, he could make out chanting now—male voices, by the sound of it, no language that he recognized.

No language anyone would recognize, he guessed, if his suspicions were correct. This tribe wouldn't have lasted long if strangers from the outside world knew they existed, where they could be found. A generation earlier, they would have been packed off to populate the freak shows of a hundred circuses and carnivals in Europe and America. These days, they were more likely to be singled out for "help" from some well-meaning agency that would invade their world with scholars, doctors, CARE packages—inevitably followed up by medical researchers, newsmen, missionaries, tax collectors and police. The military would be coming, too, when they got wind of weapons-grade uranium.

There goes the neighborhood.

One corridor led Remo to another, on and on. He memorized the twists and turns, took care as he approached each corner just in case another group of sentries might be waiting for him on the other side. But there were none, and soon the throbbing in the ceiling overhead told Remo that he was below the drums and chanting throng. He found a narrow staircase, carved by hand, and scaled it, moving without a sound.

The staircase was blocked off by a hatch made of wood and relatively new, as if—unlike the gates outside—it had been recently replaced. He raised it cautiously, a half inch at a time, prepared to turn and flee if it made any noise at all.

From the trapdoor, Remo had a rat's-eye view of an expansive dais, with a terraced amphitheater in front of it, the stony benches packed by what looked to be scores of tribesmen. Remo didn't bother with a head count, since he was more involved with an examination of their faces and the various mutations they displayed. Except for tentacles and trunks, they could have been the barroom cast from *Star Wars*, turning out in costume for the grand premiere.

Onstage were Dr. Stockwell, Sibu Sandakan and Chalmers. They were kneeling, arms behind their backs, wrists bound to ankles so they could not rise, hand-woven ropes around their necks tied off to rusty metal rings set in the dais. Standing over them, the honcho of the tribe commanded full attention from the audience.

No wonder, Remo thought.

The guy was tall enough to make an NBA scout promise him the moon—if not eight feet, distinctly pushing it. Where several members of his audience had only one good eye, the chief had three—two normal ones, plus what appeared to be an embryonic orb set in the middle of his forehead, raised an inch or so above the others. Woolly hair was visible beneath a headdress fashioned from a large iguana's carcass, with the lizard's face protruding from above its wearer's, while the dorsal skin and tail hung down his back. Bright feathers had been thrust into the reptile's skin as decoration, to create the likeness of a mythical winged lizard, but the chief was otherwise entirely nude. No loincloth to disguise the mammoth genitalia, which, when added to his stature, clearly marked him as the biggest man in town.

It's quality, not quantity, thought Remo. Sure, and I'm a tenor for the Mormon Tabernacle Choir.

He tore his eyes away from Mr. Big and made another circuit of the room, saw that a portion of the roof was open to the sky, so moonlight aided the illumination of the torches set into the walls at ten- or twelve-foot intervals. In back, behind the ghastly audience, a pair of massive doors was closed against the night, and Remo guessed the courtyard lay in that direction, with the wall and outer gates beyond.

He was considering a move, convinced that he could drop the chief and liberate at least one prisoner before the audience responded in a screaming, killing rush, when there was a disturbance in the back rows of the amphitheater. Someone was pounding on the massive doors, and two sentries hastened to check it out. These doors were easier to handle than the outer gates, but they still needed muscle, with the two guards getting help from those outside.

As Remo watched, a squad of six more tribesmen trooped in to join the others, every eye in the assembly turned to follow them, weird faces scowling at the interruption, then displaying disapproval as they got a look at the captive boxed in by her guards.

Audrey Moreland.

Remo cursed himself and let it go—no more time for recriminations at the moment. He would have to think of something fast, before the party started heating up.

And from the looks of Mr. Big, his visible reaction to the struggling blonde, there would be little time to waste.

17

It was all too much for Audrey's mind to process, pouring in on her without a breather. Being decked by Renton Ward and waking up to find herself alone, trussed up like Grandma's Christmas turkey in the middle of the godforsaken jungle. Struggling to get free and picking up the trail, only to find herself surrounded by a gang who could be poster children for the next Wes Craven movie. Marching through the darkness to an ancient, obviously undiscovered city, where her captors led her past a glowing fountain—the uranium?—to reach a kind of Stone Age auditorium. Her traveling companions kneeling on the stage, tied up, while an ungainly three-eyed giant with a schlong the size of Baja California, shouted gibberish to an assembled audience of living, breathing nightmares.

What was she supposed to do?

Scream, baby, scream—and fight as if her life depended on it, which it obviously did.

She gave a fair impersonation of a grown-up temper tantrum, kicking, screaming, spitting,

scratching at her captors. She stopped short of biting them, since they were smeared from head to
foot with mud or something worse that came from
God knew where, but her resistance had its impact.
Her fingernails plowed bloody furrows down the
cheek of Mr. No Nose, after which she kicked him
in the loincloth, hard enough to leave him gasping
on his knees. The pygmies tried to stick her then,
but Audrey grabbed one of the spears and swung
the first runt hard into his stubby buddy, dropping
both of them.

She had a weapon now, and was prepared to use
it, but she never got the chance. Someone came up
behind her with a club and tapped her skull just
hard enough to dim the lights, turn her legs to
rubber, while a swarm of mud-caked hands reached
out to grab the spear away from her, pin down her
arms and legs.

One chance, she thought. I had one chance, and
that was it. It's gone.

They dragged her toward the stage, boots scuffing on the stony floor, where Three Eyes waited for
her, showing signs of interest that a naked man had
difficulty hiding. Hell, with that equipment, his excitement would have been apparent in a suit of ar-
mor.

Others noticed his reaction, too, and as the sleeping giant rose to full attention, certain members of
the audience began to chant, a rhythmic, off-key
dirge.

She reached the dais, borne on eager hands, and was deposited at Long John Silver's feet, his fleshy cudgel aimed directly at her face. No way, thought Audrey. Where the hell is Linda Lovelace when you need her?

Giant drums had fallen silent when the raiding party entered with their captive, but the beat resumed now, throbbing in the amphitheater like some great, cosmic heartbeat. Someone found a length of rope and bound her hands behind her, tied off to her ankles as the others were secured. If Audrey struggled now, she had a choice of four directions she could fall in: right, left, backward or directly on her face.

The three-eyed giant and his one-eyed buddy had begun to sway in front of her, a jerky little dance that matched the rhythm of the drumbeats more or less. She closed her eyes, preferring not to watch, her mind already focused on the prospect of what former generations had described—and accurately, she decided—as "a fate worse than death." There could be no "relax and enjoy it" with this freak, or those who might line up behind him if worse came to worst.

I wonder, Audrey thought, if you can will yourself to die?

The morbid train of thought was interrupted by a new sound, emanating from outside. Behind the chanting of the audience surrounding her, she heard one man, and then another, shouting frantically, their shouts resolving into screams of pain or panic. There was a distant sound of old wood groaning, screeching, splintering, but even that wasn't what riveted her full attention.

Something else.

A loud, unearthly snarling, as of some fantastic beast enraged.

THE SNARLING, roaring, air-stirring sound had barely died away when the assembled natives went berserk. As one, they leaped up from their stony seats and rushed into the aisles, stampeding for the nearest exit. Some of them were shouting, and while Remo didn't speak their language, he could make one word out loud and clear.

"Nagaq! Nagaq!"

There was no time to hesitate or wonder what in hell was going on. He bolted through the trapdoor, charged across the stage and met the three-eyed giant just as Mr. Big turned back to face him, his impressive scepter thrust out like a weapon.

Remo saw his opportunity and seized it with a clutching, twisting move that left his eight-foot adversary standing in a pool of crimson, hitting high notes for the first time in his life. A crushing backhand silenced the soprano aria and closed the three-eyed stare forever. Remo stepped past the chief before he fell and moved on to free the hostages.

A number of the tribesmen saw their leader fall, and three of those were bold enough to leap onstage, despite their panicky reaction to the noises emanating from outside, and try to dish out instant justice. They walked into a whirlwind of destruction, fists and feet they never saw before the lights went out forever. Their bodies sprawled on the dais while their mud-caked countrymen bailed out with all deliberate speed.

"Nagaq! Nagaq!"

Outside, the noises that had prompted the stampede were getting louder, closer. Remo couldn't place the snarling—it reminded him of King Kong talking tough in Dolby stereo—but something large and angry was advancing on the temple, obviously giving hell to anyone who crossed its path. He wondered if the drums—all silent now—had summoned it, and whether this kind of intrusion was a normal part of tribal gatherings.

From the reactions of the audience, he guessed that it wasn't. Apparently, no evacuation drill had been prepared, no chants or prayers designed for the occasion. They might worship great Nagaq, but they were plainly unaccustomed to its putting in a personal appearance in the middle of the ceremony.

Now they had a party crasher who—from what was audible outside—could really crash a party when it wanted to. The screams outside were frantic, terrified, some of them cut off sharply, like a chicken's squawking severed by a hatchet blade. And over all, the snarling bass tones of Nagaq provided background music for a waking nightmare, echoing inside the amphitheater as the creature from hell drew ever closer to the open doors.

Professor Stockwell gaped at Remo, evidently stunned to see him. "Dr. Ward! Where did you come from?"

"No time for a recap," Remo told him. "Do your legs work?"

"Pardon me?"

He reached down and snapped the ropes that shackled Stockwell. "Can you run like hell?"

"I think so. Yes."

"Be ready, then. We haven't got much time."

"I understand."

He moved on to the next in line, freed Sibu Sandakan. Pike Chalmers glared at Remo, stubborn pride at war with the survival instinct, but he didn't pull away when Remo stepped around behind him, pulled the ropes apart as if they were flimsy threads.

And he saved Audrey for the last, unfastening the rope around her ankles, hesitating for a beat before he freed her hands and helped her to her feet. She wore a dazed expression, no defiance visible as he took her by the arm and steered her toward the trapdoor in the stage.

"This way," he urged the others.

"Sod that!" Chalmers snapped. "Those bloody wogs have got a thing or two to answer for. They have my rifle and my trophy, Dr. Ward, and I'm not leaving here without the lot!"

That said, he leaped down from the stage and

sprinted toward the exit, bowling over several of the pygmy types who blocked his path. He made it halfway there before a giant, looming shadow fell across the threshold, blotting out the night.

"My God, what's that?" asked Audrey.

Down below, the natives were yammering, "Nagaq! Nagaq!" Some of them knelt and pressed their foreheads to the floor, while others scattered for their lives.

"It can't be!" Dr. Stockwell said. "What's that...?"

"I don't know," Remo said, "but something tells me we're about to meet the big kid on the block. And from the sound of it, he's pissed right now."

CHIUN WAS still a half mile from the hidden city when he heard the drums, a muffled, throbbing beat that seemed to give the very jungle life. His huge mount hesitated, grumbling, but plowed ahead when he dug his heels in, snapping orders in his most authoritative tone. It made no difference what he said; he could have shouted, "Dog shit! Saxophone!" for all the pachyderm would know. It was the tenor of his voice, the aura of command, that left the Master of Sinanju in control.

It had been simple to follow his quarry once he steered the elephant back to the trail and got it headed eastward. Even in the darkness, he could easily keep up with twenty men who took no pains to hide their tracks. They may as well have blazed the trees or planted signs along the way to guide him.

Chiun had been concerned at first, in case their seeming negligence turned out to be a ruse, some crafty scheme to undermine his vigilance, prepare an ambush, but he quickly put his mind at ease.

The men he stalked were clumsy idiots.

The drumbeats told him that, if nothing else. Chiun could only marvel that the tribe hadn't been hunted down much sooner, since they were so careless with security. Of course, they dealt primarily with whites and Malays, which would make a difference. If a Korean had come looking for them, all the world would know their secrets now.

A quarter mile before they reached their destination, Chiun's mount was distracted by a new scent on the trail. It was a gamy, pungent odor that reminded Chiun a little of the snake farm he had visited in Bangkok years ago.

The elephant was trembling, scuffing at the ground with giant feet, but there was less fear than anger in its attitude. Chiun urged it forward, and the beast responded with the barest hesitation, trotting faster as the unidentified reptilian scent intensified. Its trunk was raised as if to trumpet out a challenge, but the only sound that emanated from its throat was the warm huffing of its breath.

Chiun wasn't surprised at the appearance of the ancient city. It made perfect sense, considering the circumstances, and he knew now where the rhythmic sound of drums was coming from. At first glance, he was worried that the looming outer wall might be a problem—not for him, of course, but for the elephant—until he saw the wooden gates, wide open in the moonlight.

Human figures milled about the open gates, as if they couldn't make their minds up whether to remain or flee. Chiun urged his elephant to greater speed, bent forward, with his hands braced on the giant's leather scalp until the gap had closed to fifty yards. Then something roared inside the city walls, a primal sound of rage and hunger from a set of massive vocal cords.

The dragon? What else could it be?

Chiun's elephant stopped short on hearing that, and actually backed up several yards before he could assert control. He thumped a fist on the behemoth's skull, not hard enough to damage anything, and dug in with his heels once more. The elephant resisted for another fleeting moment, but its will posed no real challenge for the Master of Sinanju. Finally, reluctantly at first, but then with greater energy, it moved ahead.

The natives clustered at the gate were unaware of Doom advancing on flank, until the elephant raised up its trunk and blared a challenge to the night. The tribesmen turned at that, and Chiun confirmed what he had surmised already from a number of their tracks. They were deformed, most of them, with a solitary normal-looking man who stood back and deferred to the grotesques. There was no time to speculate on how they got that way, no pity in Chiun's heart when three of them stood fast instead of taking to their heels as any sane man would have when confronted with a charging elephant.

The beast crushed two of them beneath its tree-stump feet before they had a chance to launch their spears in self-defense. The tallest of the three screamed once as he was lifted with the trunk coiled tight around his rib cage, emptying his lungs. Instead of goring him, the elephant released him with a quick toss of its head that flung him headfirst toward the wall. There was a crunch on impact, and his lifeless body tumbled ten or twelve feet to the ground, where it lay twitching in the mud.

The gates were tall enough that Chiun wasn't required to duck as they passed through. Where he had expected sentries on the wall, it was deserted. Something had distracted them before the Master of Sinanju put in his appearance, and the sound of human screams, with loud snarls overriding them, led him in the direction of the battle.

Maybe not a dragon, thought Chiun, but it was something he had never seen before, and that alone could make the trip worthwhile.

The Master of Sinanju spurred his mount to greater speed, his lips turned upward in a beatific smile.

KUCHING KANGAR hadn't been with his brothers in
the Hall of Ceremony when Nagaq arrived. It was
forbidden for the normal ones to take direct part in
a sacrifice, since they weren't considered pure. It
galled him sometimes when he thought of the humiliation he endured to serve Nagaq, but it wasn't
his place to argue with tradition.

Not when it could get him killed.

Still, none of them had counted on Nagaq appearing in the flesh. Nagaq always waited for the
sacrificial offerings to be prepared and taken outside, to a clearing where the stakes were planted.
You could hear it from the City, growling as it fed,
but there were few among the tribe who claimed
that they had actually seen the dragon god. The
chief, of course, and several of his close advisers,
but no one else.

Tonight was different, somehow. Perhaps Nagaq
was hungrier than usual, or maybe it could tell they
had three offerings instead of one. Kuching Kangar
could no more read a god's mind than he could
predict the future, but tradition told him it would
mean something momentous for the tribe if great
Nagaq should ever deign to come inside the City.

From the sound of things, momentous massacre
would be more like it. Great Nagaq was surly at
the best of times, but if its snarls were any indication, then it must be positively rabid at the moment.
Men were screaming in the courtyard, some of them
in mortal pain, the rest in fear.

Kuching Kangar, emerging from his quarters, was uncertain how he should react. There had been no rehearsals for this moment, nothing to prepare them for a house call from the forest god.

He frowned and took his spear along for comfort. Just in case.

A hundred yards separated Kangar's sleeping quarters from the courtyard of the shining fountain. There was no sign of Nagaq when he arrived but there were several bodies—and parts of bodies— scattered in the courtyard, as if some gigantic child had run amok and torn his toys apart. Fresh blood was everywhere, its sharp, metallic scent strong in the night.

Where was Nagaq?

The temple doors were open, wild screams issuing from those inside. The drums were silent now, but something had replaced their background noise. A rumbling sound, much like the purring of a giant cat.

The whisper of Nagaq.

Kuching Kangar was moving toward the temple when a babble of excited voices from the gate distracted him. A small group of his fellow tribesmen had collected there, wanting to flee the City, but something seemed to block their way. As Kangar stood watching, he was treated to a new and wholly unexpected sight.

An elephant came through the gate, trunk furled, tusks flashing in the moonlight, bellowing a high note to announce itself. Astride the gray behemoth's neck, a slight man with snow white puffs of hair and flowing robes sat watching with a smile as his mount trampled one of Kangar's brothers, then scooped up another with its trunk and flung him far across the courtyard.

Great Nagaq would have to wait. This stranger had the gall to trespass in the City with his elephant, slay members of the tribe as if they were insects. It was every tribesman's duty to defend their sanctuary from the Outside, make sure the secrets of the City were preserved for future generations. Even normal members of the tribe, excluded from its sacred rituals, were still expected to lay down their lives, if necessary, for the common good.

Kuching Kangar knew what he had to do. He didn't hesitate, but took a firm grip on his spear and charged directly toward the elephant, lips drawn back from his sharp white teeth as he unleashed a fearsome battle cry.

He couldn't kill the elephant, perhaps, but that wasn't important. Given time, sufficient spears and arrows, they would bring it down or chase it back into the forest. No, it was the man who mattered, one who could betray their secret to the Outside.

The toss was perfect. He could actually see the spear arc toward its target, silent, deadly—

No!

Somehow the scrawny man had snatched his spear out of the air before it struck. Kuching Kangar stood speechless, stunned. Could such a thing be possible? Should he believe his eyes, or was the whole scene a hallucination, prompted by the lethal aura of Nagaq?

Before he had a chance to ponder that, Kangar observed the old man toss his six-foot spear into the air, reversing it, and catch it, primed for throwing, with the point directed back from whence it came. His feet refused to move somehow, and he was rooted to the same spot when the lance burst through his chest and out his back, below one shoulder blade. The impact knocked him over backward, and he would have fallen, but the three-foot shaft protruding from his back was jammed into the dirt. He screamed as gravity took over and his body started sliding down the wooden shaft by inches, creeping toward a rendezvous with Mother Earth.

He never made it, though, because the elephant stepped forward, following instructions from its master, and a large, round foot came down on Kangar's lower body. His last coherent thought, before eternal darkness, was a quick prayer to the only god he knew.

Avenge me, great Nagaq!

A LIVING NIGHTMARE stepped in through the open temple doors. Or rather, hopped in, since the movement was distinctly birdlike, even with the new arrival's bulk and clear reptilian aspect.

Remo thought it most resembled re-creations of

Tyrannosaurus rex, except that this one had a blunt horn on its snout and bony knobs above each eye. A quick guess made it twenty feet in length, with half of that devoted to a heavy, twitching tail that helped the creature balance on its stout back legs and three-toed feet. The forelimbs looked a bit like chunky human arms, except for the four-fingered hands with wicked claws designed for holding lively prey.

"Ceratosaurus!" Dr. Stockwell blurted out. "Extinct since the Jurassic period!"

"Why don't you tell him that?" said Remo, looking for a weapon that would let him keep some distance between himself and what appeared to be one pissed-off prehistoric carnivore.

"This is incredible!"

"You'll think so, while he's snacking on your ass," said Remo, scooping up a fallen spear. It felt more like a toothpick in the presence of their snarling enemy, but it would have to do.

Pike Chalmers recognized the better part of valor, in the circumstances. Dodging to his left, he grabbed a quaking pygmy, scooped him up and threw him at the monster like a basketball. Nagaq, or whatever the hell it was, snapped once and caught the offering in midair, chomping down a time or two before it shook its head and spit the mangled body out.

No sale.

By that time, though, Pike Chalmers had a lead

and he was out of there, arms pumping as he ran. The Brit ran true to form. True-blue to himself, that was. Women and children last.

The snarling dinosaur was momentarily distracted by some stragglers from the audience, a couple of them kneeling down to worship him, while others had the good sense to evacuate. The suppliants were first to die, pinned down with giant three-toed feet and shredded with a set of teeth that looked like sharpened railroad spikes. That done, Stockwell's ceratosaurus started checking out the temple, looking for more agile prey.

"We'd better get a move on if we're going," Remo said.

Behind him, Sibu Sandakan and Audrey were intent on emptying the contents of their stomachs, gagging at the sight of mutilated bodies down below. Professor Stockwell stood erect and glassy eyed, as if he had been hypnotized.

"Incredible," he said, and then repeated it for emphasis. *"Incredible."*

"Unfortunately, we are not inedible," said Remo. "I'm afraid we have to leave right now."

With Audrey's help, he hustled Stockwell off the dais, toward the wings, with Sandakan behind them, bringing up the rear. Nagaq let out a screech that sounded like Godzilla dragging claws across a chalkboard, and you didn't need a special training course on dinosaurs to recognize the sound of big feet slapping on the stonework, gaining on them in a rush.

It would be snack time any moment now, and Remo felt a little like an appetizer, destined to be eaten raw.

One thing about this morsel, though, he thought. Nagaq might choke before getting it down.

18

Remo passed the trapdoor up deliberately. They were already short of time, with an alarm in progress, and he didn't care for the idea of getting ambushed on the stairs—or in the winding corridors that led back to the exit, either. It was a deliberate gamble, since he didn't have another way out of the temple readily in mind, but with the rush of tribesmen to escape their hungry god, he reckoned something would present itself.

The natives weren't just running, though. Enough of them still had their wits about them to remember who they were and who they were supposed to serve. Nagaq might be a bit disgruntled at the moment, snacking down on some of their compatriots back in the amphitheater, but what else could be expected from a demented, jungle-dwelling lizard-god? For a believer, it was only logical to think their god would be even more pissed off if it got done with the hors d'oeuvres and found out that its acolytes had let the main course slip away.

A couple of the pygmy types were waiting for

them as the party made its way backstage. It felt like fighting children, but in this case both tykes carried six-foot spears and knew exactly how to use them. Remo put himself between the sawed-off warriors and his onetime traveling companions, bracing for the rush he knew was sure to come.

It came.

The runt on Remo's left went with a feint to try to throw him off before the other pygmy made his move straight down the middle. Remo turned the lance into a yardstick with a sharp flick of his wrist, then grabbed the shorter part and used it as a lever, yanked the pygmy close enough to kill him with an open-handed blow against his knobby forehead.

His companion could have run for it and saved himself, but something—call it courage or stupidity—made him stand fast, the spear poised out in front of him as if he were about to prod a hornets' nest. The point was darkened, maybe dipped in something lethal.

Instead of waiting for the pygmy to attack him, Remo went in for the kill, deflected an impressive thrust with no real effort and removed the long spear from his adversary's grasp. He could have let it go at that, but this was life-and-death, no substitutions, no time-outs. He gave the pygmy time to bark some kind of curse, a final gesture of defiance in the face of certain death, then ran him through.

Behind him, Audrey grappled with another bout of nausea; the others simply stared.

"Let's go," he said. "We haven't got all night."

They followed him past massive columns, all carved out of jade. The raw material in just one column would have kept a hundred Chinese sculptors busy for a decade, but there seemed to be no shortage where the tribesmen did their shopping.

Tribesmen.

It occurred to Remo that he hadn't seen a woman or a child so far, since entering the ancient city. They were obviously somewhere, but he hoped his luck would hold, remembering that females were among the most ferocious members of some primitive tribes, from early North America to "modern" Venezuela and Brazil.

They reached a spiral staircase leading down to what must be the ground floor near where he entered, though he didn't recognize the stretch of corridor that he could see. He had no trouble recognizing the committee gathered to receive them, though: eight warriors armed with clubs and spears.

"Stay close and watch yourselves," Remo cautioned his companions, starting down the stairs to meet their enemies.

One thing about the locals, while they might be crafty with an ambush in the jungle, they were pitiful on strategy for stand-up fights. If Remo had to guess, he would have said they didn't get much practice, having no real neighbors, but for now he would be satisfied to take advantage of whatever weakness they displayed.

They started up the spiral staircase three abreast, spears held in front of them, prepared to skewer him before he could resist. It would have worked with most opponents—Remo gave them that—but warriors lived or died on their ability to cope with an exception to the rule.

These died.

He stepped between the thrusting spears, gripped one in either hand and used the long shaft on his right to block a thrust from number three, the farthest out of reach. A swift kick dropped the tribesman on his right and left Remo with his weapon. He turned the spear on the others, nailing both of them and leaving them to wriggle like a pair of insects pinned on a dissecting needle.

The survivors were advancing with a bit more caution when a sudden babble in the corridor behind them reached his ears. And Remo saw the women now, God help him, some holding babies, others herding small, misshapen forms in front of them like livestock. They were shouting at the warriors on the staircase, managed to distract a couple of them from the work at hand.

It was enough.

Without another glance, Remo cleared a path like a whirlwind sent by the wrath of God.

PIKE CHALMERS FOUND his nerve again somewhere between the amphitheater and the deserted courtyard. He came charging through the exit, snapping the neck of a native in his way, looking for a way to save himself. The others had evacuated, though, and that was fine with Chalmers, since he didn't feel like taking on an army when his only weapon was a bloody spear.

His guns were somewhere handy, if he just knew where to look. But he didn't speak the lingo, and they had only met one member of the tribe who had a grasp of English. And from what he saw, across the courtyard, poor Kuching Kangar was well past giving interviews.

Pike guessed the bloody lizard must have had him, though his corpse didn't display the kind of rip-and-render damage common to the others strewed about the courtyard. It would be more accurate to say their former guide looked broken, as if he had fallen from a lofty height, but that made no sense whatsoever, since he lay an easy fifteen paces from the nearest wall.

Forget it, Chalmers told himself. Not your problem.

He was gunning for a dinosaur, without a bloody gun, but now that he had found his guts again, all he could think of was the money he could make from packing home the monster's head—hell, any part of its anatomy at all. Live capture was a hopeless case, and it would take a cargo helicopter to transport the bloody carcass in one piece. Chalmers calculated that the head alone must weigh two hundred pounds or more, but he would settle for a jawbone and some bits of skin if he had to. Any egg-head worth his salt could tell the specimens were fresh, and if that didn't do the trick, then he would lead them back to view the rotting carcass.

For a hefty fee, of course.

In fact, he saw a whole new profit angle on the site itself. He could run walking tours of the city, point out spots of interest for the visitors who could afford his services. The local wogs would want a piece of it, he realized, and they might cut him out entirely if they started getting greedy. In the meanwhile, though, there should be ample time for him to walk a film crew through the ruins, cut a deal with some fat-cat producer out of Hollywood—hell, why not Steven Spielberg?—for the movie rights.

But first, he had to bag his specimen.

He turned back toward the temple, moving toward the open doors, and made it halfway there before the elephant appeared. Not just an elephant, however, but an elephant with some ancient personage riding on its back. From the look of it, perhaps Chinese or Japanese.

Now, what in bloody hell?

The goddamned circus never ended—that was obvious. It wasn't bad enough that he had human mutants and some kind of prehistoric throwback to contend with; now they threw an ancient Oriental and a frigging elephant at Chalmers, just to see if he could handle it.

Too bloody right he could.

Chalmers broke into a trot, then sprinted all out for the open doorway, anxious to be out of sight before the old man or his elephant got wind of him.

And made it by a nose, as far as he could tell.

The bloody lizard-thing was wreaking havoc on its worshipers, just swatting one with its enormous tail as Chalmers barged into the temple. Not a pygmy, either, but he may as well have been, the way he flew across the room and landed in a heap some fifty feet away.

I'll have to watch that, Chalmers told himself, advancing cautiously along the central aisle. A crocodile could drop you that way, but its jaws still did the butcher work. This bloody thing was big and strong enough to kill a human being with its tail, the way your average man would splat an insect with a flyswatter.

Not for him, thank you very much.

He glanced around the spacious room, half-hoping he would find his weapons standing in a corner, but the guns were nowhere to be seen.

The decision had been made for him, then. He'd have to use the bloody spear or give it up.

There was a way to do it, Chalmers knew. In Africa, the pygmies hunted elephants with spears and arrows, but they had to hit a vital spot, and sometimes they lost a few men in the process. Chalmers didn't have a few spare helpers, at the moment, so he had to do the bloody job himself.

Which meant he had to get it right the first time, or be damned.

From what he saw and guessed about Nagaq's anatomy, his only hope would be a clean thrust to the brain. That meant he would be forced to go in through an eye, or through the great lizard's palate. The latter angle was a risk, since Chalmers didn't know if reptile skulls were even built the same way as a mammal's, but if that turned out to be his only option, he would have to do his best.

He stepped across a fallen tribesman, knowing he had to get a move on now, before the bloody gargoyles found their guts again and started back to find out what was going on between their lizard-god and any hapless stragglers in the amphitheater. Experience told Chalmers that a tribe of savages could stand for almost anything where their half-baked religion was concerned, and he had no doubt they would go for him before they ever tried to show Nagaq the gate. If he could top the lizard off before they got there, though, he might pick up some points for heroism.

Hell, he might wind up as some kind of a god himself!

A few more yards, and he could smell the damned thing now. More to the point, it caught a whiff of him and turned to face him, big jaws dripping mucus streaked with blood. The rumbling sound that issued from its throat was somewhere in between a belch and snarl.

And when it moved, Nagaq was lightning fast, not slow and plodding like a movie dinosaur. It ran, instead of walking, eight- or ten-foot strides that caught Pike Chalmers by surprise and left him no time to escape. The monster jaws were yawning over him before he even had a chance to raise his spear in lame defiance.

When the five-inch teeth clamped down on his body, there was nothing he could do but scream inside the reptile's suffocating gullet.

CHIUN WASN'T CONCERNED about the white man who eluded him. It was not his job to protect or punish members of the Stockwell party, and he felt no urge to do so, since he wasn't being paid to baby-sit. He was concerned for Remo, but the Master of Sinanju had faith in his pupil. None of the deformed, pathetic creatures who inhabited this city was a match for Remo, even if they came at him in numbers—but the dragon was another proposition altogether.

It required a Master's touch.

Three tribesmen came around a corner of the temple seconds after the ungainly white man ducked inside, two armed with spears, the tallest of them carrying a bow. The archer nocked an arrow, aimed and fired, his one eye gaping in surprise as Chiun reached out to snatch the shaft in flight and snap it like a toothpick, smiling as he tossed the broken halves aside.

He spurred the elephant and ordered it to charge. The great gray beast responded like a born Korean native, lowering its head and rushing at the savages, a screech of fury rising from its throat.

Chiun's adversaries tried to bolt then, but they weren't fast enough. The elephant was on them, slashing with its tusks and stamping with its big round feet before they could escape. It almost felt too easy, killing this way, but the Master of Sinanju told himself his enemies deserved no better. They were not Korean, after all, and there was not an emperor or king among them worthy of a more elaborate death.

Chiun would save himself to face the dragon any moment now.

He turned his mount back toward the savages' temple, with its open doors. The snarling, snuffling sounds that emanated from inside there told him that the dragon had found something to amuse it and to quench the legendary reptile's thirst for blood. Chiun wondered if the other expedition members had been sacrificed, but didn't really care, as long as Remo wasn't found among the human offerings.

Impossible.

His white adopted son was far too swift and clever for these stepchildren of nature. If a hundred of them tried to corner him, Chiun would bet on Remo to emerge victorious.

But even skilled assassins sometimes made mistakes, Chiun realized, and no one was immortal. It was always possible that one of these creatures would creep up on a distracted Remo from behind and unleash an arrow while his back was turned.

A spark of anger flared inside Chiun, caught on and burst into a flame that seared his heart. No dragon god would save these savages if they were rash enough to harm his chosen son and heir. The very walls of jade would tumble down upon their heads before he finished with this miserable city of the damned. Chiun would wade waist deep in blood and shout his fury at the sky if Remo came to harm.

He caught himself before his mood affected the behemoth he had drafted as his warhorse. It was better to be calm around wild animals, lest excitement drive them mad and make them run amok.

In seconds flat, his pulse and respiration had returned to normal, while the burning fury in his gut was replaced by icy calm. He was prepared to face the dragon, and teach it that a Master of Sinanju had no peers where killing was concerned.

His mount stopped short outside the temple, peering through the open doors, its trunk raised, sampling the gamy air. Instead of trying to retreat, it trembled with a kind of urgency that told Chiun it would fight. A challenge issued from its tiny mouth, the bold note amplified by lungs like giant bellows, summoning the dragon out to war.

A moment later, Chiun beheld the monster's shadow, looming dark across the threshold. He wasn't sure what form it would take, if this one would have wings or blow fire through its nostrils, but he kept his seat and waited for his adversary to emerge.

The creature that appeared a moment later was familiar from a television program Chiun had seen, with Walter Cronkite. It was not *Tyrannosaurus rex,* but a smaller relative, and the most peculiar thing about it—aside from its very existence—was the pair of human legs that dangled from the monster's wicked jaws.

Chiun saw the blood-soaked khaki trousers, ankle boots, and knew what had become of the ungainly white man who had run inside the temple moments earlier.

With a sharp kick of his heels, he urged his mount to the attack.

THE NATIVES WERE almost ready to defend themselves as Remo vaulted down the spiral stairs. Almost. But there is a world of difference, though, between a fit of mindless anger and cohesive strategy in crisis situations. Charging pell-mell toward an unknown adversary doesn't always do the trick. In fact, it can be self-defeating, as his adversaries quickly learned to their regret.

The leader met him with another of their carbon-copy handmade spears, the darkened point outthrust. It snagged a piece of Remo's shirt, but missed his flesh by inches as he went inside the thrust, deflected it and snapped the warrior's neck with an explosive straight-arm shot. The flaccid body tumbled over backward, down the stairs, and set the other tribesmen scrambling as they tried to get out of the way.

They never got the chance.

Still moving, homicidal poetry in motion, Remo closed the gap between them, striking left and right at his discouraged challengers. The tribesmen had already seen four of their comrades die, and while they might have happily retreated, there was nowhere left for them to go, with Death among them, reaching out to touch each man in turn.

One tried to vault the staircase railing, heedless of the drop below, some twenty feet between his perch and the unyielding floor of jade. A punch from Remo helped him get there, snapped his spine just where it joined the pelvis and converted what might otherwise have been an awkward leap into a deadly cartwheel, ending with the warrior's skull exploding like a shattered egg.

A long spiked club hissed past his face, and Remo countered with a swift kick that collapsed his adversary's rib cage, driving bony spikes into his heart and lungs. The warrior went down, spouting blood, already dead before his body reached the bottom of the staircase.

That left two, and neither one of them had any great enthusiasm for the fight, but neither could they run away. One tried, and Remo caught him with a short jab to a point below one shoulder blade, which stopped his heart and sent another dead man body-surfing down the spiral stairs.

The sole survivor had no options left. He came at Remo, shrieking through a set of crooked, fang-like teeth, and slashing with the thick shaft of his lance. It was a simple thing to block the downward blow, disarm him, hoist the scrawny figure overhead and toss him twenty feet across the hand-carved banister. The native went down screaming, flapping arms that wouldn't serve as wings, and hit the floor with a resounding thud.

The three surviving expedition members stared at Remo, wide-eyed, Audrey with her mouth agape. If she had closed her eyes, thought Remo, the expression would have been familiar, but she wasn't high on sex right now. Instead, like Stockwell and their Malay chaperon, she seemed both amazed and repulsed.

"How...?" she began, choking on the words. "I mean—"

"I took some classes," Remo told her. "Can we go now?"

Angry voices from a another corridor, somewhere below them and to Remo's left, provided all the motivation they required to scramble down the stairs past the pair of crumpled bodies, down a hallway that he hoped would lead them to the open air. If they were forced to double back, it meant another confrontation with the palace guards. While he had no doubt of his ability to cope with the resistance, Remo couldn't guarantee that one or more of his companions wouldn't stop a spear or arrow in the process.

If he had been saddled with a lone companion, Remo could have simply carried him or her and run as fast as necessary to the nearest exit. As it was, though, progress was effectively restricted to the top speed of their slowest member—meaning that Dr. Stockwell set the pace. Protesting all the way, demanding that the others leave him, save themselves, the weary academic could do little better than a shuffling jog by now. They were losing precious time.

Somehow they found an exit and got out of there before the rabble in pursuit caught up with them. This door, like all the others, was constructed out of wood; it opened outward on a patio that seemed to join the courtyard proper somewhere to their right, around a corner of the temple. Remo dug his fingers deep into the wooden door and ripped a six-inch wedge-shaped portion free before he slammed the door and held it shut. The wedge went underneath, a solid kick ensuring that the hostiles on the other side would have their work cut out for them if they intended following this way.

"Come on," said Remo to the others. "We're already out of time."

They followed him through darkness, toward the

open courtyard, where the awesome sounds of mortal combat told them that a battle from another age was taking place.

19

Audrey Moreland's mind was racing as she followed Renton Ward—or whoever the hell he was—in the direction of the courtyard. From the sounds, it was apparent that the dinosaur these tribesmen worshiped as Nagaq had left the temple, made its way outside, where it was raising hell. Its snarling, roaring voice was readily identifiable before she glimpsed the monster—and, Audrey suspected, she would hear it in her dreams for months to come.

It was the other sound that puzzled her right now. A kind of trumpeting. Some other animal perhaps…or were the natives trying to distract their killer god by blowing horns?

No, that was wrong. The sound was something she had heard before, if she could only place it, drag the necessary sound bytes from her memory and bring them forward into conscious thought. It sounded like…

An elephant!

Sherlockian deduction played no part in Audrey's sudden breakthrough. Rather, she had reached the corner separating her from the main courtyard, and she saw the looming pachyderm in front of her.

Not just an elephant, at that. It was an elephant complete with rider, and a queer old duck he seemed to be. A slight figure with white puffs of hair and wearing what appeared to be a jet black robe. An Asian of some kind, she realized, and clearly not a member of the local tribe. He held no staff or riding crop, as was the normal practice with most handlers, yet the elephant appeared to understand and willingly obey his orders...to a point.

The creature was distracted now, of course, by the ceratosaurus pacing back and forth some thirty feet away. From all appearances, the two great beasts were strangers to each other, nothing in the way of species recognition visible on either side. The reptile's attitude combined suspicion, anger and a kind of raw malevolence rarely associated with nonhuman species in the wild. The elephant, for its part, seemed determined not to give its snarling enemy the satisfaction of displaying fear. As Audrey watched, it raised its trunk and screeched another challenge at the prehistoric hunter.

The ceratosaurus hesitated briefly, rocked back on its haunches, great tail twitching, then shot forward, massive jaws agape and hissing. If the elephant was startled or intimidated, nothing showed. Instead of bolting for the open gates, it put its head down, furled its trunk to clear the long white tusks—and charged.

Before the two behemoths came together, Audrey saw the rider leap to safety, his kimono flared around him like a vampire's cloak open to the night. He made a perfect three-point touchdown, scrambled clear and turned to watch the jungle giants as they met with a resounding crunch of flesh and bone.

All eyes were on the grim, primeval contest, Audrey's no exception, but her thoughts were not confined to the potential fate of two inhuman gladiators. In the background, when their lurching bodies cleared the way, she had a fair view of the courtyard's phosphorescent fountain, shining like a beacon to her fortune.

The uranium was down there, somewhere underneath this city of grotesque inhabitants. Her contact with the rebels had been broken permanently, thanks to Renton Ward, but there was nothing to prevent her passing map coordinates along to the Chinese, fulfilling her part of the contract to ensure that she received the second payment of five hundred thousand dollars. She would walk into the Chinese embassy in broad daylight, if necessary, and concern herself with consequences afterward.

When she was wealthy and retired.

It crossed her mind that there might even be a bonus in the deal if she could block the Malay government from finding out about the lode before her

Chinese sponsors had a chance to make their move. As far as she could make out, only Renton and herself knew anything about the city's radioactive foundation so far. Dear old Safford was off in a dreamworld, watching the ceratosaurus like a child with a new toy on Christmas morning. Sibu Sandakan might work it out if he had time, but it was still a long way back to Kuala Lumpur. Anything could happen on a trip like that—assuming Sandakan escaped the ancient city with his life.

And that left Renton Ward. From what she had already seen, there would be no point trying to surprise him or knock him on the head. Some kind of kung fu expert, for heaven's sake, from the damned New Orleans Serpentarium! That cover wouldn't hold for long, once he got home and started spouting off about their find.

If he got home.

She might get lucky, see an elephant or dinosaur step on him yet. It would be quite a waste, considering his talents in the sex department, but a million dollars would ensure that Audrey Moreland never lacked for male companionship again. Not that she couldn't find a man these days, but something told her she would meet a better class of lover on the Riviera, maybe down in Rio de Janeiro—or Tahiti. Sure, why not?

The first step was to get away from her companions, find a decent place to hide. And with the contest going on in front of them, she knew that there would never be a better time to make her exit.

Next stop, Audrey thought, the land of milk and honey.

REMO MARKED a flash of movement from the corner of his eye. He turned in time to catch a glimpse of Audrey running toward the wall that marked the ancient city's boundary line. The massive gates were sixty yards to her right, but she didn't veer off in that direction. Rather, she appeared intent on getting to a kind of lean-to shed that stood against the inside of the wall, its wooden door ajar.

"Stay here!" he told the others, hoping they would follow his instruction, less concerned about their fate just then than with the prospect of the ringer making good her getaway.

He spared a glance for the immense combatants, ducked a spray of blood as the ceratosaurus raked the elephant across one ear with four sharp claws. It left the ear in tatters, but the elephant wouldn't back down. If anything, the sudden pain appeared to galvanize the pachyderm, propelled it forward, slashing with its tusks. The reptile scuttled backward, snarling, but a long gash opened on its flank before it hopped out of range.

Remo was in full motion now. On the far side of the jade arena, he saw Chiun, a tiny, black-clad witness to the clash of titans. Chiun saw Remo, too, and raised an open hand. From the expression on

his face, they might have met by accident, outside
a restaurant in downtown Seoul, instead of on some
blood-smeared battleground where living nightmares dined on human flesh.

He kept on after Audrey, knowing Chiun could
take care of himself in any given situation. Remo
didn't have a clue as to where Chiun had found an
elephant, but from the trail of broken corpses leading to the open gates, he knew the beast had paid
its way before it ever caught a glimpse of old Nagaq.

As for the outcome of the present contest, Remo
figured it was still too close to call.

Across the courtyard, Audrey was within a few
strides of the lean-to, gaining fast, when she
stopped short, recoiling in apparent fear. The door
flew open, and a hulking, mud-caked tribesman
leaped out to confront her, brandishing a spear. Her
scream was audible above the snarling, grunting
sounds of mortal combat at his back as Remo
poured on speed.

CHIUN WAS HUMMING softly as he watched the contest that no living man had witnessed heretofore.
Brute creatures lacked finesse, of course, but it was
still an honor to observe their efforts from a ring-
side seat. His sympathy lay with the elephant, since
it had served him well with no reward, but it was
difficult to see the dragon as a loser, with its nimble
sidesteps, wicked claws and flashing fangs.

Still, it was something of a disappointment when he thought about the great scrolls of Sinanju. Chiun had hoped the dragon would have wings, perhaps breathe fire—in short, put on a better show. It would have made the combat hopeless, stolen any chance the elephant might have, but there was something in the preservation of tradition that appealed to him.

Chiun doubted whether this big lizard even had an eye for gold and gems.

A sudden jabbering of voices from his flank distracted Chiun, and he was turning to confront the natives when the first spear whispered past him, struck the elephant and pierced its shoulder. Two more lances followed swiftly, striking home, and while they were no mortal threat to the behemoth, it was clear they irritated him. He shook himself, dislodged one spear, but the other two held fast.

Chiun was not amused.

He counted seven natives—three of whom had foolishly disarmed themselves—with two more poised to hurl their spears. They shouted for Nagaq as if they were a group of drunken white men watching football on a Sunday afternoon and rooting for the quarterback.

The Master of Sinanju moved against them, killing two before they seemed to recognize the threat. Nagaq's surviving acolytes turned their attention to Chiun, but it was already too late for them to save themselves.

Too easy, thought Chiun as he swept through
their ranks without resistance, cleaving flesh and
bone the way a butcher opens lifeless carcasses.
There was no contest, and he finished swiftly, picking up one of their fallen spears and hefting it, considering its usefulness before he frowned and cast
it to the side.

Chiun did not feel pity for his enemies. It had
been their choice to attack, when they could just as
easily have run into the jungle and concealed themselves. If they elected to do battle with the Master
of Sinanju, it was understood—by Chiun, at least—
that they would die in sundry violent and humili-
ating ways. There was no dignity in foolishness,
and Chiun felt nothing but contempt for those who
threw their lives away in hopeless causes.

He returned his full attention to the clash of giants in the courtyard. It wouldn't be long, pure logic
said, before a winner was revealed.

His heart was with the elephant, but if he had
been forced to bet, Chiun would have put his
money on the reptile.

REMO WAS a dozen paces from the lean-to when
the tribesman drove his spear through Audrey's ab-
domen, below the ribs, and hoisted her as if she
were a fish, still wriggling on the tip of his harpoon.
She screamed—a wild, unearthly sound, half pain,
half disbelief—and Remo saw the warrior tilt his

head back, opening his mouth to catch the first warm drops of blood that showered on his face.

It was the moment something snapped inside him, and a red haze blurred his vision for perhaps two heartbeats. Remo had been sent to kill this woman, and he would have done the job without complaint, but there was something so barbaric in the act of her impalement, something so inhuman in that thirst for blood, that Remo voluntarily let go of his reserve, felt fury energize him as he closed the final distance to his prey.

The tribesman saw Death coming through his one good eye, but there was little he could do about it. The man's first instinct was to drop the spear, drop Audrey and retreat in the direction of the lean-to.

He never made it. Remo caught him by the nape and hauled him back before the tribesman reached the threshold of his sanctuary. Simple pressure at the point where skull met spine would do the trick, but Remo didn't let his adversary off that easily. Instead, he hauled the native back and set him on his big, splayed feet, stood waiting for the guy to make his move.

The cyclops blinked twice, muttered something in his native tongue and threw a roundhouse punch at Remo's head. It was the final voluntary move his body ever made. His arm was snapped like kindling at wrist and elbow, twisted from the shoulder socket with a gruesome sucking sound. Before the native even knew he was disarmed, before the agony could register, his own arm whipped around and struck him in the face with force enough to crush his nose and cheekbones, shearing off his front teeth at the gum line. One more stroke before he fell, and that was all it took to split his skull, the lifeless body falling next to Audrey.

Remo knelt beside the woman, cradling her head without a sudden motion that would fire new jolts of pain off through her body. He didn't remove the spear or otherwise disturb it, understanding that her wound was hopeless from the dark blood soaking through her denim shirt in front and back. A modern hospital with trauma surgeons standing by might just have saved her, but there was a shortage of facilities in the Malaysian jungle. Even with a helicopter on the scene right now, she would have bled to death or died from shock within the first few minutes, miles away from any kind of help.

So Remo, helpless, brushed the hair back from her face and asked her how she felt.

"Like shit," she told him honestly. "It isn't fair."

"What is?"

"Goddamned philosophy." She grimaced, fighting with the pain. "I don't suppose you've got a neat trick up your sleeve for this?"

"'Fraid not," he said.

"I didn't think so. Shit! Don't leave me like this, Renton."

"No."

She forced a smile in spite of everything. "I guess this means you win."

"Two different games," he said. "I won't be getting rich and fat, if it's a consolation."

"Screw your consolation," Audrey hissed. "Somebody ought to make a dollar off this deal."

"I have a feeling someone will."

"Not Beijing, though."

He shook his head. "Not this time."

"Just as well. You need five hundred thousand dollars, Renton?"

Remo didn't have to think about it. "No," he said.

"You sure? I'll tell you where it is, how you can get it, if you promise—"

"Never mind," he interrupted her. "It's on the house. Just close your eyes now."

Audrey Moreland did as she was told, and Remo finished it, a light stroke to the temple, blotting out her pain, replacing it with darkness.

Remo hoped that she was warm.

Across the courtyard, primal sounds of pain and fury snapped him out of it. He rose and turned back toward the huge combatants, saw them lurching in a grim ballet of death.

And Remo left the newly dead blonde behind him as he went to join Chiun.

IT WAS THE GREATEST battle of the century, of any century, thought Stockwell. You could keep *Juras-*

sic Park, with all its clever animation and effects. The scene in front of him was real, no miniatures, stage blood, blue screens or stop-motion photography involved.

So real that he could smell it. The metallic scent of blood was overwhelming; some of it had even spattered Stockwell's face, run down his cheeks and neck into the open collar of his shirt. A musky odor from the great ceratosaurus, doubtless similar to odors certain snakes produced when caught or taken by surprise. The elephant had urinated sometime in the early moments of the fight, and the ammonia smell was strong enough to open up a dead man's sinuses.

It was illusory, thought Stockwell, but he could have sworn he felt the earth tilt underneath his feet. No man on earth had ever witnessed anything like this before—except, perhaps, some member of the local tribe—and he, Professor Safford Stockwell, would be first to share the story with the outside world.

Then it struck him that their gear—the cameras, everything—had been stripped from them by the natives when they reached the city. Christ, had it been only hours earlier? He didn't have a single photograph or videocassette to document what he was seeing, nothing that would prove his case once they escaped.

If they escaped.

There would be witnesses, of course. Poor Chalmers was a write-off, but he still had Sibu Sandakan and the amazing Dr. Renton Ward.

And Audrey. Where in God's name had she gotten to this time?

There was no time to search for her just now. He was preoccupied to the exclusion of all else with the display of sheer brute force in front of him. Each move of the ceratosaurus felt like poetry, his dusty textbooks with their sketches come to life upon command.

He saw the elephant lunge forward, jabbing with its tusks, but the ceratosaurus sidestepped, bobbed its head and clamped down on its adversary's back with jaws agape. Blood fountained from the new wounds, streaking dusty hide and pooling on the ground, producing rust-colored mud as it was trampled under massive feet.

The elephant was lurching, bucking almost like a horse, to shake its ancient foe. The reptile lost its grip, but kept a ragged hunk of flesh clenched in its jaws as it fell over sideways, sprawling in the dirt. Before it sprang erect once more, the elephant closed in and hooked the carnivore with one long tusk, a piercing wound beneath its left arm, through the ribs.

Ceratosaurus shrieked in pain and rage, leaped backward, leaving bloodstains on the elephant's right tusk. Instead of hesitating, though, it circled to the left, then doubled back, the change-up smooth enough to be a practiced move. The elephant was forced to follow, facing toward its enemy, but dizziness and steady loss of blood combined to make its steps unsteady, tremulous.

The reptile saw its opening, rushed in and dodged the flashing tusks to clamp its jaws behind the elephant's great skull. Ceratosaurus gave a stiff shake of its head, teeth grinding into flesh and bone, blood streaming, and the elephant began to squeal, a weird, almost unearthly sound. Its trunk thrashed helplessly as it dug in with all four feet, but weight and bulk alone were not enough to save it. With its enemy beyond the reach of either tusk, the elephant could only lurch from side to side and try to pull away.

Too late.

The snap of separating vertebrae was loud enough that Stockwell had no trouble hearing it above the other noises of the two combatants. Instantly, it was as if someone had punctured an immense balloon, as the elephant collapsed, its treetrunk legs giving way. It landed belly down, with the ceratosaurus still on top, still clinging to its neck, but in another moment, even a diminutive reptile brain could tell the fight was over.

Grudgingly, the dinosaur released its grip and tottered backward, favoring its injured side. The puncture wound was bleeding freely, with no way to determine from a distance whether it was mortal. It was obviously painful, though, since the Jurassic predator didn't take time to sample so much as a mouthful from its latest kill.

In fact, as Stockwell watched, the ceratosaurus turned back toward the gates and the darkness of the rain forest outside the city walls. It was escaping! In a few more seconds, it would be beyond his reach forever!

Safford Stockwell moved like someone caught up in a dream. He scarcely realized that he was stepping forward, rushing toward the giant prehistoric reptile as it turned away from him. He felt hands clutching at his sleeve and threw them off, determined. If he could not photograph the reptile, could not cage a specimen, the very least that he could do was touch it, for his own sake.

Now!

He reached out for the flicking tail and saw it coming back to meet him. The ceratosaurus never saw him—or if so, it paid no more attention to him than a grizzly bear might pay a gnat. In retrospect, what happened next was probably an accident, more Stockwell's fault than anything.

He tried to duck at the last instant, raise a hand to save himself, but it was already too late. The hard tip of the reptile's tail struck him a glancing blow, peeled back a six-inch strip of scalp and knocked him sprawling to the ground.

His world was reeling, upside down, and it was difficult to see with fresh blood in his eyes, the night stained crimson. Even so, Professor Stockwell saw the creature of his dreams lurch out of sight, away beyond the massive open gates.

And something else.

Behind it, running like the wind, he could have sworn he saw a frail old man, dressed all in black.

"WE NEED TO LEAVE right now," said Remo, "or we won't get out of here at all."

Their Malay chaperon had Stockwell on his feet, and while the scalp wound bled as if there were no tomorrow, Stockwell seemed to be in no real danger. He would slow them down, of course, but that was nothing new.

"And Dr. Moreland?" Sibu Sandakan inquired, voice trembling as he spoke.

"She won't be coming."

"Audrey?" Stockwell had enough sense left to recognize the name, but he had trouble focusing his eyes.

"We'll see her later," Remo lied. "This way."

A handful of the locals had begun to gather near the fallen elephant, some of them prodding it with spears, while others watched the strangers, pointing, mouthing threats, and Remo swore softly under his breath.

It would be pointless, running, with the natives primed to follow them. While he could give them the slip or double back to kill them in the dark, he would be gravely handicapped by Sandakan and Stockwell. Better, he decided, if they finished it right here. It could mean wiping out the tribe, but Remo didn't plan to spend the next few days in hiding, dodging spears.

A group of six or seven tribesmen was advancing, muttering among themselves, and Remo was prepared to meet them, when an arrow sprouted from the leader's chest and dropped him in his tracks. At once, a second shaft cut down the warrior on his left, and then a third picked off the gangly cyclops standing just behind the fallen leader.

It was all they needed, sending up a frightened shout in unison and taking to their heels. In seconds, Remo and his traveling companions were alone with one dead elephant and several dozen mutilated corpses.

"Fairly decent shooting," Remo told Chiun. "You took your time, though."

"I was otherwise engaged," the Master of Sinanju answered, "with a dragon."

"Oh?"

"I did not kill it," said Chiun. "It had no magic and no treasure. There was nothing for Sinanju."

"Maybe next time," Remo said.

"You found what you were looking for, at least." The old Korean nodded toward the phosphorescent fountain as he spoke.

"Somebody else's problem, Little Father. Thanks for joining us."

"I had to satisfy my curiosity," Chiun said. "This is a strange part of the world."

"You can say that again."

"Unnecessary repetition is the trademark of a moron."

"Sorry, my mistake."

"We must be going," said Chiun. "I've missed too many of my programs as it is."

"Sounds good to me."

He took the small transmitter from his pocket, pressed the button once and left it on the ground beside the elephant. It made no sound that he could hear; there were no flashing lights.

If it was broken, it was someone else's problem.

The others were already fifty yards ahead of him when Remo turned and started for the gates.

20

They heard the helicopters churning overhead two hours later, with the ancient city well behind them. Sibu Sandakan glanced upward at the sound of engines, but the forest canopy was too thick for a glimpse of aircraft overhead. Dawn had not broken yet, and even running lights were hidden by the forest giants towering around them.

"Sounds like the natives have company," said Remo, winking at the Malay deputy.

"But how?"

"Would you believe the power of positive thinking?"

They marched back the way they came, no longer frightened of pursuit. Remo had given passing thought to the ceratosaurus as they left the city, but Chiun was quick to show him where the reptile had struck off among the trees, due north, with an impressive trail of blood to mark its passage. Even if it managed to survive, he thought, the city would be poison for a while, with memories of pain and chaos.

Did a dinosaur have memories?

In any case, there would be no more drums to beckon great Nagaq, no human sacrifice to whet his appetite. The reptile would be forced to get its meals the good old-fashioned way, by stalking them. Survival of the fittest.

They stopped to rest at dawn, with Dr. Stockwell verging on collapse. The loss of blood had weakened him, and Remo would have bet his meager salary on a concussion, but it sounded more like shock when the professor spoke.

"We must go back!" he blurted out while Sibu Sandakan was tending to his wounded scalp.

"Don't hold your breath," said Remo.

"But it's absolutely vital, don't you see?"

"Relax, Professor. We're already past the point of no return."

Chiun sat watching from the sidelines, frowning to himself as Stockwell ranted on. It wasn't necessary to speak Korean or read minds to guess at his opinion of the expedition's erstwhile leader.

"More!" raved Stockwell, lurching forward onto hands and knees. "There must be more!"

"Don't sweat it, Doc. We're out of range. They'll never catch us now," said Remo.

"Not those freaks, you idiot!" Professor Stockwell sounded frantic now. "More dinosaurs!"

"How's that?"

"You can't believe one specimen has lived for over sixty million years," said Stockwell, biting off a giggle. "That's preposterous! They must be breeding, don't you understand? A dinosaur needs parents, just like anybody else."

His giggling got the better of him then, dissolving into high-pitched cackling, like the sound track for a film about a lunatic asylum. Remo stared at Stockwell, felt his flesh crawl as the snowy-haired professor fell apart before his very eyes.

"There could be dozens!" Stockwell ranted. "Maybe hundreds! Why not thousands? Don't you see?"

"The man's insane," Chiun said to Remo, speaking in Korean as an act of courtesy to the deranged. "Time has no meaning to a dragon."

Maybe not, but Stockwell's words had started Remo thinking. If your reading matter was restricted to the supermarket-tabloid press, it was conceivable there might be one Bigfoot, one Loch Ness monster, one Abominable Snowman. Any working knowledge of biology, however, would dictate that even freaks of nature had to come from somewhere. There was no great monster warehouse, where a fickle Fate could shop around for oddities to populate the globe. In that respect, he knew that Stockwell must be right.

Even a dragon needed parents somewhere up the line.

The very notion challenged Remo's sense of logic. He had gone into the jungle looking for uranium, convinced the dinosaur hunt was nothing but a cover—or perhaps an aging academic's last-ditch fantasy. His guess had been correct where Audrey Moreland's motive was concerned, but totally amiss with reference to Dr. Stockwell and his quest.

What did it mean? What could it mean?

Would there be travelers' advisories about the risk of tourists being eaten by a dinosaur when word leaked out? No one with any sense went tramping through the Tasek Bera, as it was, but a confirmed report of living prehistoric animals would change all that. Green Hell would rapidly become a must-see spot for every scientist with strength and nerve enough to hoist a backpack, not to mention wealthy dilettantes and "sportsmen" who would give up next year's Porsche to catch a glimpse of—or take a shot at—living monsters from a bygone era.

Once the word got out...

He glanced at Chiun, saw understanding in the Master's eyes and nodded. Remo turned to Sibu Sandakan, ignoring Dr. Stockwell as he said, "We need to talk."

ON TUESDAY MORNING, Dr. Harold Smith met Remo in his office at the Folcroft Sanitarium, in Rye, New York. It was Remo's first full day back from Malaysia, but he had caught up on sleep in airplanes, thirteen hours crossing the Pacific and another six across the continent, with downtime in the San Francisco and Chicago airports.

"You'll be glad to know the government has laid claim to the new lode of uranium," Smith said.

"Which government is that?" asked Remo.

Dr. Smith blinked twice, a curious expression on his lemon face. "Why, the Malaysian government, of course," he said. "Did you believe we had an interest in the ore?"

"It crossed my mind," said Remo, "since you sent me out to find it."

"That was simple self-defense," Smith told him, rocking backward in his swivel chair. "And justified, as it turned out. The last thing anybody needs right now is more bombs in Beijing."

"We're happy, then," said Remo.

"Absolutely. The United States has excellent relations with Malaysia."

"Could it be that they'll be selling part of the uranium to mining interests in the States?" asked Remo.

Dr. Smith responded with a shrug. "That won't concern us here. We're problem solvers, Remo, you and I."

"Sure thing. I meant to thank you for your great help in the jungle, Doc."

"Chiun was there, I take it. What else did you need?"

"A tour guide to the twilight zone, as it turned out."

Smith frowned and spent a moment shuffling papers on his desk before he spoke again. "There's something else we need to talk about," he said at last.

"Do tell."

"About this dinosaur..."

"Ceratosaurus," Remo said, correcting him. "I did some reading on the plane. It's a Jurassic meat eater, assuming that it's still alive. I guess it didn't read about the great extinction in the papers."

"Most amusing." There was clearly something on Smith's mind. "I understand that Dr. Stockwell is convinced there may be...well..."

"More dinosaurs," said Remo, finishing the sentence for him.

"Yes."

"Is that a problem?"

"Not for us, specifically," Smith said. "I mean, it's hardly national-security material. Unless..."

"Don't tell me."

"If he's right, it stands to reason someone may go looking for them. I mean, it's hardly something that the scientific world could manage to ignore."

"If anyone was listening," said Remo. "I was told you had the situation under wraps."

"Our end," said Dr. Smith. "Professor Stockwell will be spending several weeks with us at Folcroft, working through his little problem. In the end, I'm confident he'll realize that he was subject to delusions. All that stress, the loss of valued colleagues, jungle fever—it was only natural that he should lose touch with reality."

"You'll have a problem holding him," said Remo. "He's an egghead with a following in Washington, you may recall."

"Georgetown enjoys the bounty of substantial federal grants," Smith said, recovering a portion of his jaundiced smile. "They're telling anyone who asks that Dr. Stockwell is recuperating from his trip in private, holding off on any monographs and statements for a while."

"So, what's the problem?" Remo asked.

"Well, as I said, that's only our end of the pipeline. There were other witnesses, Malaysians, who could spill the beans."

"I've taken care of that," said Remo.

"Oh? How so?" asked Dr. Smith.

"I had a word with Stockwell's baby-sitter," Remo said. "Chiun helped. Between us, we persuaded him that any mention of a living dinosaur would cause more problems for his country than it solved."

"He bought that?" Dr. Smith was clearly skeptical. "I would imagine they're already printing tickets for a new exhibit at the zoo."

"Not quite. They're anxious to avoid discussing how one of their crack commando squads wiped out the last survivors of a previously undiscovered tribe and let the dinosaur escape. Bad ink in that, you know? I would imagine they could catch some heavy flak from the United Nations, not to mention various environmental groups. You mention genocide in certain circles these days, and you're talking automatic tourist boycotts."

"It's something to consider, I suppose," Smith said. "Still, news like this is difficult to bury. Even if it only leaks out through the tabloid press…"

"Forget it," Remo said. "I can't see any redneck housewives flying to Malaysia for a dinosaur hunt."

Smith frowned and shook his head. "My point is that eventually someone's bound to spill the beans, you see? And when that happens, there will be investigations."

"Maybe so. I'm betting we're retired by then."

"Retirement's looking better all the time," Smith said. "Have you considered what could happen if a living specimen wound up in other hands?"

Smith spoke the last two words as if they left a foul taste in his mouth. The strained expression on his face made Remo smile, despite an effort to restrain himself.

"Can't say I've given it much thought."

"We could be faced," Smith told him sternly, "with a dinosaur gap!"

"You're sending someone," Remo said. It didn't come out sounding like a question.

"No," Smith said. "Not yet, I mean. We'll have to think about it. Wait and see."

"Chiun won't be happy."

"Chiun?"

"He wanted me to give you some advice," said

Remo, rattling off a burst of rapid-fire Korean with the accent of a native.

"May I ask what that's supposed to mean?"

"Let sleeping dragons lie," said Remo, "or they just might turn around and bite you on the ass."

TAKE 'EM FREE
4 action-packed novels plus a mystery bonus
NO RISK
NO OBLIGATION TO BUY

Don't miss out on the action in these titles!

<u>Deathlands</u>

#62527	GROUND ZERO	$4.99 U.S.	☐
		$5.50 CAN.	☐
#62530	CROSSWAYS	$4.99 U.S.	☐
		$5.50 CAN.	☐
#62533	ECLIPSE AT NOON	$5.50 U.S.	☐
		$6.50 CAN.	☐
#62534	STONEFACE	$5.50 U.S.	☐
		$6.50 CAN.	☐

<u>The Destroyer</u>

#63210	HIGH PRIESTESS	$4.99	☐
#63218	ENGINES OF DESTRUCTION	$5.50 U.S.	☐
		$6.50 CAN.	☐
#63219	ANGRY WHITE MAILMEN	$5.50 U.S.	☐
		$6.50 CAN.	☐
#63220	SCORCHED EARTH	$5.50 U.S.	☐
		$6.50 CAN.	☐

(limited quantities available on certain titles)

TOTAL AMOUNT	$
POSTAGE & HANDLING	$
($1.00 for one book, 50¢ for each additional)	
APPLICABLE TAXES*	$ _____
TOTAL PAYABLE	$ _____
(check or money order—please do not send cash)	

To order, complete this form and send it, along with a check or money order for the total above, payable to Gold Eagle Books, to: **In the U.S.:** 3010 Walden Avenue, P.O. Box 9077, Buffalo, NY 14269-9077; **In Canada:** P.O. Box 636, Fort Erie, Ontario, L2A 5X3.

Name:_____

Address:_____ City:_____

State/Prov.:_____ Zip/Postal Code:_____

*New York residents remit applicable sales taxes.
 Canadian residents remit applicable GST and provincial taxes.

GEBACK18A